BEYOND

PROMISE

Karice Bolton

DEDICATION

Always to my husband and mom. Love you both
so much.

And thank you to the readers of the Beyond Love
Series. I'm so grateful to you all for reading about
Brandy, Gabby, and Lily. They have been so much
fun to write, and I can't thank you enough for
reading about these women and their lives.

BOOKS BY KARICE BOLTON

ISLAND COUNTY SERIES
FINDING LOVE IN FORGOTTEN COVE
LOVE REDONE IN HIDDEN HARBOR
TANGLED LOVE ON PELICAN POINT
FOREVER LOVE ON FIREWEED ISLAND
TEMPTING LOVE ON HOLLY LANE
CHANCE AT LOVE ON MYSTI BAY
IRRESISTIBLE LOVE AT SILVER FALLS

BEYOND LOVE SERIES
BEYOND CONTROL
BEYOND DOUBT
BEYOND REASON
BEYOND INTENT
BEYOND CHANCE
BEYOND PROMISE
BEYOND the MISTLETOE

LUKE FLETCHER SERIES
HIDDEN SINS
BURIED SINS
REDEMPTION
MIA

V MAFIA
BLAKE
DEVIN

MORE BOOKS BY KARICE BOLTON

JAXSON

THE WITCH AVENUE SERIES
LONELY SOULS
ALTERED SOULS

RELEASED SOULS
SHATTERED SOULS

THE WATCHERS TRILOGY
AWAKENING
LEGIONS
CATACLYSM
TAKEN NOVELLA (A Watchers Prequel)

WHISPER SERIES
WHISPERS IN THE WOODS: The Camp
WHISPERS ON CAMPUS: The Dorm

AFTERWORLD SERIES
RecruitZ
AlibiZ
UprisingZ

ACKNOWLEDGMENTS

I want to say a simple thank you to Amazon, iBooks, Kobo, Barnes & Noble, and all of the other avenues available to the indie publishing world. It allows the art of storytelling to continue to flourish in unexpected ways!

Cover Design: Phatpuppy, Typography: BB Designs, Female model: Anya Kod, Male Model: Steve Alario, Makeup/Hair artist: Nadya Rutman, Photography: Teresa Yeh
DepositPhotos: © Subbotina

Chapter One

I glanced around the back room of Gabby's Goodies and felt at home as Gabby worked away on a wedding cake, and I sat sipping tea and doing absolutely nothing. Even though the outside air was frigid, Gabby had the door propped open to let the heat from the ovens escape the small space. I'd tucked myself in the far corner and breathed in the sugar scent that permeated the air. There was nothing better than being best friends with a baker. I took in a deep breath and smiled a happy smile. Between the almost caramel smell of the falling autumn leaves and Gabby's sugary confections, I was in my own version of heaven. Not to mention as wonky as my sniffer had been lately, I was relieved to be where scents didn't torment me.

"That's it," Emily said, walking through the door of the workroom. Emily had quickly

1

become Gabby's right hand around the shop and they made a great team. Plus, we all loved Emily. "I've had it. I think there is some sort of secret, underground network for single men where they all get together and figure out who they can torment next and somehow they pick me again and again and again. Oh, hi, Lily."

Emily's fiery—and often unruly—red hair and olive complexion made most men and women take a second glance because she was just that stunning. Of course, she never stood still long enough to notice others' reactions, but we did. Emily had been divorced for almost six years, and she'd only recently started to try online dating. So far she wasn't singing any praises.

Emily gave me a quick kiss and tied an apron around her waist.

"Good morning," I said, giving her an understanding nod.

"So the morning coffee date didn't go well?" Gabby asked.

"What made you say that? It went fabulous." Emily gave a doleful laugh. "As fabulous as my dates always go."

She grabbed a tray of already rolled biscuit dough and began cutting each dough circle out.

"It couldn't have been that bad," Gabby prodded.

"Within seconds of meeting him, he asked if he could call me Kitty going forward."

My brow arched. "Kitty? Why Kitty?"

Emily's lip curled in disgust. "Apparently, the fine fellow has a cat fetish and prefers his redheads to be named Kitty."

Gabby burst into laughter, "At least he didn't ask to call you Garfield."

I bit my lip and tried to keep in the eruption of giggles that wanted to come out because Emily looked purely miserable.

"What does a cat fetish entail?" I asked, completely fascinated.

"You know, I didn't stick around long enough to find out." Emily winked.

"Good call." I nodded in approval.

"I'm actually wondering if maybe some people aren't meant for love. Like maybe there's a batch of us that are predisposed to hunt out and distract the bad seeds so others don't get stuck with them. Maybe it's part of evolution or genetics. Or a public service designed by the man upstairs."

"I doubt that," Gabby assured her. "Although it is an interesting theory."

Emily smiled and placed the dough on the cooking sheets, but we could tell she was disappointed. "In all honesty, I noticed that once I started this online dating thing, my paintings got angrier. I used to paint pretty things— flowers, gardens, and birds. Not now. I've got so many paintings with furious storms and crashing waves, I don't even know what to do with them."

"It must be therapeutic," Gabby offered.

"Maybe, but I think as of this morning, I'm officially off the market. I'm pulling my profile off the websites, and I'm shutting down shop. I'm tired of dating all these donkey asses," she said it with a grin, but we knew she was serious.

"Aren't a donkey and an ass one in the same," Gabby muttered.

Emily chuckled and shoved the first tray in the oven.

I knew how hard it was to date and how easy it was to shut down. All I had to do was think of the nightmare that was my ex-boss's son—that some had the nerve to call Portland's Most Eligible Bachelor—and it left me shivering just thinking of how horrible he was. Not to mention my high school boyfriend. But I also knew if I'd thrown in the towel, I wouldn't have fallen for Ayden, and he was the best thing that ever happened in my life.

I adjusted myself on the stool and leaned my back against the wall. I hated to see someone give up on love. I rested my hands on my belly and let out a sigh.

"You know, Emily, if the donkey throws you off, you get right back up and get yourself on a different one. Not the same one, of course. That would be foolish. Possibly find one that is a little taller, a little more muscular, and isn't into cats quite as much. Maybe don't even try a donkey, try a stallion the next time around."

"So you're saying not to set my sights so low?" Emily grinned.

"Exactly what she's saying. Stay away from the asses and find yourself a stallion," Gabby chuckled.

"I appreciate the pep talk, ladies, but I need a break," Emily said, feigning exhaustion.

"How long have you had the profile up online?" I asked, intrigued with the process.

"Two weeks," Emily said.

"And why don't you tell her when your last date was prior to uploading your profile?" Gabby prompted.

Emily rolled her eyes and a huge smile tugged at her lips.

"Well?" I encouraged.

"Three years. I hadn't been on a date for three years."

My mouth fell open. "Really? And you only gave your online profile two weeks?"

"I'm not lying when I say I've had a long line of duds in that department, but enough about me. Tell me all about this beach wedding you have planned. It's in Bermuda, right? Are you nervous?"

I nodded and a flutter sprang through me, but it wasn't because of the wedding.

"The wedding planning is going perfectly. That's the easy part. No nerves there."

"Well, that's good. So many brides are stressed beyond belief."

"Tell me about it," Gabby laughed. "Carla has more ideas than I do about my wedding, and I seem to have to hear about every single one of them."

Carla was Gabby's stepmom, and she was one of the most well meaning event planners out there.

"Since it's so far away, I mostly only have to approve items the planner at the hotel emails me, like flower colors and dinner options."

"That's the fun part," Emily agreed. "So what's got you nervous?"

I traded glances with Gabby and let out a deep breath. "Ayden's got a huge fight coming up. He says it's his last, but from what I've heard about his opponent I'm a nervous wreck. The guy is like a beast. Ayden's undefeated and an amazing fighter, but I—" I stopped myself. I didn't want to say it out loud. I didn't want to jinx his winning streak, but the truth of it was since Ayden and I found out we were pregnant, my priorities shifted and my worries became more pronounced. Since we hadn't announced that I was expecting, I didn't detail why I was more worried than usual. Emily already knew I always got nervous when Ayden stepped in the ring.

"When is the fight?" Emily asked, wiping down the counter with a cloth.

"It's three weeks prior to Bermuda. On the off chance that he doesn't dodge a fist, he should have enough time to heal up before our big day," I laughed nervously. That was actually the least of my worries. There was something primal driving me to not want him to get into the ring again.

But I also didn't want to be one of those fiancées who made their partner change everything about who they were before the relationship. I hadn't asked him to stop fighting. It was Ayden's idea.

"Well, I can understand your worry, hun," Emily said, shaking the cloth off outside. "But he's got it down."

Gabby nodded in agreement as she worked on rolling the fondant. She'd already managed to place the fondant twigs along the first two layers and was focusing on the third. The cake, like usual, was spectacular. Fondant cherry blossoms canvased the cake, creating an elegant yet natural theme.

"I wish you were doing my cake," I told Gabby, trying to change the topic.

I hated thinking about the fight. It almost made me ill when I thought too long and hard about it.

"I'm sure the hotel will provide a beautiful cake," Gabby assured me.

"Won't be the same."

"Well, you could cancel your tropical wedding and have it right here in the middle of rainy season." She smiled. "I'm sure Mason's girlfriend would love to host a beach wedding in Forgotten Cove in the middle of November. Sounds just as wonderful as the sun soaking into our bones in Bermuda."

Emily brought over a croissant and set it down in front of me. "Go ahead. You look hungry." She eyed me suspiciously so I returned the favor, giving her a once over with a wry grin firmly planted on my lips.

"What?" I asked.

"Nothing at all." Her eyes dropped to my hands that were resting on my nearly flat stomach and I rolled my eyes. To prove my point that I had no idea what she was getting at, I reached over and took a bite of the croissant. The flaky crust melted in my mouth as I stared blankly at Emily.

"This hits the spot. Thank goodness I ran those five miles this morning," I lied.

"Would you like me to make you a triple mocha?" Emily asked. "I know how you love your caffeine and you must be exhausted after the run."

Playing dirty, I see. "No, the tea is perfectly fine."

"What kind of tea?" Emily asked.

"Passion fruit."

Emily nodded "Interesting. No caffeine. Have you gotten your wedding dress yet?"

Nice try, my friend, but I wasn't going to let it out. I hated to keep secrets and was possibly the worst at it in the world, but I wasn't going to say a word, regardless of the fact that Emily already guessed. It was actually nice sharing this news with only Ayden for as long as we could. It was our own private moment that happened to extend over several months.

I stood up from the stool and stretched as Emily scooped cookie dough onto a metal tray. I was supposed to meet Ayden at his brother's house on Fireweed Island. Actually, it wasn't exactly his brother's house. It was a home Mason shared with his new girlfriend, Tori. I really wasn't sure who owned what. There were a lot of complicated things that went down between the two of them, and I didn't really follow the dirty details, but the important part was that they had a guestroom and didn't mind us spending a weekend now and again. Mason had remodeled the entire home and it was beautiful.

"I should get going so I don't miss out on lunch. I'm starving."

"You just had a croissant," Emily replied smiling.

"Lily's appetite always amazes us all," Gabby said, and I knew the unsaid secret was no longer a secret, but I refused to confirm or deny.

I gave Emily a quick hug and walked over to Gabby, squeezing her in between twigs.

"Enjoy your weekend on Fireweed."

"I will. Ayden's been out of town all week at a trade show and I've missed him like crazy."

"That's right," Gabby said, forming the next twig. "Weren't you supposed to go with him?"

I nodded. "Yeah, but there was a bit of a distribution issue on our latest launch so I needed to stay back and get that straightened out. Nothing like sponsoring a party and having no product to hand out. Anyway, I got some trucked in from a different distributor and all was saved. And I have to admit the party was pretty fun."

"Where was it at?" Emily asked.

"The actual party was at the convention center in Seattle. They were holding a women's science and technology fair and we sponsored the after party."

"You never cease to amaze me," Gabby chuckled. "I didn't even know there was a women's science and technology fair."

"That's what I do."

And I loved my job, but I couldn't wait to see Ayden. We'd originally planned a week together in Boston while we attended the trade show so I was kind of annoyed I didn't get to go, but I had my own fun at the party we hosted back in Seattle. It was a CosPlay party where people could dress up as their favorite video game or comic book or anime characters. I was a little out of my element, but I loved every second of it. I might even have to put my costume back on for Ayden this weekend. If he was lucky.

My gut said he was going to be very lucky.

I gave a quick wave to Emily and Gabby and walked through the bakery and out to my car. The chill in the air made me tighten up my scarf as I stood and looked out over Puget Sound. The water glittered in the October haze, and my heart skipped a beat at the thought of seeing Ayden. I loved that even though we were quickly approaching our one-year anniversary of being together, I literally couldn't keep my hands off him or my mind pure of thought when he popped in. I glanced at my phone and was surprised to see a missed text from Ayden.

Are you tormenting me on purpose by keeping me waiting? Can't wait to see you. X

My entire body warmed and I quickly texted him back. I thought back to the very first time I saw him in a different light. No longer just my best friend's brother, but someone more

10

endearing, layered and complex who wanted to know me and try to understand me. Another flutter flitted through my body, and I knew that the weekend was going to be incredible.

Chapter Two

Ayden was standing on the front porch, his blond hair getting tousled in the wind as his eyes connected with mine, and I wanted nothing more than to be held in his arms. I spotted his brother in the garden on the side of the house, trimming dead perennials, while his girlfriend pruned one of the shrubs. It made me chuckle to see Mason so in his element. I was happy he'd found someone, and Tori was a lot of fun to be around.

"You look sensational," Ayden almost growled. His arms snaked around my waist.

He brought me tightly into him, and I felt the strength of his embrace. There was no reason to worry about the fight, yet it was at the tip of every conversation and on the surface of every thought.

"What's wrong?" he whispered, sensing my unease.

I shook my head. "Sorry. Nothing."

The worst thing I could do was convey my fears and make him lose focus during training. The contracts were already signed. He was stepping in the ring regardless, so the least I could do was keep quiet and allow him to concentrate on winning.

"I almost let the secret out," I whispered.

"You know, I think it's fine to tell people now."

"Yeah...I guess. But I like you and I sharing this little secret."

He smiled and it felt like we were the only two people on Fireweed Island as he held me tightly. "Big secret, you mean."

I tilted my head and looked into his gaze. "Big, little secret."

He gave me a devilish grin and my insides stirred as if it were the first time he held me.

"Hey, Lily," Tori called from the garden. "Thanks for coming over."

Ayden let me go and I waved. "Are you serious? Thanks for letting us hang out all weekend. It was much needed after the last few weeks at work."

"Ayden's that hard to work for, huh?" she teased.

"Yeah. It's brutal. Some mornings he forgets to bring me coffee at the office, and then there are those days where I have to go get my own lunch. As an assistant, he's really got a thing or two to learn."

"Just like this one." Tori thumbed Mason and he laughed. "We've got some lunch in the crockpot, if you two are hungry."

"I'm starved."

"What's new?" Mason shouted from behind Tori.

"Hey, now. Is that polite for a potential sister-in-law?"

"Not potential." Mason started walking our way. "As far as I'm concerned it's a done deal, and before you know it, I'll be calling you knucklehead and pounding the top of your head."

I shook my head and chuckled. Poor Brandy still had to endure endless brotherly shenanigans. Between constant ribbing and impromptu wrestling sessions, I didn't know how she managed not to thump Mason or Ayden. But I was definitely looking forward to becoming a Rhodes.

Ayden slipped his hand in mine and led me up the steps.

"I need to get my bag," I told Ayden.

"No problem. I'll get it for you," Mason said from behind us.

"Wow. Such service. I tell one twin my request and the other fulfills it."

Ayden beamed as he opened the door, and I walked in underneath his raised arm. Tori was right behind and took my coat and scarf from me and hung it in the closet. The most delicious smelling aroma of cooked tomato and onion wafted through the house.

"What smells so amazing?"

"Stew," Tori said, closing the door. "I found the recipe in one of my mom's recipe boxes and now it's Mason's favorite."

"Yum. One of my favorites too."

"Let's be honest," Ayden said, releasing my hand. "What's not your favorite?"

"Good point." I took a couple steps forward and without warning a wave of nausea hit me at full impact. My entire body got clammy, and it felt like my insides were suddenly about to make their way to the outside world. I spotted the rustic bench only two feet away and quickly made my way over and took a seat.

Locking my elbows into place so my arms held me up, I stared at the wood floor in front of me. I'd only encountered nausea like this a handful of times during pregnancy, and lucky me, it hit again.

"Babe, you okay?" Ayden asked, kneeling next to me.

I nodded. "Totally, just need a second."

"Is she okay?" Tori asked Ayden.

He must have nodded because I didn't hear a response.

"Let me get you a cool washcloth," Tori offered, trundling off to the powder room.

Within seconds, Tori returned with a damp cloth and Ayden pressed it on my forehead. The coolness drifted over me, and my stomach settled as quickly as it had become unsettled. I took in a deep breath and brought my gaze to Ayden's.

"You okay? We can go to the doctor," he whispered.

I smiled and touched his cheek. Seeing the

concern in his eyes unleashed a sense of apprehension and worry for the decisions we were making as a couple. Were we in over our heads? While my pregnancy certainly hadn't been planned, we were both over the moon with excitement. Was that normal? Shouldn't we be petrified?

Okay, sometimes we were beyond petrified.

"I'm fine. I think it was the ferry ride and the onion."

I glanced up at Tori. "Sorry. I don't know what came over me."

Tori grinned. "No worries. I have some soda crackers if you'd like."

I bit my lip and looked over at Ayden and now Mason, who was holding my overnight bag, and looked quite concerned.

"Everything okay?" Mason asked, setting down the bag.

"Nothing a few soda crackers won't fix," Tori explained.

I stood up. "Sorry. Feeling totally fine now. Honestly, I think I just got up too early and had too many sweets at Gabby's."

Mason and Ayden traded glances before Mason picked the bag back up and walked it down to the guest room without saying a word.

Tori was already in the kitchen rummaging through the pantry to find the soda crackers when Ayden and I walked in.

"I can't wait to have some stew." I grabbed a bowl and Ayden started laughing.

"Are you sure you should have some right

now?"

"Totally."

Tori turned around from the pantry cupboard with a box of soda crackers. "These are always nice to have with stew anyway."

She carried them to the dining room and said nothing else on the subject. We all filled our bowls and sat around the table. I glanced out the window and quietly took in the shimmering waters beyond the bluff. The house was perched on a cliff overlooking Forgotten Cove, giving way to a picture-perfect view of the water. There was a trail that led down to the beach. It was probably too cold to attempt a canoe trip over the weekend, but it would be nice to wander down and roam the beach.

I took several bites of the stew and enjoyed the delicious goodness. It was as if the other little issue never happened at all and my taste buds were back in order.

"This is the best stew I've ever had."

Tori's expression softened as she took a bite. "Thank you. I always remember my mom making it for us in the winter."

"It's delicious," Ayden agreed.

Mason didn't say a word. Instead, he stirred the stew endlessly, bringing none of it to his lips. Considering it was supposed to be his favorite meal, I had no idea what was happening between these two until he finally broke his silence.

"I don't like what's going on one bit." Mason's gaze steadied on Ayden.

"What's going on?" Ayden asked, his brow

quirked.

"You know exactly what's going on. Does anyone know?" Mason asked.

My heart started racing. What in the world was he talking about? Had Mason figured out I was pregnant? But why in the world would that bother him? My chest tightened as I watched Mason glare at Ayden. It was as if some silent brotherly standoff was transpiring, and Tori and I were stuck in the middle.

"No one knows," Ayden replied. "We haven't announced it yet."

"I'm sure mom already knows," Mason replied.

I watched Mason and Ayden stare at each other without saying anything else, and I could no longer take it.

"I'm sorry, but what is going on between you two?"

Mason didn't answer. Rather, he directed his question to Ayden.

"So how long have you known?"

"We found out a week after the fight was booked, if that was what you're getting at," Ayden replied.

My stomach knotted.

"And you're still going through with it," Mason stated, shaking his head.

"We signed a contract. Besides, it will be my last fight."

Tori flashed me an uncomfortable smile. "Congratulations," she mouthed.

"Thank you," I whispered back.

"Is that supposed to make me feel better about this one?" Mason asked. "This guy is coming in from Russia, Ayden."

"Exactly. There is no turning back since the contracts have been signed. We'd owe a quarter million if we back out," Ayden said, his finger tapping the table.

"Don't act like you can't afford it. It's a small price to pay to ensure..." Mason stopped.

I glanced at Ayden. The panic raced through my system. I'd never seen Mason this worried over a fight before. In fact, I'd never seen Mason worried. Ever. He was the more easy-going brother and his reaction scared me.

"If a person makes a few mistakes where a quarter million doesn't seem like a lot, there will be nothing left in very short order," Ayden replied coolly. Very rarely did this side come out of Ayden, and it usually only involved business dealings when it did.

I understood Ayden's point, but seeing Mason this riled up did nothing but frighten me. No amount of money was worth Ayden getting hurt or worse.

"What do you know about this fighter?" I asked. I didn't even know he was from Russia so obviously I had a lot of catching up to do. I assumed he was an American fighter because they always had been.

Mason's jaw twitched, and he shook his head as he stared at his brother.

"What?" I demanded. "What makes this fight different?"

"The prize is three-quarters of a million," Ayden said, wrapping his hand around mine.

"So it's the largest pot yet?" I glanced at Mason and back at Ayden. I knew that wasn't what made it different.

"Yes, it's the largest pot to date with the potential to bring in even more since we're the organizers and promoters," Ayden said, taking another bite of stew with his free hand. It was like he thought holding my hand would calm me down, but it didn't.

He still wasn't telling me something and that alone had me concerned. Money had never been what made Ayden step into the ring. Fighting started as a way to help his brother pay off debt and turned into a passion for Ayden. He loved the training. He loved the winning. He'd always won.

"This isn't quite how I imagined sharing the good news with your brother," I said, eyeing Ayden and all he did was nod.

The tension in the air was intense, and the emotions inside of me were boiling over. I didn't understand why Ayden was being so evasive. He was never like that. We were always open and honest about everything. He knew I worried about him stepping into the ring. I didn't hide it completely. I might not have ever told him how I couldn't sleep the night before, but he knew it was rough. Why wouldn't it be? Watching someone you love step into a ring where his safety was at risk was even more grueling. But there was something different about this match. I could sense it. I sensed it even before Mason brought it up today, and that had me concerned.

"Is this because you don't really want it to you be your last fight?" I asked. "I've never asked you to stop. It makes you happy, and we all need to do what makes us happy."

Ayden shook his head and let go of my hand. "No. It's not that. It's time for me to throw in the towel after this. I've got bigger and better things coming my way." His smile melted me on the spot, but Mason's voice broke through my temporary moment of swooning.

"I'm not going to let you get in the ring," Mason said softly.

"You really don't have a say in the matter."

Tori's eyes connected with mine, and I knew she even knew the reason or reasons behind Mason's worry and that only angered me more. I'd done well over the months with my fiery temper. I'd really done a good job of keeping it under control, but everyone had limits and I was about to reach mine.

I adjusted in my seat so I could get a better look at Ayden. I wanted to see what was driving him to make whatever decision it was that even had his brother frightened for his safety.

Ayden took a sip of water and relaxed into his seat. He knew he had merely seconds before I was about to blow, and neither of us wanted that for our weekend away.

One-one-thousand.

Two-one-thousand.

Three-one-thousand.

"The last person the Russian fought wound up in the hospital," Ayden said, sensing I was about to lose my cool.

My pulse rang in my ears and my world began to spin. Why in the world would he have agreed to fight someone like that? I didn't understand. Even before knowing we were expecting, why would he be willing to do that to himself? What was he trying to prove?

"And you'd risk that?" I whispered.

"Why don't you tell her the rest?" Mason asked, narrowing his eyes at his brother.

"There's more? What do you mean there's more?" My blood pumped wildly through my veins. I knew it wasn't good for the baby so I tried to center my breathing. I needed to calm down. I needed to be told the full story.

Ayden took a deep breath in. He flashed an unsettled gaze at his brother before bringing his eyes back to mine.

"The man died from his injuries three days later."

Chapter Three

Tori and Mason stood up, glancing at both of us. Probably worried red horns were about to grow out the top of my head. But I only saved those for special occasions and usually not for people I cared about.

"We'll let you have some privacy," Mason replied.

I shook my head. "Nah. We'll go outside. A walk along the trail will let me digest the news better. It's not fair to chase you two out of your own home."

They nodded and smiled nervously as they walked to the family room that overlooked the Sound. I sat at the table in a fog, wondering how and why Ayden didn't tell me something that was this important.

Ayden draped his arm over my shoulders and brought me in close. He brushed a kiss along the top of my head and whispered an apology, but I wasn't sure for what in particular.

I let out a sigh and patted his knee. "Let's go for a walk."

He agreed and slowly got up from the chair as if he was afraid I might pounce on him. My expression must have been conveying how I felt quite accurately. Ayden's hand linked with mine, and we walked out of the house, not saying a word until we reached the path that led down to Forgotten Cove.

It was a peaceful place to think and talk, but as we wandered down the trail, words didn't even come to mind. I was in shock that Ayden would keep something like this from me, and it was almost like I didn't actually care what his excuse was. The secret of it hurt more than anything.

We walked past the garden where Mason and Tori were working when I arrived. Most of the flowers had been cut down to the ground with only a few woody stocks sticking out of the ground that Mason missed while trimming.

"I'm sorry I didn't tell you," Ayden said softly.

I nodded and continued trudging down the rocky trail. His arm snaked around my waist, and the cool breeze nipped at my cheeks. I imagined a carefree weekend with Ayden, one where we could regroup before his fight, and before we flew to Bermuda to get married on the beach. Now, I was dealt a blow that made every inch of me hurt with worry.

The earlier haze of the skyline had lifted as I stared over the glistening water. Ayden's steady breathing calmed me as the cove welcomed us to a quieter place, away from it all. The water lapped against the shore as Ayden and I stood waiting for the other to begin. We were both stubborn, but we weren't stupid. We knew anything we said could help or hurt the situation. I didn't want to accuse him and he didn't want to be accused. So silence hovered thick between us until I couldn't take it any longer.

"I've never been someone who needed to be protected from the truth," I said, looking into Ayden's blue eyes.

He pushed his lips together as he thought about what to say, his expression softening.

"No, you never have," he agreed. "That's what I love about you. You're strong, independent, beautiful."

"Keep it coming," I teased, kicking one of the beach pebbles away.

Humor was one of the many things I valued about our relationship. No matter what we faced as a couple, there was always a way to bring levity to the situation. After all, life was too short to get tangled in the weeds.

Ayden's mouth broke into a smile and he shook his head. "Funny, brilliant..."

"What a catch I am."

"You have no idea," Ayden said, resting both his hands on my hips. "There isn't anything I can say that will change the fact I didn't tell you. And I'm sorry."

I nodded.

"But, honestly, I'm new at this whole thing."

His mouth puckered, and he blew out a gust of air.

"What whole thing?"

His gaze fell to my stomach.

"You don't have to treat me differently because I'm pregnant." I almost laughed, but I saw the tender look in his eyes, and my heart actually broke slightly.

"I love you so much, Lily. The thought of anything happening to you or..." He shook his head and combed his hand through his hair. "I read that stress is really hard on pregnancies. I didn't want to do anything to jeopardize you or the baby. I wish I hadn't signed up for this fight."

I let his words sink in. It was true. It wasn't only about me any longer. There were two of us along for this ride, but my personality wasn't one to sit back and watch life go by.

"I think that's very sweet of you, but the stress of you keeping secrets from me is far worse than any truth you could hand me. I don't do well with secrets, big or small."

Ayden tilted his head as his eyes focused on mine.

"I know what kind of fighter you are. I know you will win. You always do." And I felt that, truly felt that. He trained like a beast. He was in top physical form, and he understood the strategy behind the fight, the psychology of it. Yet fear traced each thought of him stepping into the ring. It always did before the fights, but this felt different. There was something at the pit of my stomach making every worry amplified.

"I will. I wouldn't step in the ring if I thought differently."

I nodded. "Hearing you'd keep something like this from me makes my mind race with what else you could be hiding. I thought no matter what, we'd tell each other everything. I thought that was what we had that a lot of others didn't."

"It is and it always will be. This is the only thing I've ever kept quiet about. I hated not telling you about this. Keeping it from you ate me alive. It really did."

"Well, that at least makes me feel somewhat better." I gave him a wry grin. "I like the thought of you suffering as you held this secret tight."

"I might as well tell you everything."

"Wait. There's more?" I asked, swallowing my surprise.

He nodded. "Not like what you're thinking, but yeah. There's more."

The breeze picked up, and I glanced toward the woods behind Ayden. Now what?

"You know the product Jason and Aaron originally created and sold to Aaron's father?" Ayden asked.

My brows furrowed in confusion. What did a security system have to do with Ayden fighting?

"Yeah, what about it?"

"I was talking to Jason about the fight, and he was asking me about my strategy."

"Okay..."

"The security software they developed included motion sensors that monitored and predicted movement."

"How can they predict movement?"

"It's not always a hundred percent accurate, but they developed a method that uses algorithms as precursors. Apparently that was one of the many things that set their product apart. It was especially useful to predict a thief's movements so when the silent alarms are going off, the police can track where they might go next in a building and meet them there."

"Wow. I had no idea, but what does that have to do with fighting?"

"All of our fights are recorded. I tracked down hours of footage of my opponent, and Jason was able to create a simulation of sorts. Using the data, he was able to show me what to expect if I were to say land an uppercut or move to the left to avoid a punch. Of course, it's not a hundred percent. No one can predict human nature, but it's a tool I'm happy to keep in my arsenal."

"So that's what you've been studying at night on the laptop?"

He nodded.

"Wow. I'm impressed, a little relieved and a little annoyed but mostly impressed." I briefly glanced over the water and brought my eyes back to his. "So you're feeling confident that you'll be able to judge his moves as they come."

"I was confident about that before the software." Ayden flashed a dazzling smile, and I couldn't help but laugh.

"You're lucky that you're so attractive." I narrowed my eyes at him.

"Is that so?" he asked, taking a step closer.

"Very so. Or you wouldn't be able to get away with so much."

"I thought it was my personality that provided me the much needed wiggle room. I had no idea the mother of my child was so shallow," he teased.

"Oh, you knew what you were getting into with me."

"Possibly. I have seen things that others haven't."

I smiled. "Who knew the one you'd end up with was the same one you had to shovel off the floor when she drank too much with your sister..."

"That was in college and not your fault."

"We might be able to get away with saying that if it only happened once, but you saved me several times."

"At least we'll have some good stories to tell our kid..."

"Yeah, right," I released a petrified yelp. "There is no way any college stories are coming from those lips of yours, especially if they're about me."

"But think how responsible I'll sound?" Ayden beamed.

"Really? What were you and Mason doing hanging around those college parties? If I remember, you're a few years older than me."

"Well... I mean that's just irrelevant."

"That's a big word."

His hands moved around my waist and up my back, pulling me into him.

"Is all forgiven?" he whispered.

"As long as you win." My mouth curled up slightly as his gaze fell to my lips.

"Never lost one yet, baby," he murmured, and it felt like the very first time he kissed me as his mouth crashed down to mine.

The feelings of need rushed through me as his mouth searched for forgiveness, and my world spun into the complicated web of Ayden Rhodes. The danger of what he was about to face created an odd sensation that made me ache with uncertainty and desire. As if sensing my longing, Ayden's kisses intensified, and I stood on my toes as if every inch closer would solidify that everything was going to be okay. A shiver ran through me, his lips slowly releasing from mine, and I opened my eyes gradually, not wanting to let go of this moment. Being on the rocky beach with Ayden made me feel safe and far away from the troubles of the world, but it didn't let me forget about the man who died by the hands of his opponent.

I truly believed Ayden would win the match.

I wanted to believe it with all my heart.

I had to believe it.

Ayden wrenched his gaze from mine and my stomach fell. Had he caught my trace of doubt? I would never forgive myself had he detected even a flicker of reservation.

"I won't let you down," he whispered, tracing his finger along my jaw. "I won't let either of you down."

And without warning a lump formed in the

back of my throat. Hearing those words come from Ayden's lips hurt my heart. I wanted nothing more than for him to walk away from the fight.

"You would never let me down. Ever. Never. Ever. It's impossible. You mean everything to me, Ayden. Everything."

He nodded.

I knew if I asked him if there was a way out, he'd take that as me doubting his abilities, and I couldn't have him thinking I held even the slightest hesitation. But with every fiber in my being, I wanted him to walk away. I wanted him to lose the money, give up the money, throw it away. It didn't matter to me. But that was the problem. The money didn't matter to Ayden either. The money wasn't what drove him, which was why I knew he would be stepping in that ring no matter what. It was for the satisfaction of the win. It wasn't about ego with Ayden. It never had been. It was about competence and being the best. He applied that way of thinking to his business and his personal life.

I had no doubt he would be the best husband and best father humanly possible. It was his drive to be better and do better that made him the man he was—the man I fell in love with—and I certainly wasn't going to ask him to change. I fell in love with all the parts of Ayden Rhodes, and we were in this together, all three of us. One way or another, we would get through this fight, and then we'd focus on our future together.

Chapter Four

I walked by the gym in our house and peeked into the large space where Ayden had been for the last hour. It never got old seeing him work out the way he did, his body glistening as he jumped rope, music cranked and pure determination running through his eyes. It was beyond sexy, and it explained how we were now planning for three. He was addicting—every square inch of him—and he brought out a side in me that threw caution to the wind.

Needless to say, throwing caution to the wind only took one gym session, a sinus infection, and two rounds of antibiotics to create the perfect storm known as baby Rhodes. Thinking back on the shock of it all made me chuckle. I'll never forget the look in his eyes when we watched the stick change our lives forever.

Fear.

Excitement.

And pure bliss.

Was it unexpected? Absolutely. But it felt right. Everything about being with Ayden felt right. My career was excelling. I enjoyed what I did during the day and I enjoyed who I did at night. Corny to say? Yeah. But I'd been around the Rhodes men far too long not to allow some of their humor to seep into my blood. It was inevitable. His jokes I used to roll my eyes at in college, were now highlights of my day.

"Love ya," I called into the gym as I passed by.

"You too, babe," he yelled back, wiping the sweat from his brow.

Ever since the weekend at Mason and Tori's, I'd been concentrating on the positives. It would be his last fight. He was undefeated. He had an entire software program on his side. He would win. He always won. He had a great trainer. And he had more to lose than his opponent.

The last thought nearly took my breath away.

He had more to lose than his opponent.

But *what if* he didn't win? My hand unexpectedly caressed my stomach as I walked down the stairs and into the kitchen. I got a glass of water and took a few swallows to calm my nerves. We would get through this. I glanced at the clock, noticing Gabby and Brandy were late. Trying to get my mind off the fight, I trundled over to the crockpot and lifted the lid. The pot roast smelled delicious, and by the looks of it, we'd have plenty for leftovers, which was good because in spite of everything I'd read about not eating for two, I swore I could now eat for ten. I placed the lid back on the pot and leaned against the counter, debating whether or not to tell Brandy and Gabby. Or maybe they already knew about Ayden's opponent. If Jason developed the program, there was a high chance Gabby knew why.

So much for not thinking about the fight.

I turned on the television and watched the news with depressing event after event flash across the screen. This wasn't helping me to get over the fight. I clicked on the channels determined to stay far away from news today. Landing on a DIY show, I placed the remote down right when the doorbell rang.

I'd been looking forward to seeing Gabby and Brandy all day. Ayden and I weren't planning to tell anyone other than Tori and Mason about our pregnancy until the wedding rehearsal dinner, but I was pretty sure they already knew.

Yeah, they knew.

I yanked on the front door and was surprised to see Ayden's trainer staring back at me instead of Brandy and Gabby.

"Hey," Derek said, giving a slight wave and tweaking his duffel bag.

"Come on in." I motioned him in and took a step away from the door. Derek was very tall and imposing to most, but inside he was a big teddy bear. I'd gotten to know him over the last several months and often enjoyed his company at the dinner table. He was in his mid-forties, divorced, and his dating stories always made for a fun night. Not that we got enjoyment from others' pain but his stories were pretty hilarious.

"He's upstairs. Staying for dinner?" I asked.

"Not tonight. I've got a date." He let out a sigh and sheepishly grinned. "I don't know why I keep trying."

"What? What aren't you telling me?" I pried.

"Nothing." He closed the door behind us.

I folded my arms and furrowed my brows. He was hiding something.

"Is it serious?" I asked. "Have you found someone?"

Derek's laughter boomed through the air and he shook his head. "Not at all. Alright. I'll tell you, but you can't judge."

"Why would I judge? I don't judge. No way sir-ee."

"It's my first match."

"Match? You met her while boxing?"

Derek focused mostly on training others, but every once in a while, he was known to step back in the ring.

His jaw tensed and he glanced around the room.

"No. My first online match." His voice was almost a whisper.

I clapped my hands together. "Oh. My. Gosh. I'm so excited for you. Those services are supposed to do wonders."

"We'll see about that. I might have another great story to add to the dinner conversation next week." He grinned.

"Way to stay positive," Ayden's voice came

down the stairs. He glided into the entry and fist pumped Derek.

"Exactly," I agreed. "You've got to stay positive or there's no point in showing up. If I was your date and felt like you didn't want to be there..."

Derek threw his hands into the air. "I get it. I get it. Enough about me. It's you I'm here for." He pointed his finger at Ayden."

"I'm all warmed up," Ayden told him.

"Yep. He's been in the gym for over an hour," I confirmed.

Derek nodded and dropped his bag onto the ground, fishing out some belt weights. "Let's get outside before it starts to rain."

Ayden gave me a quick kiss on the cheek.

"Whatever you say." Ayden opened the door and there stood Brandy and Gabby. They were grinning from ear to ear and looked suspiciously inside as they eyed Ayden, who was still shirtless.

"Did we interrupt something? We can come back later." Gabby started giggling.

"Very funny," I hollered over Ayden's shoulder. "He's training. Derek just got here and they're headed outside."

"Sure he was," Brandy yielded a wry laugh.

Gabby and Brandy came inside and set their purses on the entry table. I noticed Brandy's slight limp had returned. She hadn't mentioned anything about her leg recently, but obviously that didn't mean anything.

"Like my decorations?" I asked, shoving the thought aside. I knew Brandy hated when we brought up anything to do with her accident, and I tried my best to respect her wishes.

This morning I had decorated the entry table with mini pumpkins and dried leaves. I was quite impressed with myself, considering I'd never really been the crafty type of person.

"It looks lovely," Gabby said, taking her purse back off the table. Brandy did the same.

"You didn't even notice, did you?" I narrowed my eyes and they both exchanged looks.

"It looks amazing," Gabby said again.

"And that's my cue to exit." Ayden gave me a wave and a quick hug to his sister, Brandy, before walking outside with Derek.

"It really does look neat," Brandy seconded.

"But?"

"But nothing. It looks amazing." Gabby reached over and squeezed my hand.

Brandy bit her lip and looked at the table. "I think that would be the perfect arrangement for an end table or somewhere a little smaller. It kind of gets lost on this huge table."

I glanced at the long foyer table that stretched the length of the wall and she had a point. The distressed wood table was probably five feet long and my arrangement, maybe, took up six inches of the table.

"I don't think she needs something that takes up the whole table," Gabby countered.

"I didn't say that, but I didn't even see it until she asked about it—"

"And size isn't everything," Gabby interrupted, and then turned bright red as she realized how that could be misinterpreted. "Okay, size is important sometimes."

I started laughing, realizing that these two had already become like sisters, arguing and all, and Brandy hadn't even officially walked down the aisle with Aaron yet.

"Alright. I've got the perfect addition," I said, remembering an embroidered table runner Brandy and Ayden's mom had given me. I walked into the dining room and opened the drawer of the hutch.

"What about this?" I asked, removing the burnt-orange table runner with embroidered pumpkins and leaves.

"That is perfect," Gabby agreed.

"I thought you said it already was perfect," Brandy laughed and Gabby rolled her eyes.

I walked it over to the table, and we all worked on the display, placing my arrangement back in the center as the final touch.

"That does look better," I announced.

"Yep. Now it says, don't put your purse here." Brandy smiled. "But back to the important stuff. What smells so delicious?"

"Pot roast. I'm making pot roast."

"I'm so impressed," Gabby said, following Brandy and me into the family room. "Our Lily is cooking *and* decorating."

"It's almost like she's nesting." Brandy's brow arched, and I smiled, not taking the bait. I knew her brother hadn't told her, and I was eighty percent certain Mason hadn't mentioned it either.

"I'm not a bird."

"No, you're not and don't let anyone tell you otherwise," Gabby assured me, and I chuckled. These two were exactly what I needed to relax. I'd been wound so tightly since the weekend I needed some comic relief.

"Seriously, though, are you doing okay? I feel like there's something beyond the obvious you're not telling us." Brandy took a seat on the couch, and Gabby sat in a wooden rocker near the fireplace. Ayden and I'd just bought it at an antique store in town. We both thought it would be perfect for when the baby came.

"You do seem nervous about something." Gabby nodded. "Is it the fight?"

I sat down on the couch next to Brandy and rested my head on the back cushion.

"Yeah." I looked at Gabby. "Has Jason told you anything about it?"

Gabby shook her head. "Nothing more than the usual."

"I wouldn't be mad if he did…"

Gabby's brows furrowed in confusion as she slowly rocked in the chair, and I realized she actually didn't know. Jason hadn't told her the details.

I let out a sigh and turned my head back and forth. "Turns out Ayden's last fight is against someone who is also undefeated in the circuit he fights in."

"He's gone against other undefeated fighters," Brandy said, resting her hand on my knee in reassurance. She wasn't thrilled about her brother fighting either.

If only that was where it ended.

"True." I sucked my lip in and blew out air, trying to keep the worry at bay.

"So that's not all of it, is it?" Brandy prodded.

"Ayden is about to step into the ring against a fighter who killed his last opponent."

Brandy and Gabby gasped before their expressions turned to horror. Gabby's gaze fell to my belly and she shook her head. "Why is he still doing it?"

"He's gotta bail. You've got to make him throw in the towel," Brandy almost whispered. "If our parents found out..."

I shook my head. "I could never ask him to do that."

"It's not a question about what you want. It's about safety and Ayden's life. This is ridiculous." Gabby stopped rocking. "Why in the world would he do this when you guys are..." She didn't continue.

"Is it the money?" Brandy asked, but she knew her brother better than anyone. It had nothing to do with money.

"Not at all. Granted, he'd lose a lot... More than any other fight they'd promoted and managed, but that's not it. His company's sales are skyrocketing, and besides the money he's already put away, I wouldn't be a bit surprised if one of the big companies didn't try to buy him out soon. So no. If it was about money, it would be easy to get him to stop. With Ayden it's all about pride and proving to himself he's the best."

"But he's already proven that time and again." Brandy looked unnerved, exactly how I felt. "I can't believe he'd do this to you. To me. To our parents."

I let out a deep breath and looked around the room. The usually cozy place felt completely chilling as the thought of Ayden losing forced its way into my mind. I'd been keeping positive, but when I saw the fear I was feeling reflected on my best friends' faces, it forced me to deal with the alternative. What if Ayden was never here to enjoy this room, this house, with me again? No. That wasn't how it worked. Ayden won every match he'd ever entered.

"I'm not trying to cause a problem between you two," Brandy began. "But it only takes one second for a person's life to be changed forever. I know firsthand..." She chewed on her cheek for a few seconds before continuing. "There isn't a day I don't wake up with pain. And there are some days that I want nothing more than to crawl under the covers and sleep my aches away. But I wouldn't do anything different. I thank the heavens above I'm here to be with my friends and family, no matter how much it hurts. But I can't understand throwing yourself in front of a speeding train. I don't understand my brother's line of reasoning. Maybe I shouldn't have been so private about my suffering. I've never wanted to burden him or Mason. It's bad enough Aaron has to listen to me."

My gaze connected with Brandy's and my heart ached for her. I didn't know she was in pain every day. If I could personally meet the man who did that to her, I didn't even know what I would do to him. And I also understood what she was saying about Ayden's desire to step into the ring.

"Aaron loves you so much, Brandy. We all do and you're never a burden. We all want to be here for you. And I do think you should tell your brothers about how you're doing."

"It's not about me right now." Brandy shook her hands. "It's about my brother who's being absolutely pig-headed. Life isn't only about him any longer."

"What if this isn't his last fight?" Gabby asked.

"He promised it would be," I said softly.

"Sometimes promises change," Gabby replied. "Would you allow him to fight after this one?"

"It's not a question of me allowing him to do anything. That's not how our relationship works. I'd be horrified if he told me I could or couldn't do something."

Brandy smiled and nodded. "It's true, Gabby, she'd have a complete tantrum and I've seen it firsthand with Ayden growing up. They're two peas in a pod."

"I suppose." Gabby eyed me and then turned her attention to outside where Ayden and Derek were training. For someone who hadn't seen it before it might look somewhat strange.

"Why in the world is Ayden twirling around by that tree?" Gabby questioned.

Brandy craned her neck to get a better view.

"Oh my word. He really is twirling. He just

needs a tutu." Brandy smiled wickedly. "If only I had my phone."

"The exercise is for balance. If he gets knocked around, he still needs to be able to throw a punch at his opponent. No matter how dizzy he gets, he needs to be able to focus. Keep watching and you'll see."

I kept my eyes steadied on Ayden. Derek grabbed Ayden's shoulders, stopping him in place, and held up a target, waiting for Ayden to throw a punch. Within seconds, Ayden's knuckles landed directly in the middle of the target, pushing Derek backward and my body filled with relief. He was going to win this fight.

"I had no idea there was such an exercise," Brandy said.

Ayden's smile was filled with accomplishment, and I knew I wasn't going to be the one to ask him to wave the flag of surrender. Derek handed him two huge ball weights, and I watched him grip them tightly and curl his arms up.

"What's he doing now?" Gabby asked.

"He's holding his arms up by his face to strengthen them so they don't get fatigued during the fight when he's blocking punches. Arm fatigue is a huge thing in fighting so they're always working on ways to keep his endurance up." A couple minutes of silence passed as we watched Ayden's expression intensify as the burn radiated down his arms and shoulders, but behind his stare sat fortitude and grit.

"You're right. There's no way of talking him

out of it," Brandy said quietly. She turned on the couch and her eyes fastened on mine. "As your almost sister and someone who loves you and my brother very much, I have to ask this. I want you to be protected no matter what."

My heart hammered inside my chest as her gaze studied mine. There was a coldness resting behind her eyes, and I understood completely what she was about to ask, and it took everything I had not to burst into tears as she and I faced the facts about what her brother— my fiancé—was about to do in less than a week.

"Has he prepared his will? If not, I can help you both with getting everything in order if he hasn't done that recently. You need to be protected."

Chapter Five

"That's how Brandy is. Straight to the point and practical. Always very practical," Gabby assured me.

"I know, and I've always appreciated that about her. But hearing her talk about Ayden's affairs so matter-of-factly was startling. It made this all seem too real."

We were sitting on a bench in the middle of Discovery Park in Seattle, overlooking Puget Sound. The late afternoon weather teetered between chilly and refreshing as the meadow grass trembled in the wind, and the red and gold leaves clutched the limbs of the maples that dotted the trail alongside of us. We were two days away from the fight, and every hour ticked by at an excruciatingly slow pace. To pass the time, I hitched a ride with Gabby to the park. She had a wedding cake to drop off near here, and

Ayden planned on swinging by later to pick me up. I'd gotten all my work done at the office in record time this morning and needed a mental break. It was hard to focus on anything other than Ayden stepping into the ring.

"It's too real. That's the problem. I understand where you're coming from, and why you don't want to tell him not to fight, but sometimes we know better."

I let out an ironic yap and shook my head. "Not in Ayden's world."

"Not in Jason's immediate world either, but with some gently nudging, it can be done." Gabby smiled and took a sip of her latte. That was the one thing I missed about being pregnant, not the wine, the coffee. "I know Jason is so used to everyone always doing what he wants. In business, what he says goes. Always has and always will. Sometimes that doesn't translate well at home though." She furrowed her brows.

"I can't imagine why not," I chuckled. "It's the same with Ayden. He's got that business running so smoothly, and the staff respects him for it. But it's kind of funny, he sneezes and someone runs to find him a tissue. I can guarantee it's not like that at the house."

Gabby nodded in agreement. She understood exactly what I was talking about.

A few minutes of silence passed as we watched people walk along the trail toward the beach.

"I understand where you're coming from, but I believe in Ayden. I know he'll take the guy down.

I've got to put it out of my mind and focus on all the amazing things ahead of us." I let out a sigh, hoping if I voiced the positive outcome one would manifest itself.

"Only you know what you're comfortable with. I guess it's like me riding my bike. It doesn't matter how many people want me to stop riding because motorcycles are *dangerous*. But I love it and I won't stop riding."

"So you understand my dilemma." I shook my head, flashing a wry grin. I was one of the many who always hoped she'd give it up.

"Perfectly. Now tell me about this wedding. I'm literally counting down the days, minutes, and seconds to get myself on that tiny island known as Bermuda. The pictures look amazing, and I can tell you after all my wedding planning with Carla, I need the vacation."

My body instantly relaxed the moment Bermuda settled into my mind. I'd sent over the final menu to our coordinator and had shipped boxes of decorations and gift bags to the hotel this morning. So far everything was coming together for this destination wedding...if we could just get there.

"The ceremony is going to be on the beach, barring any hurricanes."

"Hurricanes?" Gabby's brow arched.

"Well, technically hurricane season lasts through November, but they're really unlikely to hit when we're there." I grinned.

Even with everything Gabby had been through in her life, there were still some topics that made her uneasy. Natural disasters were high on that list. It didn't matter what the statistics said, she focused on the what-if scenario. I wasn't sure it was healthy.

"Why oh why did I ask about the wedding?" she teased. "And let me remind you how our luck usually goes."

I chuckled and took a sip from my water bottle.

"I looked up the weather on the extended forecast for when we're supposed to arrive, and there isn't even a hint of rain in the forecast," I assured her.

Gabby wrapped her arm around my shoulders and squeezed. "Now what in the world makes you think the weatherman who can't predict tomorrow's forecast can predict weeks in advance."

"Valid point, I'll admit, but I happen to know there will be no hurricanes during our wedding or vacation. There just won't!"

"Whatever you say," Gabby yammered.

"So like I said, our ceremony will be on the beach, and the reception will be at a small restaurant near the water that we'll be taking over for the night. The pictures look amazing. The building is open to the outside and the deck sits on the sand, overlooking the ocean. Perfect for storm watching."

"Hardee-har-har." Gabby rolled her eyes and freed her arm from my shoulders. "Well, one thing I already love is our bridesmaid dresses. I think you picked out the very first amazing bridesmaid dresses in the history of bridesmaid fashion. And for that, I'm forever grateful."

"What's that saying about yours?" My brow rose. "You picked yours out months ago."

Gabby's grin turned evil. "I'm one of those brides who doesn't wish to be upstaged by my best friends, and there are only so many options to make sure that doesn't happen. Simple as that."

"Is that what happened with those dresses?" I teased. I playfully smacked her shoulder and she shrugged. "That's evil. Pure evil."

"Not evil, strategic."

"The evil genius strikes again," I said, ignoring her. "Well, I think Brandy and I will look stunning in our emerald green dresses," I told her. "So your strategy might have backfired."

"I can assure you that you two won't look as stunning as Brandy and I will in the ivory maxi dresses we get to wear in Bermuda. Come on. I mean we even get to wear flip-flops? We scored and I can't thank you enough."

"It's not too late for me to change what you'll be wearing." I narrowed my eyes at her. "Maybe I'll make it so you have to wear a giant conch shell on your head or something."

"You wouldn't."

"Oh, but I would. Just keep talking. Besides, Brandy and I were discussing how we always wanted to dress up as a living Christmas tree and now's our chance. So thank you for that."

Gabby's laughter echoed through the air, and for a brief moment, I felt at complete peace. My only hope was that it would last until after Ayden's match.

"At least I'm not asking you to wear tinsel in your hair." She grinned.

"Was that an option?"

"I'll never tell."

I shook my head and let out a sigh. "This was what I needed today."

"Glad I could be of service. You know, Katie is so excited about being the flower girl in your wedding. She's been practicing nonstop."

Hearing that made my heart melt. We all adored Katie, and she was the best little girl to have ever graced the planet. I was sure of it. Something told me that I needed to embrace the calmness of Katie because I wasn't sure that's what we'd have in store for us. Between Ayden's taste for danger and my fiery temper, I couldn't even begin to imagine the ride we were in for.

"Well, are you making Katie dress up like a polar bear for your wedding or how about an elf? I'm sure she'd look cute in red and white striped stockings."

"For your information, Katie's flower girl dress is beautiful. It's white tulle layered over ivory lace and there are tiny satin red roses at the hem."

"Can we get matching dresses?" I begged, clasping my hands together. "Hers sounds way better than ours."

"Seriously?"

"Heck yeah, I'm serious."

My phone buzzed, and I looked down to see a

text from Ayden. He was in the parking lot.

"Time for dinner. Ayden's here."

Gabby's brows furrowed. "Have you guys started hitting up the early-bird specials or something?"

"No. Thank you very much. We're headed to a happy hour by our house."

"Huh?"

"It's all-you-can-eat wings, and their potato skins are like $2.99." I stood up gathering my coat and purse. The reds and oranges of the vanishing sun highlighted the skyline. It would be dark in less than an hour, and by then, hopefully we'd be snuggled into a booth snacking on appetizers.

"Well, good. I'm glad to see you're eating healthy for your—"

"For my what?" I asked, unable to hide my grin.

We all knew. But I really didn't want to relinquish my telling of it until the day before our wedding. I'd already packed the little announcements and shipped them to Bermuda with everything else.

"Nothing." Gabby flashed a knowing smile and gave me a hug. "Absolutely nothing. Enjoy your chicken wings and potato skins."

"I will, and you know, I very well might try to eat my way out of having to wear that green dress."

Ayden was walking through the park, and he gave a quick wave when he spotted us roaming toward him.

"Lily said you're off to hit the early-bird specials."

A smirk fell across Ayden's lips, and he shook his head, giving me a big hug. I melted in his embrace and felt him lift me off the ground slightly, my feet dangling a few inches above the grass. I wondered how much longer he'd be able to do that.

Ayden placed me back down and slid his hand into mine. "It's happy hour."

"Sure. Tell yourselves that. I think you're just one step away from blue poodles and pink Lincoln Town cars."

"You're making it easier and easier to change your bridesmaid dresses," I teased, as we all walked to the parking lot. "You wait and see."

"I dare you," Gabby sneered. She stood next to her car and smiled.

Gabby looked so at ease and happy. I loved seeing how well she'd settled into her life with Jason and Katie. It made me long for that same sense of contentment.

Ignoring Gabby's last jab, I climbed into our car and Ayden shut the door. I heard him tease Gabby a little more, and then he waited until she got into her car before he climbed into ours.

"Did you have a nice time?" Ayden asked, turning on the ignition.

"It was great. I didn't know how much I needed to get away from the office."

Ayden pressed his lips together and nodded. He pulled the car onto the main street that would eventually lead us to the chicken wings. I hadn't realized how hungry I'd gotten until the thought of food getting closer popped into my mind.

"You've been working like you're on speed since the weekend," Ayden said. He put his hand on my knee, and I immediately covered it with mine, holding it tightly. It was like I wanted to capture every little touch and glance from Ayden and that worried me. It made me feel like my subconscious knew something more than I did about the upcoming event.

"I think it's all the nervousness. I can't sit still, and once I'm at the office, I dive in so I don't have to think about the fight."

"I never meant to do this to you," Ayden said softly. "I wish my brother hadn't brought it up."

"Wrong answer, buddy. If I found out after the fact, there would've been hell to pay." I eyed him and wondered if he meant it. If he had that would send us backward in this whole conversation from the weekend, not forward. "I thought we established the whole *not keeping* things from one another pact at Mason's."

He nodded. "We definitely did. I don't know. I guess I hoped things would turn out differently. I wanted to tell you on my own terms."

The anguish in his voice worried me. I didn't want him to be focused on us or fret over anything that would distract him from the main goal in front of us, which was to win the fight and get us to our wedding.

"Truthfully, my suspicion is that your own terms would've included waiting until after you stepped out of the ring declaring victory. Then you'd smother me with kisses to distract me and it'd all blow over," I blabbed.

He threw me a sideways glance, and he shrugged his shoulders. "Maybe you know me better than I realize."

"I hope so since we'll be stuck with one another for the next ninety years."

"Ninety? That's a lot. Are you sure about ninety?" he teased.

"I don't think I like the alternative so ninety it is," I countered.

"True. There's nothing wrong with being a hundred and twenty. I'm sure there's plenty of activities we can do to keep us young at heart."

"Like get out of the bed every morning?"

"Not quite what I was thinking, but yeah. I guess at a hundred and twenty, getting out of bed is a good goal."

"Probably one of the most important ones of the day."

Ayden smiled and squeezed my knee.

"Listen, don't think about it for one more second. You're going to do what you always do when you step into the ring, and I'll be there rooting for you every step of the way. We all will. And before you know it, one of us will be sipping cocktails while hanging out on a beautiful beach. Sand between the toes, warmth cascading over our skin, and amazing food morning, noon, and night."

My stomach growled again and Ayden chuckled. "I'm going as fast as I can. I promise, I'll feed you soon."

I nestled into the seat and grinned.

"Can you believe we'll be married by Thanksgiving?" I asked.

He shook his head. "Hey, did you know we are going to Bermuda during hurricane season?"

"Argh. Why does everyone keep bringing that up?" I rested my head on the seat. "It's very unlikely that a hurricane will happen during our wedding."

"It was also very unlikely that you'd get pregnant while on antibiotics." His smile widened and I couldn't help but laugh.

A truer statement could not have been said.

Chapter Six

Brandy figured out I hadn't asked Ayden about his estate planning so she took it upon herself to talk to him about it that night after he came in from training with Derek. It was good they were such close siblings. A conversation like that would never happen in my family without wild accusations. Come to find out, Ayden had already been in touch with his attorneys, and things had been updated over the last few weeks.

Hearing the news did nothing to settle my worries. Instead, it made me realize Ayden, too, had doubts and concerns he hadn't shared with me about the outcome of the fight. I actually wished I hadn't heard that he'd updated his affairs. Granted, it was the responsible thing to do, but it painted an alternative ending I refused to think about.

And here it was the night before he was about

to step into the ring, and I was deliberating whether I even wanted to go to the match. I was almost sick to my stomach with fear and apprehension.

"I promise you this time tomorrow, we'll be home in front of the fire, watching a movie. Me stepping into the ring will be a thing of the past, and we'll never have to—" Ayden began.

I shook my head and placed my fingers on his lips. "Enough talk about the fight. I've spent too much time over the last week focusing on it. I want us to have a nice, normal night without some epic battle going on in my mind about you fighting that monster."

We were sitting in the family room, and he'd just shut his laptop down and sat next to me on the chaise. My guess was that he'd run a few more scenarios through Jason's program while he'd been sitting there glued to his laptop.

"You know, you're absolutely glowing," he interrupted my thoughts.

"I think it's a hot flash. I'm burning up from the fire and hormones," I confessed. "Not to mention this flannel nightshirt I've got on."

He laughed, shaking his head.

"Sorry. Not very romantic." I looked around the room. The light was low with only the table lamp beside me turned on so I could pretend to read the book I'd been holding all night. "I'll have to work on that."

"You don't have to be romantic to get me to fantasize about having sex with you." He grinned. "But let's get those PJs off. I don't want you to overheat."

"Yes, I'm sure that's what you're worried about," I teased.

His fingers gripped the hem, and he gently tugged it over my head and tossed it on the floor. His eyes fell to my chest and he grinned.

"What?" I grabbed a pillow and playfully swatted his head.

"The perks of this whole nine month process are pretty appealing." He flashed a wicked grin and moistened his lips.

I glanced down at my bra, which was overflowing, and I whistled.

"Guess it's time to go up a size."

"Or three," he murmured, lifting his gaze back to mine. "Lily, I know I promised I wouldn't bring up the fight, but I need you to know I'd never put myself or our future in jeopardy. I know I'll pummel him. I'd never do anything to put our dreams at risk. I promise you that. I promise you that more than anything. I see our future together and it's a happy one."

I nodded slowly as he touched my cheek softly, and the heat that had been washing through my system turned to chills. A wave of goose bumps ran across my flesh, and I suddenly wished I had my flannel nightshirt back on. His words were comforting, but they didn't erase the fact that tomorrow he'd be doing exactly what he said he wouldn't do. He was putting our future, our dreams, in jeopardy, and I couldn't fathom how he didn't see that.

I reached for a throw and wrapped it around

my shoulders, leaving enough of a glimpse so he didn't forget about the very future he was talking about.

"Do you still want to wait until our rehearsal to tell everyone?" he asked.

"I think so. It might be kind of fun to see everybody's reactions at once. And I sent the little favors I made that announce it. If we spill the beans sooner, it would lose something."

"Good point. It will be pretty special."

"It will," I agreed, but the emptiness inside of me was growing. Every second closer to tomorrow made me want to crawl under a rock and not come out until it was all over.

"I love you more than you'll ever know," Ayden said quietly.

Enough to not step into the ring? I wondered, but I pushed the thought away as quickly as it came and steadied my eyes on his.

"I love you too."

"Have I ever told you I fell in love with you the first time Brandy brought you around?" he asked.

"You've mentioned it a time or two..." I grinned.

Ayden traced his finger along my leg, and I felt the electricity run between us.

"Well, it's true. I knew one day I'd be with you. I didn't know how or when, but I was willing to wait."

Now was the time. If I was going to beg him to stay home tomorrow, now was the time. Now was the moment to confess that tomorrow scared me to death, and I wanted him to bow out.

Ayden's hunger-filled gaze locked on mine, and I took in a deep, shaky breath as he moved toward me. His hands slid along my sides, and he pulled me onto his lap in one quick, fluid motion. A quiet wall of hesitancy went up around me before his mouth collided with mine, and I knew I wouldn't be saying a word.

My arms wrapped around his neck, and my body pressed against his, feeling the need in him demand something from me.

Understanding.

And I gave it to him. I relinquished the panic that had knotted itself up inside as my fingers tangled through his hair. The coolness of his lips excited me as our kisses intensified, hungrily searching for approval and strength to get through the next twenty-four hours.

Being denied the comfort of knowing Ayden was going to come out okay thrust itself into a raw, almost painful, desire to be with him. My kisses deepened as his hands drifted along my skin, fueling my need for him. His lips broke free, but his gaze stayed on mine while he unfastened my bra and drew the straps down my arms. The heat running through his expression made my entire body warm with excitement. He threw the pink lace on the chaise and ran his fingers up my back, cradling the back of my head in his palm as his tongue slowly traced down my throat, sending staggering sensations of want through my body.

He greedily teased and taunted with his

tongue as he worked his way around my breasts, never stopping, demanding more of me as my body arched into his. Resting his fingers along my panties without his hands moving in the slightest bit was torturous.

"You're being cruel," I whispered, as he trailed his mouth back along my neck. I wiggled my hips deeper into him as I continued to straddle his lap.

"Is there something you want?" Ayden murmured, skimming his fingers across the lace.

"Yes," I said, my voice almost breathless as he edged his finger along the inside elastic of the lace.

"What do you want, Lily?" I knew he was watching my reaction, waiting for me to plead with him, but I was stronger than that. His fingers flitted across the lace, tormenting me more with every light stroke and playful touch, and I held in a gasp, tightening my thighs around his waist.

"Tell me what it is you want," he repeated, skating his lips across my chest.

I let out a slight moan and shook my head.

"You're impossible," he almost growled, as his hands quickly cupped my butt. He stood up with me, and I attempted to secure my legs around his waist. I slid my hand in between his jeans and waist, and his breath caught. To prove my point, I slowly trailed my fingers back the way they came and grinned.

"Two can play this game," I whispered. "But should we wait until after the fight?"

"Absolutely not. It's never been a problem before, baby."

He spun us around and placed me back on the chaise. This time kneeing my legs open as his fingers edged under my panties. Propping himself up, with one arm and stroking me with the other made my entire body feel as if I were hovering between fantasy and reality.

He fit his mouth over mine and kissed me in a way that told me he wanted to savor every second of now. My body tensed with the realization the only way to retreat from the pain and fear of tomorrow was to give myself fully to Ayden just as he was doing with me. I moaned into his mouth as our kisses slowed, but my blood remained wild with anticipation. His mouth broke away from mine, and he sat up, his eyes scanning my body.

"I love you more every single day," Ayden murmured.

"I love you more. Period."

"Impossible."

My pulse pounded madly as he pushed my legs wider and knelt between them, his fingers unbuttoning his jeans and sliding them off. He turned his attention back to me and slid his hands up my legs, bringing a wave of shivers with his touch. Ayden slowly worked my panties off and leaned back over me as our need grew for one another. Fueled by an unknown tomorrow, I felt him push inside of me, and I locked my legs around him as he thrust into me. His fingers stroking the warmth between us as our bodies rocked as one, and my world spun with ecstasy. I opened my eyes to see Ayden's jaw tense and his teeth grit as the pleasure we shared overcame us both, and the problems of our world slipped away for another day.

Chapter Seven

The paved parking lot was slick with rainwater from a passing summer shower. I surveyed the lot packed full of cars, and my pulse quickened. By the looks of everything, this was one of the biggest fights I'd been to, and that revelation didn't help my worries one bit. Ayden, Mason, and Derek had arrived several hours earlier, and I came with Brandy and Aaron. Jason and Gabby were going to meet us.

I climbed out of the car and stretched as I looked at the warehouse where the fight was about to take place. The fights were always held in a vacant building, generally in an industrial part of a city, and this location was no different. A chain-link fence circled the property and rusty "For Rent" signs barely clung to the metal building. Weeds sprouted alongside the fence, and the sidewalk leading to the front of the warehouse was cracked and barely holding together. A pile of old, rusty junk was heaped in the far corner of the land. I'd be thrilled to leave here quickly.

"Should we get going?" Brandy asked, looping her arm through mine. "I know I'd never be forgiven if I didn't get you inside to see Ayden before the fight."

I nodded and slowly walked toward the entrance as people trickled inside. I didn't want to hurry to tell him good luck because that would only bring the event quicker. As we got closer, the chatter became louder and their words clearer. I glanced nervously at Aaron as he held the door open for us. He gave a slight nod as we made our way over to another door where a security guard stood tall. I recognized him and felt slightly more at ease. He'd been at several of Ayden's fights. The moment we slid into the hallway, I turned around and looked at Aaron.

"Did you notice most of the people coming inside weren't speaking English?"

"I did," Aaron confirmed.

"It sounded like Russian."

"That would make sense considering who he's fighting," Aaron laughed.

"Captain Obvious strikes again." I nodded and climbed up the long flight of stairs, tamping down the fear that was threatening to boil over as I got closer to seeing Ayden.

Ayden's fights usually had a crowd siding with him or at least evenly divided between the fighters, but if the group in the parking lot and downstairs were any indication, this could be the first fight where the crowd was siding with Ayden's opponent. The nausea spun through my system when I reached the top of the steps and waited for Brandy and Aaron. I kept my eyes focused on the dingy wall to keep away the dizziness. I couldn't let Ayden see I was worried. I needed to get my emotions under control before I went inside.

Brandy was looking at her phone and glanced up at me. "Gabby and Jason just parked. They'll be up in a second."

My fingers wrapped around the cold metal handle, and I pushed open the door to see Ayden in the far corner of the room. Mason was peering through the window that overlooked the growing crowd below while Derek was giving Ayden some last minute pointers.

"You know, I think after you clobber this guy we're going to have to get you out of here as quickly as we can," Mason said, his thumb and forefinger squeezing his chin.

"Why's that?" Ayden asked, turning his gaze to Mason.

Derek started wrapping Ayden's hands, and I took that first step into the room, the one that fully committed me to this situation. Ayden turned his attention from his brother, and his eyes connected with mine. He smiled and my heart raced with nervous anticipation. I wanted this fight to be over.

Ayden walked away from Derek with one hand left to wrap and made his way over to me.

He had the familiar glint in his eyes he'd get right before a fight, which was blazing determination mixed with fierce agitation. He wanted in the ring as badly as I wanted him out of it.

"You look stunning," he rumbled so close to my ear only I could hear.

Ayden wrapped his arms around me, and I nestled my head against his chest, feeling the strength of his hold on me. How I prayed nothing would happen to him. I forced the thought away and whispered to Ayden.

"Stretch pants are always known to be sexy." I'd also put on one of his sweatshirts that fit more like a dress on me, but it was cold outside, and the sweatshirt had proven to be good luck at his other fights. "I figured I needed lots of room when we go out to eat later to celebrate your victory."

He nodded and released his arms from our hug, and I suddenly felt extremely alone in a room full of my best friends. I glanced around the space and saw the worried expressions on Gabby and Brandy, while I forced down the lump that was about to evolve into a full meltdown of tears and anger. Jason and Aaron were doing their best at keeping the conversation rolling over by the door so that Ayden wouldn't see their expressions, but I was certain Ayden felt something different in the air today. He knew he shouldn't be getting in the ring.

"Hey, we've only got about ten minutes," Derek called. "Let me get your other hand wrapped."

Ayden brushed a soft kiss along my lips, and I kept my eyes closed until he turned and walked toward Derek. If he'd looked in my eyes, he'd have seen the fear running rampant, and I couldn't do that to him.

Ayden strode toward Derek and stood directly in front of him, glancing down toward the ring, his expression hardened. I wondered what he saw, but instead I focused on the physical features of the man in front of me. His bare, broad shoulders exposed the sleekest of muscles as he held out his hand to be wrapped, and I continued to analyze Ayden as a machine, which was what he had turned himself into. His strong shoulders angled into his muscular back. Even the smallest of muscles were built into a powerful device. Ayden's slender waist was corded with strength along his sides, and his lean, hard abdomen provided the shield from his opponents' fists. He had constructed a finely-tuned instrument that was built for throwing punches and resisting impact from others' power. He was a modern day warrior. The logical side of my brain understood that fully, but my heart whispered another story.

Brandy's hand softly rubbed my back, and I jumped in place, startling us both.

"I know the feeling," Brandy whispered, and I rested my head on her shoulder. As his sister, she probably did understand more than most—the teetering between nightmare and reality that wouldn't end until he stepped out of the ring.

Derek tossed the tape in his bag and nodded.

"We're golden."

Ayden flashed a look at Mason, and I knew we were getting painfully close to the event. I lifted my head off of Brandy and let out a quiet sigh. Prior to finding out about Ayden's opponent, I was purely excited that this fight was possibly going to be his last. I actually dreamed about how we'd all be here, cheering him on. He'd win and then take a bow, and we'd all be off to a celebration dinner.

Now I tried to focus on him surviving, and I cursed myself for allowing my thoughts to venture there.

Derek smeared some Vaseline around Ayden's mouth and cheeks, and I walked over to the window and peered down into the crowd. Besides the obvious, there was something different in the air. The electricity from the crowd wasn't running in the right direction, and the realization scared me to death. I wondered if that was what Ayden noticed. I watched as people waved more cash in the air as they placed their final bets, and my heart plummeted. There was no way out.

I had to keep it together. I couldn't let Ayden see the fear in me, not even the slightest tremor.

Behind me, Jason and Aaron were giving Ayden some last minute advice, which had them all laughing, and I heard Brandy tell her brother she loved him, giving him a big hug.

"We'll meet you outside the door," Derek instructed, as he gathered the group and led them out of the room to give Ayden some privacy.

I didn't need to turn around to know Ayden was directly behind me. I was frozen in place and time. He slid his arms around my waist, resting them on my belly, and he nuzzled his chin into the crook of my neck, the whiskers tickling me as he hugged me tightly.

"Thank you for always being there for me," he whispered. "I don't think anyone else would be."

I rested my hands on his and took in a deep breath.

"I know it's what you love to do." My voice caught in my throat.

"It'll be over before you know it," he whispered.

"It will and you'll be the victor." I nodded my head as if for reassurance, feeling the tears well in my eyes.

He gave me a soft kiss on my neck and let out a deep breath. "It's time."

"I know." My eyes were focused on the crowd below. "Do you feel that?"

He rubbed my stomach and shook his head.

"Not that." The building was vibrating.

Within seconds more of the crowd began stomping their feet in unison as if they were demanding their fighters enter the ring. As the building shook, the feeling that spread over me felt visceral and daunting. This wasn't like any other fight. The steady beat got louder, and hands went into the air, stirring the restless air between the spectators. Chanting that had begun slowly became louder with each passing second.

A knock on the door, followed by Derek sticking in his head, told me it really was time. I turned to face Ayden, and he rested his forehead on mine.

"Get to him first," I whispered, and Ayden shook his head, swiping a kiss along my cheek before leaving the room.

I wanted to give him time to get down the stairs before I left. I needed to regroup. Seeing the unconcerned expressions on the men below made my worst nightmares seem like child's play. I heard the door click shut down the stairs and took in a deep breath.

Everything was going to be fine.

"Aaron's got our area reserved downstairs," Brandy said softly from behind. "Jason will walk us through the crowd."

I gave a slight nod and turned to see the same look of fear running through her gaze.

"We'll get through this, and then we'll both beat him up for putting us through this," Brandy vowed.

I half-laughed as Brandy clutched my hand and led me out of the room to where Jason and Gabby were waiting. There was nothing about this fight that was similar to any of the others we'd been to. Gabby wasn't chatty. Jason wasn't offering anecdotal humor. We were all silent as if we were about to head into the lion's den of things you wished you could change.

We walked down the stairs and pushed open the door to find the chanting almost deafening, and the thunderous stomps even louder than moments before as the spectators waited for the main attraction. We weren't even in the room where the tournament was being held and the noise was earsplitting. Jason opened the metal doors and a blast of warm air hit me. The room was so packed, it didn't matter that the building had no heat.

I scanned the crowd, seeing nothing but heads bobbing, hands waving, and rowdy patrons yelling for the match to begin. Jason began clearing the way through the aisle that had been closed in by gawkers. My heart hammered in my chest as Jason pushed a couple raucous individuals out of the way and led us to where Aaron was waiting. We were right next to the ring. I skimmed the room, hoping to get a glimpse of where Ayden or his opponent would be coming from, but the crowd was so dense it was impossible to tell.

It wasn't until a man climbed into the ring with a microphone that the audience fell silent. I scouted the room for the ring girls that were at every fight and saw none.

"Two undisputed champions going head to head, knuckle to knuckle. No gloves in this match, only taped hands. We've got Ayden Rhodes..."

The crowd burst into a round of boos and jeers, interrupting the announcer, and my heart fell to the ground. This had never happened. Ever. I glanced at Brandy whose eyes were locked on Aaron, hoping for some hint he couldn't give.

Aaron and Jason stared straight ahead, not making eye contact with any of us, which told me that something was definitely wrong.

The heckling stopped, and the announcer continued by introducing Viktor, Ayden's opponent, and the crowd immediately erupted into cheers. I glanced around us and saw the ravenous eyes of individuals waiting for nothing more than to claim their winnings.

Music exploded from the speakers as the MC extolled Viktor. I looked around the room until I saw a door open and a massive figure appeared across the room. He seemed to be a good head taller than most of the crowd. The spectators parted immediately as he made his way down the aisle toward the ring. The fighter's head was shaved, and his body looked like he'd stolen it from the *Jolly Green Giant* as he lumbered toward the square in front of us.

I saw brute force behind his shoulders, but I saw a lack of quickness. Ayden had both qualities. He was not only quick but, also, strong. I took in a deep breath, watching him climb between the ropes, and I prayed that his fist would never connect with Ayden. The electronic music continued blaring through the speakers as the MC announced Ayden's entrance. A loud mix of cheers and jeers could be heard around the room, and my chest tightened. It killed me to hear to the negativity, and I couldn't even imagine what it had done to Ayden. My hope was that he didn't hear them.

To my right, doors swung open, and Ayden

took a step into the room. His stare was focused. He looked intimidating and determined. Watching him stride down the aisle took my breath away. He was elegant, demanding, and controlled. He was a machine.

I watched him climb into the ring, and Brandy squeezed my shoulder and didn't let go as Derek and Mason started giving him instructions as the MC read the rules. My pulse quickened as Ayden's gaze connected briefly with mine before looking across the ring.

Before the beginning bell even chimed I saw Ayden's opponent charge at him, and I knew this was unlike any other fight I'd ever witnessed.

Chapter Eight

Ayden lunged from his stool in an instant, his fists in the air. He'd anticipated his opponent's preemptive attack as if he'd planned it himself. Dodging from Viktor's left hook, Ayden swung his fist into the abdomen of his opponent. The sound of his fist hitting his opponent's flesh was a welcome one.

The glint in Ayden's eyes was focused as he dodged an uppercut and threw a jab back at his opponent, knocking the man's chin to the left. Anger flashed through Viktor's eyes as he returned a fist into Ayden's stomach. The sweat sprayed onto the mat as the crowd went crazy with the contact, and my stomach knotted with every new swing.

I gasped as Ayden's opponent repeated his move and landed another punch into Ayden's side, more liquid spraying toward the crowd.

Ayden didn't even wince as the man's fist moved away. Ayden's feet shuffled around the ring waiting for his opponent to come to him.

My heart raced as I watched these two men maintain their distance, their control. The cheers from the crowd quickly turned to hungry cries for more blood, more sweat. Ayden's opponent drove a punch through the air, and I held my breath as I saw his fist miss Ayden's chin by less than an inch.

Ayden didn't let the close call distract him. He bobbed his head and plunged his fist directly into the unguarded side of the other fighter. Ayden's right fist smacked beneath his opponent's ribcage, and he let out a wheeze as Ayden swung his left fist to land a powerful crunch to Viktor's cheek. His skin split, and his head lolled to the side as he took a step backward to gain balance, but Ayden didn't miss a beat.

Utilizing the split second advantage, he rammed his left hand into the jaw of his opponent, flooring him almost immediately. I knew better than to think this was the end. His opponent's eyes were still open, cagily looking around as he thrashed his legs on the mat attempting to get back up. The majority of the crowd began chanting "Viktor" into the air, which overshadowed Ayden's cheers.

Warily, I scanned the crowd and saw something I'd never seen before: a place full of people who genuinely seemed to hate the man still standing inside the ring, Ayden. My hands got clammy as I watched them demand that

Viktor get back up. Crawling to the ropes, he hung on each and pulled and steadied himself upward.

After a few more seconds Viktor stood up and straightened his back, focusing on Ayden. Disdain and hatred ran through his gaze as he glared at Ayden and motioned with his two fingers to come forward. Ayden didn't take the bait. Instead he took two steps back, and Viktor came zooming through the ring, his fist crunching into Ayden's stomach. The power behind the throw would've done most in, but Ayden's abdomen clenched, blocking the brute force behind Viktor's punch.

"He's a body puncher," Jason whispered softly. I could barely hear him over the crowd.

"I'm assuming that was something Ayden trained for with the software."

Jason gave a nod, his eyes not leaving the ring. I returned my eyes to the ring and saw Ayden's gaze become crazed as he threw a flurry of punches at his opponent. It was as if his stamina was refueled, and the energy running through his veins had supercharged with each new punch landing on Viktor's cheeks and jaw.

"Ayden's turned into a headhunter," Jason muttered.

"By the looks of it, I'd say that's a good thing," Brandy almost yelled.

Viktor's head was hanging as he attempted to evade each punch thrown by Ayden, and as I looked into the ring, the voices inside my mind finally quieted. Watching Ayden throw jab after jab at his opponent with such vigor and power showed me why Ayden would win this match and any other match in front of him.

Ayden had heart. It was Ayden's heart that brought his opponent down time and again. He was absorbed in the act of fighting. Dynamism drove every punch, every jab, and the intensity only grew as time went on. My pulse picked up speed at the sight of him dodging Viktor's punches. It was an art form, of sorts, as these two swayed in and out of one another's range, but it only took a second to realize how quickly it could change.

Viktor delivered another blow into Ayden's side, but Ayden took a step back and dismissed the infliction of pain as if it were nothing more than a fleabite. The crowd was getting antsy as it became obvious who was going to win the fight, but I wouldn't allow myself to get my hopes up. Things could change on a dime. It only took a fleeting second where the smallest distraction could change everything.

I blinked and opened my eyes to see Ayden hook Viktor in the jaw with such raw force that Viktor spun toward the ropes, bouncing from one to the next until his body slammed onto the mat, but he scrambled to his feet immediately.

The sparring turned into a ritualistic dance between these two fighters, but the power continued to shift toward Ayden. It was undeniable. Ayden had been a student of the game, always learning, striving to do better, and here he was excelling in a warehouse full of people who wanted to see him fail. Needed to see him fail to get their money back.

I was engrossed with what I was seeing in front of me and knew I'd made the right choice by letting him step into the ring. If I'd asked him to not to step into the ring, he would've respected my wishes, but then he wouldn't have left the circuit knowing he was truly the best. There was no fighter capable of beating Ayden Rhodes, and now everyone fully understood that.

Ayden landed a punch across Viktor's nose, and the infliction of pain could be felt in the crowd as the blood trickled down Viktor's face. I slowly let out a breath as I watched Viktor unleash a punch with such devastating power that when it landed on Ayden's jaw, his entire head flew backward. I jumped on my toes as fear pummeled my system. Ayden took a few steps back. It was like slow motion as I watched Viktor soar across the ring attempting to connect his fist with Ayden's chin once more. Something I'd never done before erupted from my gut as I screamed for Ayden to come alive.

And come alive he did.

Ayden arced his body away from Viktor's fist and landed his own punch right in his opponent's gut, and it didn't stop there. I watched a rapid-fire assault take place on Viktor's already abused body. Ayden landed a right hook, followed by a straight punch into Viktor's jaw, a power shot like no other. Viktor attempted to steady himself, but it was too late. Ayden landed a haymaker into his opponent's jaw. The unnerving amount of force behind Ayden's punch sent a chill up my spine as the pain radiated from Viktor's gaze. The quick-fire assault of Ayden's fist as he jabbed and grabbed Viktor to finish him off gave me hope that the fight would end soon.

Viktor's stamina was running out. The fight had taken its toll. There was no denying the hazy look sitting behind his expression as he attempted a couple missed swings that resulted in nothing more than slaps. Boxing was a science, and it seemed all the fights leading up to this one were Ayden's experiments.

The smacking of skin on skin echoed through the air as the crowd quieted down to an astonished murmur as Ayden threw his final punch. Viktor's head lolled about before he took one step back and fell to the mat. Ayden had floored him again, but this time there was no getting up for Viktor.

The world around me fell away as I watched Ayden declared the victor, the MC holding up his arm. Everything around me was nebulous as I watched the man of my dreams fulfill his own, and I was here to experience it. Ayden's gaze buzzed with excitement as he scanned the crowd.

His eyes found mine, and excitement ran through me as I saw the look in his eyes. His hunger for the fight had been sated. But truthfully I wasn't sure how long that feeling would last for him.

Ayden bent under the top rope and left the ring almost unblemished. His gaze connected with mine as he climbed down, and a flurry of emotions ran through me. I wanted to hug him, kiss him, and never let go. The fight had been grueling, but the victory had made his spirit soar.

In my haze of staring at the winner, I hadn't noticed how unruly the crowd had gotten until Mason grabbed Ayden's arm and shook it. I saw the two trade glances, and my pulse quickened with the realization that a lot of people had lost a lot of money. There was always security at every fight, and this event was no different. I watched the men descend from all corners of the building and quickly create an aisle for us to exit. I glanced behind me toward the ring and saw Viktor, now standing, glaring at us as we left the makeshift arena. We climbed the stairs quickly and guards stood post at each door.

"You were like a machine out there," I whispered to Ayden when we reached the top of the stairs. "You were amazing. Incredible, really."

"Thank you, babe," Ayden said. His intense gaze locked on mine as he pushed the door open, and I wished that we were alone.

The excited chatter from Brandy and Gabby broke our silent moment as everyone piled into the room, amazed at what they just witnessed. Everything we'd worried about earlier was absent, leaving us all relieved and excited for our future, any future.

"You'll polish right up for the wedding," I teased, touching a slight cut above his brow. "Nothing a little Neosporin won't fix."

"My ribs might be a little sore so I might not

be able to carry you over the threshold on our honeymoon," he laughed.

"That might not be the only reason," Mason teased.

I gave him a dirty look but had to agree.

We wandered over to the window that overlooked where the match had been only moments before. The crowd was clearing out quickly and there was no sign of Viktor. I saw a group congregating near one of the exits, and my stomach tightened as I watched them survey their surroundings.

"That's weird," I said, tapping Ayden and pointing to the group.

Ayden nodded. "Probably nothing."

"It pays to be the underdog," Mason blabbed, coming up behind us. "Our take is turning out to be insane."

Never once had Ayden been the underdog.

"How so?" I asked.

"The odds were against us and the pot grew and grew."

"That might make the sting of this whole thing hurt a little less," I teased. I knew he didn't do it for the money, but come on. Getting some certainly didn't hurt anyone's feelings.

"And just when I'm ending it all, you get the hang of this promoter thing," Ayden joked with his brother.

Mason rolled his eyes. "Tori's got our table waiting at the pub."

"I'm starved," I announced.

"I never would've guessed," Brandy teased.

"I'm gonna rinse off, and I'll meet you all there," Ayden said, pointing at the small washroom.

"Nah. We'll wait for you in the parking lot." Mason shook his head. "Probably not the wisest of ideas to be wandering around alone after you cost a lot of people a lot of money."

I nodded in agreement. "He's got a point."

Ayden smiled and shook his head as he wandered toward the washroom. Gabby and Brandy's expressions were free of worry as they trundled my direction.

"You look like the weight of the world has been lifted," Gabby said, reaching for my hand.

"It feels like it has." I smiled.

"Do you believe he's through?" Brandy asked. "Like really finished?"

"I'd like to believe he is, but seeing the look in his eyes when he lands those punches..."

"I know." Brandy pressed her lips together and shook her head. "But let's pretend he is and enjoy what's to come in the next few weeks."

"Let's drink to that," Gabby said, holding up an imaginary glass.

Mason and Derek caught my eye over by the window. They were looking down below, talking about something in hushed voices.

"What's going on?" I asked, almost shouting to get their attention.

Derek turned around and smiled. "Just listening to the reports from the security guards. A couple of fights broke out in the parking lot."

"Oh, great," I mumbled.

I'd been to plenty of fights since I started dating Ayden, and there'd never been one fight in all those times.

Mason caught the worried expression running through my gaze and smiled. "It's nothing to worry about. Security has already cleared out most of the lot."

Ayden walked out of the bathroom. His hair was still wet, and he looked squeaky clean in a pair of jeans and a flannel shirt. Most wouldn't even be able to tell he'd just been in a grueling match if it weren't for some pinkness along his jaw, and how he walked carefully, protecting his bruised ribcage. He came over to me and slid his arm around my waist. I immediately melted in his arms as relief flooded through me. My shoulders instantly unknotted, and my body felt like a wet noodle as the tension finally flooded out of my system. I thought I'd done a good job keeping the anxiety at bay, but I was obviously quite wrong about that.

Mason walked over to the door and swung it open. "Let's get going, or my girl will think we abandoned her."

I hid my smile. Mason had fallen completely head-over-heels for Tori, and it was fun to see. Jason, Gabby, Brandy and Aaron all filed through the door. We followed behind and Derek and Mason turned off the lights and shut the door behind us while we all trundled down the stairs.

The place had really cleared out. I heard the clangs and bangs of the ring being dismantled in the other room. A few more minutes and no one would even know a fight had taken place here.

We walked into the crisp air, and the metal door closed with a thud behind us as we made our way through the almost empty parking lot to our cars.

"Let's get our undefeated fighter some grub," Gabby said, giving me a quick hug. "We'll see you in a few."

Brandy gave me a hug as well and then climbed into her car. Ayden rested his hand on my back and rubbed it softly as we watched our friends climb into their cars and start the ignitions. I took a deep breath in, finally feeling free of stress, and I turned to face Ayden.

He flashed me a devilish grin and brought his lips close to mine.

"I love you, Lily," he whispered.

He took a step back and from out of nowhere I watched in horror as Viktor landed a punch to the side of Ayden's head. I saw the pain flash through Ayden's gaze before he fell unconscious, his body crashing to the pavement. My heart stopped as I tumbled to the ground with him, screaming for help, and begging for Viktor to stop, but he didn't.

Chapter Nine

Viktor's expression was primal and animalistic as his fist continued to pummel Ayden's cheek. He attempted to drag him away, and I instinctively threw my body across Ayden's as my sobs and screams grew piercing. Mason and Jason pulled me off Ayden, while Derek and Aaron attacked Viktor, but I refused to release my grip from Ayden's hand. I would not let go no matter how far my arm was stretched.

Brandy's cries surrounded us, and I slowly crawled closer to Ayden the moment Mason went to help Derek and Aaron take care of Viktor. The world went into slow motion as Gabby called 9-1-1. Jason tried to hold me back, but I squirmed away and made it next to Ayden. The tears stung my lids, but I refused to shed any. Ayden was going to be okay. He'd been knocked around before.

I slid my shaking finger along his neck, feeling for a pulse.

I couldn't find one.

There wasn't one.

There had to be one.

I cradled Ayden's head in my lap, refusing to look at what the others were doing to Viktor. It wasn't enough.

"Why isn't he moving?" Brandy sobbed, running to us.

I shook my head, unable to speak. I just kept stroking his cheek over and over again.

"Ambulance is on the way," Gabby said, her voice hoarse.

"We need two of them," Jason said, his voice calm.

I shook my head. "Let Viktor die." I felt the burn of hate building inside of me, my eyes falling to Ayden's battered and bloodied face.

Brandy's whimpers echoed into the air, and I listened for the nonexistent sirens.

"Come on, baby," I whispered, bending down to his ear. ""You've got this."

"There's a pulse," Jason said, his fingers pressed to Ayden's wrist. "It's faint, but it's there."

I nodded, stroking my hands along his cheeks.

"Let him go," Jason hollered over to Mason and the others. "He's not going to come back for more."

"Kill him," I whispered. "Kill him."

Brandy rested her hands on her brother's abdomen, praying quietly as I stayed focused on the man in front of me.

The fury running through me kept me going and was as vital as the blood that fed my body. I didn't understand what happened. Why this would happen? I heard the footsteps behind me surround Ayden and me. Mason knelt down next to us. His eyes filled with tears and a look I'd never seen before. It was what happened when hate was no longer enough. I knew I wore the same expression.

"I never should've let him fight," Mason murmured.

The sirens blared in the distance and I shook my head.

"None of us could've predicted this," I said, but the words never left my lips.

I felt Viktor's poison reach every single one of us as we watched a man we all loved fading away from us. We weren't helpless. We were useless.

A car engine started somewhere in the parking lot.

"Looks like we didn't do a good enough job," Aaron muttered to Jason. "Viktor's buddies got him in the car."

I closed my eyes and prayed hard—so hard it hurt—until the sound of sirens arriving in the parking lot interrupted me. Ayden's skin had turned cold and clammy. Did that mean something?

A commotion erupted behind us as Jason and Aaron led the medics to where I was holding Ayden. They explained a man attacked him. That was enough explanation. The crunch of the gurney wheels along the pavement came closer, but I was afraid to let go. Afraid I'd never get to hold him again.

Three medics surrounded us while a fourth secured his head and neck in a brace before removing me from him. Brandy stayed, sitting on the cold pavement, staring at her lifeless brother. I kept shaking my head in protest as if I'd shake enough and wake up from this never-ending nightmare. One medic was taking vitals, while another found a vein and shot something into his body. I watched the same medic open a bag and take out tubes and a mask.

"What are you doing?" Brandy cried.

"Preparing to intubate," a medic responded. "We ask that you please step away."

Aaron came over to Brandy and wound up almost dragging her away before he was able to scoop her up in his arms.

The medics opened Ayden's mouth and snaked a tube down his throat and my knees went weak, but I refused to be weak. Ayden needed strength.

They quickly lowered the gurney and hoisted him onto the long stretcher. There was no recognition. He didn't twitch. He didn't move. He was far away. The medics pushed the gurney as they continued to squeeze the pump that breathed for him. They quickly relayed where they were taking him to Aaron and Jason who were on their heels. I tried to follow, but I was frozen. It wasn't until Brandy hung her arms around my shoulders and lowered her head that

I knew I needed to press on.

"He's going to be okay." She sniffed in. "We'll get him all patched up by the wedding."

I hadn't even thought about the wedding. I just wanted Ayden back. No matter his condition. We could face whatever was handed to us together.

The ambulance doors slammed shut, and the sirens immediately switched on. I heard Jason and Aaron talking as Mason came over and hugged me.

Before I even knew what had happened I was in a car on the way to the hospital. The sequence of events was a blur even while I stood in the emergency room waiting to hear news. I didn't know how I got there. I didn't know where Ayden went. I knew the others were with me, but I didn't remember seeing them or having them come with me. I just wanted news about Ayden.

Any news.

Time stood still and so did I.

I watched countless people come in with coughs, scratches, and back pain. Brandy was in a daze and Mason stared directly in front of him. There was nothing we could do except wait.

Every time the door opened, our heads would turn, praying we'd hear some news. Time and again, we were disappointed.

"You need to have something to eat and drink," Tori whispered. Mason had called her once we arrived at the hospital, and she'd arrived shortly after we did.

I shook my head, and Mason snapped out of

his fog.

"You need nutrients," he said, standing up and walking over to me. He took a seat in the empty chair next to me that Tori had vacated. "Ayden's gonna want a strong baby when all is said and done."

I gave a slight nod as Tori unscrewed the lid and handed me orange juice. It tasted like nothing as I gulped it down. She took the empty container from me and handed me a granola bar. I shook my head, but Mason took it from Tori and ripped the top off before pushing it into my hand.

"I'm serious," he whispered.

I took a bite and forced the scratchy cardboard bits down my throat. What was taking the doctors so long? Why hadn't we heard anything?

The door swung open, and a woman I didn't recognize stood at attention, scanning the waiting room.

"Rhodes family," she called. All eight of us stood up and the woman promptly shook her head. "Only immediate family, please."

It felt like a million stabs to my heart. Mason kissed Tori and nodded, clutching my hand, leading me and Brandy toward the woman.

"And you are?" she asked Mason.

"I'm his brother and this is my sister and Ayden's fiancée."

The woman shook her head.

"She's pregnant with his child. They're going to get married in a couple weeks in Bermuda."

Mason's jaw clenched at the bureaucracy of it all.

The woman sighed and pressed her lips to form a slit, giving us a slight nod as we walked through the door.

"I'm the nurse that will be looking after him. We're still waiting on results from the initial tests, but we've moved him to intensive care."

"Intensive care?" Brandy's voice gave out.

The woman nodded and led us to a bank of elevators. She pushed the button, and the carriage in front of us immediately opened.

"Is he going to be okay?" I asked.

The nurse chose the floor, and the doors shut with a thud.

"We're doing everything we can," she replied, offering nothing more.

I glanced at Mason, who looked completely defeated as the elevator delivered us to the fifth floor. The doors opened spilling us out onto another sterile floor.

The white linoleum flooring with grey flecks ran as far as the eye could see. A set of white metal doors with only a sliver of rectangular glass on each was visible to our right. There was a bright red sign asking visitors to stop in at the nurses' station.

We followed the nurse as she pushed through the doors. A tall counter directly in front of us housed one male and one female. I didn't know if they were nurses or administrative staff. The space was designed as a square. Down each wall, a row of windows looked into each of the patients' rooms. The center of the floor was taken up with nurses' stations, a visiting room, and restrooms.

We followed the nurse down the corridor to our right. She walked us to the last room before the hall continued to the left.

My eyes fell to Ayden. They'd cleaned up his wounds, removing the dried blood that had covered his face and neck. He had a few sets of stitches, but most appeared in his hairline or behind his ear. His cheeks were glossy pink from the swelling. I trailed Mason and Brandy as they slowly walked into his room. The nurse shoved the curtain to the side with a startling rattle. She opened up a closet door, removing a metal chair from inside and plunked it next to the other two.

"The doctor will be in as soon as we know more," the nurse said, leaving the room almost as quickly as she'd entered.

I slowly walked over to Ayden. He looked so peaceful, too peaceful. It worried me. His arms were underneath the lightweight blanket they had pulled up to his chin. I saw the definition of his arms under the fabric. I wanted to hold his hand, but I wasn't sure it was okay. I didn't have an instruction manual for this.

I glanced across the bed where Mason and Brandy stood quietly, watching their brother. Brandy wiped a tear from her cheek and looked up at me.

"Sleeping Beauty was determined to get his rest before the wedding one way or another," she said softly.

I mustered a smile and looked at Mason

whose expression made me want to break down. I could tell he was internalizing everything that happened to Ayden from the moment he stepped in the ring. I wanted to tell him it wasn't his fault, but he wouldn't believe me anyway. The Rhodes men were stubborn.

"We're waiting for you to wake up," I said, touching my finger to Ayden's cheek. "And I'm getting hungry. I still haven't had dinner."

Mason chuckled and clamped his sister's hand.

"It's true, man," Mason seconded. "This whole thing kind of waylaid our celebration dinner. And I have no idea how to deal with a hungry Lily." His voice cracked on my name, and his gaze fell to Ayden's blanket.

"You were amazing this afternoon," I tried again. "Well, you're amazing all the time."

I searched Ayden's face for some hint of recognition, some sign of life. I lifted the thin blanket and ran my hand along his arm, dodging the IV cords until I found his hand.

"I still haven't heard back from mom or dad," Brandy whispered. "They need to be here."

"They need to be here to watch him wake up, more importantly," Mason corrected.

"They were going to dinner and a movie. You'd think they'd check their phone."

"They probably turned it off for the movie and forgot to turn it back on," I said.

Brandy nodded. "Probably."

"I'm sure Jason or Aaron can go meet them at the house," Mason said.

"I think that would almost be worse. They'd have no time to absorb what was going on. They'd see those two and know something was wrong."

"I'm sure they'll call any minute," I assured them both.

"What should we tell our parents?" Mason asked Brandy.

Brandy shook her head and released her hand from her brother's.

"The truth, Mason. We need to tell them the truth."

Chapter Ten

The act of moving. We take it for granted until it's gone. We expect it will always be there to carry us through life. It's moments like these when the fragility of life becomes painfully evident.

The small flick of an eyelid or the wiggle of a brow.

A grin so wide, the eyes smile.

A lick of lips.

Breathing.

Swallowing.

Brandy finally reached her parents, and they were on their way over. We were told a doctor would be in to speak with us in about ten minutes. That was twenty minutes ago.

I sat in the metal chair next to Ayden's bed and listened to the machines click and hiss in a rhythmic pattern. Rubbing my temples, I let out a deep sigh. This entire event didn't seem real. Even with Ayden lying in a hospital bed next to me, it didn't seem real. None of this made any sort of sense. If anything were to happen to him, logic said it would be in the ring.

Not after the fight. Not on the way to a celebration dinner. I let out another sigh and hung my head in my hands. Brandy and Mason were out in the hall trying to track down the doctor.

So far since we'd gotten here, we'd heard enough to frighten us and not another word since. I stood up and ran my fingers along his jawline.

"You're an amazing man, Ayden Rhodes, and I can't wait to be your wife." I swallowed the lump in the back of my throat. "You'll make an amazing father. I know it."

A light tap on the door got my attention. The doctor was standing in the doorway with Mason and Brandy. He motioned for me to come out into the hallway. I leaned over and kissed Ayden's cheek before heading into the hall.

The doctor shut the door behind me and motioned for us to take a seat near the nurses' station.

"Ayden is a very lucky man," the doctor began.

"I doubt he'd agree at the moment," Mason replied.

The doctor nodded and continued. "If the punch that rendered him unconscious had been a centimeter to the left, it would've been immediate death."

My breath caught, but I stayed focused as the doctor kept talking.

"As it stands now, he has only a slight skull fracture, and there is no evidence of bleeding on the brain. The TBI—"

"What's a TBI?" Mason interrupted.

"Traumatic brain injury," Brandy responded. It was sometimes easy to forget that Brandy experienced much of this with her accident.

"It's a concussion. However, we're not out of the woods yet. I feel it is my obligation to be honest about his recovery. We've not induced a coma. There is no need since we saw no indication of swelling of the brain, but he does remain comatose. The MRI shows no sign of severe brain injury. But we need to be extra vigilant over the next forty-eight hours to monitor for bleeding between the dura mater and the skull. That type of bleeding is often slow to appear. We will keep a close watch on him through the night. Until he wakes up, we won't know what all we're dealing with." He stopped. "How extensive his injuries are."

I felt the numbness start in my toes and slowly work its way up my body until I was completely emotionless. I no longer had the luxury to let my emotions get the better of me so it was better to deaden them all. I glanced at Brandy, whose expression lacked the hopeful glint I'd seen when the doctor first started talking to us.

"Like what in particular?" Mason asked.

"Fatigue, blurry vision, nausea, impaired

motor and verbal skills, amnesia."

"You're saying he could have amnesia when he awakes?" Mason questioned, standing up.

"That was a risk for me, and I woke up just fine," Brandy said, attempting to calm her brother down.

Mason shrugged Brandy's touch away and sank back down into the chair, holding his head in his hands.

"Do you have statistics?" I asked. "Percentages of head injuries like his that have resulted in any of the problems you listed?"

The doctor shook his head. "Unfortunately, head injuries are far too unpredictable to be able to gauge accurately. What might impair one individual doesn't scathe another."

I nodded and saw Mr. and Mrs. Rhodes coming up the hall between us. They hadn't noticed us. They were concentrating too hard on which room Ayden was located in. I stood up and motioned toward them, trying to get their attention, but they were too focused on finding their son.

"Your parents are here," I told Mason and Brandy.

Mason lifted his head and stood up quickly.

"Can you please fill my parents in?" Brandy asked the doctor. He bowed his head slightly, and we watched his mom run into Ayden's room.

A bellowing sob came from the room and my chest tightened. I couldn't do it. I couldn't go in there. Not right now. I glanced at the doctor and took a seat back down as Brandy and Mason walked over to the room to meet their parents.

"Is talking to him okay?" I asked the doctor.

"Touching him and talking to him are imperative. We don't know how much patients hear, but we know it helps." He nodded and turned around, making his way to the room.

I sat back in the chair and forced away the wave of tears that threatened to overtake me. The numbness I'd built up was failing, and emotion I wasn't ready for began working its way into the cracks.

For the first time, I let myself think about our child.

Our child.

I'd dreamed of Ayden holding our baby, smothering the bundle in kisses, and changing diapers, and now the thoughts took my breath away. This wasn't how our life was supposed to go.

He won that fight. He trained for it and won the match fair and square. The anger started flowing freely again, and I closed my eyes to calm myself down. It was no use. There was nothing that could be done to change the past.

"Lily."

I looked up to see Ayden's mom, her arms outstretched toward me. I stood up and without hesitation, I fell into her arms as our tears began to flow. I felt Brandy wrap her arms around us both as we leaned on one another for the strength that would get us through the night.

There was no word for this kind of pain. It hurt so badly. The agony melted into our blood and pumped through our hearts, minds, and souls. Each memory was a sting of what was, and an aching reminder of what might never be again. Dreams were replaced with nightmares, and the twinge of tomorrow's promise long lost in sorrow.

But we had to remain strong.

No more tears.

Ayden was going to get through this.

I took a deep breath in and sniffed away the last of my tears until Ayden woke up, and they were tears of joy. I felt Brandy's embrace soften, and she took a step away as her mom and I broke free.

Brandy blotted her eyes with tissue and so did her mom. I used my hand.

"I feel much better," I whispered. "We'll get through this, but most importantly, Ayden will get through this."

"I don't understand," Ayden's mom began. "How did this happen? What kind of monster would attack my son?"

I looked over at Brandy's startled expression and sucked in a deep breath. There was no good way to tell her that her son was involved in illegal fighting.

"What aren't you two girls telling me?"

My gaze fell to the white linoleum, and I wondered if it was my place. I felt like a traitor each time I almost opened my mouth, but seeing the pain in her eyes killed me. She deserved the truth.

"He was attacked in a parking lot after a fight,"

Brandy said.

"What kind of fight?" Her brow rose.

"It was a fight that Ayden had entered."

"He did this to himself?" His mother's anger bounced on every syllable.

Brandy and I both shook our heads.

"Absolutely not. He won that fight fair and square," I said, my pulse pounding. Ayden didn't bring this on himself in any way, shape, or form.

"Then how did he end up here?" she questioned.

"Ayden's opponent was angry he lost. We were all getting in our cars when he attacked Ayden," Brandy said softly.

"You were there when it happened?" She crossed her arms and Brandy nodded.

"We all were. We go to all of Ayden's fights."

His mom's shoulders sank at the latest revelation, and my heart ached for her. I understood the power of secrets.

"Please don't be mad. It was something he loved to do," Brandy began. Her mom took a seat and placed her head in her hands, slowly rubbing her temples. Brandy's dad came out of the room, wiping a tear away. He beelined toward us.

"Did you know your son was a fighter?" Ayden's mom asked, lifting her head to stare at her husband.

"A damn good one," his father replied.

"You knew and never told me?" his mother whispered.

"When did you find out?" Brandy asked, crossing her arms.

"I've known since his first fight." He turned his attention to his wife. "And the reason I never told you was to not worry you. I knew he had no intention of giving it up, and I wanted to keep the peace between the family."

She shook her head. "I want to be mad at you," she looked at her husband before turning her attention to Brandy, "And you, but you're right. I would've made things a living hell had I known."

Ayden's mom stood up and let out a deep breath. "Let's go visit our son. He needs us all united now more than ever."

I glanced at Brandy who seemed somewhat relieved but still tentative. I think she knew once—if—Ayden woke up there'd still be hell to pay from his mom, but until that moment, we were going to act as if nothing was wrong. I let his parents go in front of us as they walked toward Ayden's room.

"That could've gone far worse," I whispered to Brandy.

"I think she's still in shock. I'm sure it's barely started. She hates being left out of the loop, and it doesn't help that my dad knew."

"I had no idea he knew, did you?"

She shook her head. I watched Ayden's mom walk to her son's bed. She pulled his hand up and placed a gentle kiss on his knuckles.

"I'll go talk to Gabby and everyone so they're not stuck in the ER waiting room not knowing," I said softly.

"Oh, I forgot to tell you. They're in the waiting room on this floor now. The doctor told Mason and me out in the hall."

I nodded.

"He also said once Ayden wakes up, Aaron can come in."

"What about the others?" I asked.

She shook her head. "Not until he's moved to a different unit."

I gave her a quick hug and watched her go into the room with her parents. I wanted them to have some time alone with their son and brother, and I needed some time away as well. Not because I didn't want to be with Ayden every waking second, but because I needed to absorb what the doctor said. I needed to lose myself in the possibilities of what our future might hold. And I say future because I knew Ayden would wake up. He was a stubborn fighter, who had a lot to live for.

I walked through the doors and spotted the signs for the waiting room, but instead of going toward the comforting faces that would embrace me, I pushed the elevator button and waited for the carriage to arrive. Exhaustion had finally settled over me, and if I couldn't have caffeine, I at least needed to fool myself into believing I was drinking it. I stepped onto the elevator and pushed the lobby button. I was sure there'd be a coffee stand or cafeteria somewhere.

As the doors opened onto the first floor, I stepped into the hallway and scanned for a sign leading me to where I needed to go.

Where I needed to go.

I needed to go somewhere to escape my fears.

I wanted to be able to forget about everything for five minutes, but I knew that was impossible. I wandered toward the espresso cart that was framed by two large ficus trees. There must've been some study that showed interior plants calmed people down with as many as they had placed around the building, but as I stared at the plants I noticed no difference.

I studied the chalkboard menu, finally deciding what to get.

"I'd like a white chocolate mocha, decaf. Please."

"Decaf?" the barista asked.

I nodded. "I'm pregnant."

I was stunned at how easily the words rolled off my tongue to a complete stranger.

She wrote on the cup and smiled. "Well, congratulations."

"Thank you," I almost whispered.

The thought of announcing our pregnancy at our rehearsal dinner, suddenly felt very far away, almost unattainable. The dreams I'd planted in my head about how we'd tell everyone were clouded over by the uncertainty of our future.

I paid for my order and waited for the drink to come out the other side as the memories came crashing into my mind like a wild storm.

Ayden working out in the gym.

Would his motor skills be impaired?

Ayden telling me he loved me last night as our bodies entwined.

Would his verbal skills be impaired?

Ayden holding me, kissing me, making love to me.

Would he even remember me?

The barista called my drink, and I wrapped my fingers around the paper cup, wishing I hadn't let myself tangle privately with my thoughts. The snare of emotion was far too raw to think logically about our relationship. I took a sip of the sweet drink and found a chair to slide into as I debated whether or not to call my parents.

I thought about the family upstairs, how close they were, and how lucky I was to be a part of it. If I lost Ayden, would I lose that too?

I slid out my cell phone and dialed my mother's cell number, and after a couple rings, she picked up.

"It's a little late to be calling, don't you think, Lily?" she asked into the phone.

I let out a silent sigh.

"I still haven't heard back if you and dad are coming to our wedding in a couple weeks. Ivy and Heath already said they weren't coming."

A sparse couple of seconds settled between us as I got my answer. They couldn't even be bothered for a wedding.

"Your father and I haven't RSVP'd because we were trying to rearrange our schedule. It's not like Bermuda is an easy destination to get to."

"Actually, mom, it's pretty simple. One flight to the east coast and a shuttle flight to the island."

"Well, it happens to be on the same night our country club auction is happening and this year, your father was chosen as the MC. It's quite an honor."

"I'm sure it is," I replied flatly.

"We'll try to make it, dear," my mom said. "But no promises."

"I gathered that," I said. "Okay. I thought I'd check before I sent the final numbers to the coordinator."

"Okay, dear. I'll talk with you soon."

And she hung up.

I gave a disgusted laugh, which warranted a few glances from people sitting around me, and I stood up. I'd known in my heart since I sent out the invite that my mom wasn't coming to the wedding, but I wanted to see if I could tell her about Ayden. Every now and then I wanted to find out if I could somehow crack through her callousness enough to confide in her, to treat her like a mother, my mother. The answer was always disappointing.

But after today, I wasn't sure it really merited any more effort. I had a family and fiancé waiting for me upstairs. I walked toward the elevator and Gabby hopped right off and threw her arms around me.

"Brandy said you'd come to see us and when you didn't, I got worried."

I hugged Gabby back and realized my life was full of family, and I wouldn't want it any other way.

Chapter Eleven

It was sometime after midnight. Aaron had taken Brandy home, and Tori had somehow wrangled Mason away from Ayden's bedside. Ayden's parents had left shortly thereafter, leaving me alone with Ayden and my thoughts.

I'd fallen asleep twice and was currently staring at my phone. I didn't even have it on. I stood up and stretched, looking out the window. Our room overlooked the emergency room entrance so several times an hour an ambulance would pull through the circle, and I'd wonder who was on the stretcher, a husband, wife, daughter, best friend? I turned around and walked over to Ayden's bed. He looked exactly how he had since he moved to this room, his body still, breathing controlled by something other than him, and a tangle of cords leaving his body.

I ran my finger along his cheek, picking up the tickle of his whiskers from not shaving yesterday.

"Not everyone can pull off the unshaven look in a hospital gown, you know?" I whispered. "But you look extremely sexy."

I glanced out in the hall and saw nurses chatting at their station. Every so often soft laughter would erupt, and they'd look around nervously as if laughter was regulated, and maybe on this floor it was.

My gaze fell back to Ayden, and I moved my hand along his chest, skirting the sensors and cords until I found his hand. I squeezed it and bent over the railing of his bed.

"I love you so much Ayden Rhodes. If you could do us the biggest favor when you wake up, please remember me—remember us. I'll be forever in your debt." I continued holding his hand and rested my head on his chest. It was a most uncomfortable position with the railing poking my ribs, and my neck craned so that I wouldn't run into the tubes from his breathing machine. I needed to feel the Ayden I remembered, the hard, muscled man I'd fallen in love with, who was now fighting for his life.

I didn't even let the weight of my head fully rest on his chest. I was so afraid I'd break him.

Imagine that.

Afraid I'd break Ayden Rhodes.

I stood back up, trying to lessen the sharp ache in my neck, as I watched him. Exactly what he would hate for me to do. Standing and staring at him like he was a zoo exhibit. No wonder he didn't want to wake up. He was afraid he'd blink open to a room full of eyes staring back at him.

"If there wasn't a nurses' station outside the door, you can't even imagine what I'd do to you."

Still nothing, not even a twitch.

The weight of not knowing crawled up my body in a huge upwelling of exhaustion. I glanced at the skinny recliner in the corner of the room and decided to haul it over to Ayden's bed. Sliding my hand from his, I walked over to the bulky chair and began to tug on it. Not realizing it was on wheels, I tumbled backwards onto the metal chair I'd been sitting on. My eyes landed on Ayden, and I chuckled amazed that even with him in a coma, I was worried he'd catch me falling on my ass. I stood up and moved the metal chair out of the way and glided the recliner next to his bed and unfolded the blanket that rested over the back.

"Everything okay in here?" a nurse asked, poking her head in.

"Oh. Yeah. Sorry. I didn't realize I'd caused such a commotion. I tripped over a chair."

She nodded and smiled, leaving me to shake out the flimsy blanket. The room felt warm, but I was freezing as I scooted myself into the vinyl chair.

Pulling up the blanket to my chin, I snaked my hand underneath and over to Ayden's and grabbed hold tightly and fell asleep.

It wasn't until my elbow was on fire, and my entire arm had gone numb that I woke up in a panic. I'd forgotten where I was and attempted to move my arm, but I couldn't. My arm zipped past the stage of being asleep and was working its way toward a tingly death. The low light of morning shone through the window, and I was shocked I'd slept this long. I quickly turned to look at Ayden, and he looked exactly as I'd left him.

Asleep.

It might have been my hazy, sleepy state, but I was starting to get annoyed with him. We had a lot to look forward to, and a lot of things to do to get ready for our wedding. I wanted him up. I needed him up.

"You're awake." A woman's voice came from the far corner.

My pulse quickened, and I saw a nurse tearing something off an IV bag to replace his almost empty fluid pouch

"How'd he do through the night?" I asked.

"Very well," she said, not offering any other hints. "You certainly needed the rest. You didn't wake up once last night, even when we came in to poke and prod."

"And I still feel exhausted."

"Would you like anything like orange juice or oatmeal?" she asked.

She switched out one bag for another and looked over at me as I tried to drag my arm away. The sensation of a million sharp needles poking my entire arm was less than pleasant as I swung it in front of me.

"I don't feel like anything, but I probably

should eat something."

She nodded. "I'll bring it in after my rounds."

"Thank you."

She turned and walked out of the room, leaving me with some version of Ayden I still didn't understand.

"Well, I have to confess." I stood up and rolled the chair back a few feet. "I'm a little annoyed with you."

I placed my good hand and arm on his leg.

"You promised that tonight we'd be in front of the fire in the family room, and so far, it doesn't seem like that's going to happen unless you speed things along." I rubbed my hand up and down his thigh as I kept rambling.

"Not to mention we're supposed to get on a flight to New York and hop on one to Bermuda in a couple weeks." I let a few minutes of silence pass between us.

"I called my mom yesterday about the wedding to see if she was going to come. And yes, I know we already figured out she wasn't coming, but I think I wanted to test her and I have no idea why. She's failed every single one I've flung her way so far. Anyway, my dad's got some country-club dinner that he's hosting, so yeah..." I rested my hand on the thin blanket near his waist. "Anyway, I wanted to thank you for allowing me to be part of your family. It's an honor and I'm really grateful, and soon we'll have our own to add to the bunch." My voice cracked, and my eyes ran along Ayden's torso to his neck and face. I took a couple steps toward the head of the bed and rested my fingertips on his shoulders.

"I love you, Ayden Rhodes. Now wake the hell up."

I saw a slight tic of his jaw muscle. "That's what I'm talking about." I slid my fingers along his shoulders and took a deep breath. "I need you, Mr. Rhodes. I need you to wake up so we can begin our life together as husband and wife."

The nurse walked in with the tray of food and drink.

"As I was talking to him, his jaw muscle kind of clenched."

The nurse set the tray down on the rolling cart and glanced at Ayden.

"That isn't unusual," she replied.

Whoosh. The wind was completely knocked out of my sails.

"Does it mean something?"

"It can but not always."

I stared at the plastic-wrap covered oatmeal and nodded. "Well, thank you for this."

She pressed her lips together while I stood drowning in emotion, mainly discouragement. I know it's their job to be realistic, but it's mine to be hopeful.

I reached for the orange juice and tore the top off when a startling honking sound blasted through the air, resulting in my dropping the open container on the tray. Panic started flooding through me as another long and drawn out honk echoed into the room.

I looked at the nurse for some sign and she

smiled. "Now that is a sound you want to hear."

"Why? What does that mean?" I asked.

"He's fighting the ventilator and attempting to breath on his own. I'll go page the doctor." And like that she left me alone in the room with a flock of geese and Ayden. My entire world went from despair to cautious hope, and all I wanted to do was scream at the top of my lungs for him to wake up. Instead, I leaned over the hospital bed and placed my mouth next to his ear.

"You're so close. Keep it coming," I whispered, swiping a kiss along his cheek. I saw his chest rise more severely with each honk of the ventilator, and I prayed for the doctor to arrive soon.

"By the way, you know that secret you've been keeping from your parents all these years?" I asked. "Your dad has known since the beginning, and he is so proud of you."

Another clench of jaw made my stomach flutter with hope.

"We're all proud of you: Mason, me, Brandy, TBD Rhodes."

The muscles in his neck tensed.

I reached underneath the blanket and found his cold fingers, intertwining them with mine.

"I've got a surprise for you in Bermuda. It's all planned down to the tiniest detail. You know how you wanted to know the gender, and I thought we should keep it a surprise until the end? A few weeks back, I realized you were right. It would be way easier to plan. So I had our doctor forward the results to our event coordinator. If you'd just wake up..." His eyelids twitched and I stopped talking as I swallowed down a huge lump of joy. We were getting close. I knew it in my heart.

"You've promised me a lot of things, Ayden, and I intend on holding you to every single one."

His hand squeezed mine, and my heart raced as my eyes stayed on his. Another chorus of honks blared from his ventilator.

"That's right," I said, squeezing his hand back. "Keep it coming. Open your eyes before the doctor gets here."

I waited for a flutter of lids, but none came, and the tension in his hand released.

"Your brother wanted to start a bet on who you'd wake up for first. None of us were really in the mood, but I have to confess that it would make me extra happy if I were the one who pulled it out of you."

His chin moved slightly.

And then nothing.

No honking.

No twitches.

I let out a sigh and glanced out the window. The sun had completely risen, and the sunlight was overtaking the room. I removed my hand from his and walked over to the curtains, scooting them closed to block out some of the light. I walked back over to Ayden and slid my hand back in his.

"We love you, Ayden, and we're here for you whenever you decide to join us."

His head turned slowly to the side, and his

eyes opened as if he'd just awoken from a good night's sleep. No words came as I looked into Ayden's beautiful blue eyes.

It wasn't until his eyes connected with mine that I realized he had no idea who I was.

Chapter Twelve

With the exception of Mason, everyone had returned to the hospital.

Ayden was awake!

And he was off the respirator.

Things were good.

Really good.

Except that he didn't remember me.

Doesn't remember me.

I saw a flicker of recognition when his mother, father, and sister came into the room. The same flicker I so desperately wanted to receive. I shoved the undeniable pain into a faraway place and tried not to be as selfish as I felt for wanting to be remembered.

I was important.

But I was so grateful he remembered his parents and sister. I really was, with all my heart, grateful. I let out a sigh and watched his mom and dad talk to Ayden as if he'd only suffered the flu, and I stayed back sitting on the recliner I had shoved back in the corner.

The doctor advised that I let him come to things naturally.

But there was nothing natural about this situation. Ayden and I were supposed to get married and have our baby.

His mom flashed me an understanding glance as she held Ayden's hand, which caught the look of Ayden so he looked over my way. He hadn't looked at me since his eyes first opened. He didn't smile. In fact, the complete opposite happened. The grin he was wearing fell from his lips when our eyes connected.

So here I sat, but it wasn't about me. It was about getting Ayden healthy.

Brandy walked over and took a seat in the metal foldout chair.

"How are you holding up?" she asked.

"Totally fine. The doctor said this happens in a lot of cases, and it's generally temporary." I let out a deep breath. "But not always."

"It's temporary," Brandy assured me, but we both knew it was an empty promise.

It was hard to imagine that I'd been deleted from Ayden's memory. Of all the events in his life, I wanted to believe our upcoming marriage would be a priority, one that was important enough to remember.

"It's all fine. Just enjoy your brother and relish the moment. It's a big deal," I said, the knot twisting tighter in my belly.

I glanced over at the door and saw Mason stride into the room, grinning from ear to ear as his eyes fell on his awake twin. He jogged to the side of the bed and snaked his arms around Ayden, almost raising him from the bed.

"That was too intense, man." I heard Mason whisper. "Too intense."

My heart stopped as I watched Mason let go of his brother, and the same blank stare canvased over Mason, his own twin brother. Ayden's gaze flashed to his parents, hoping to be informed about who this stranger was that nearly pulled him out of bed. I took a deep breath in and let it out slowly.

"This is your brother, Mason," their mom said. Her voice was calm, soft, showing no hint of concern.

Mason's brows furrowed and his neck snapped to look at his dad. "What? He doesn't remember me? That's ridiculous. It's like he's looking in a mirror when he sees me."

"He hasn't looked in a mirror recently," Brandy said quietly.

The defeat in Mason's eyes wrapped around every cell in my body, and I knew his plight was much worse than mine.

"I'm sorry," Ayden muttered.

Sorry?

The words killed me and, by the looks of it, did the same to his family.

"Mason, why don't you take Lily to get some coffee?"

"She can't." His gaze met mine as he corrected

119

his blunder. "Sounds like a good idea."

I nodded and stood up, giving a hug to Brandy before I followed Mason out the door. Once we reached the hall, I gave Mason a big hug.

"He doesn't remember me either," I whispered.

Mason's embrace tightened around me as we both let our new reality settle around us in the middle of a hospital hallway.

Somehow, we'd get through this.

Together as a family.

This was a slight bump in the road followed by a rather complex detour, but we'd get to our destination one way or another.

Mason and I slowly released one another. He slid his finger along his cheeks, wiping away the dampness from his face. Mason was also always full of boisterous one-liners and lively comebacks. Not now though. What we faced left us both speechless.

We walked silently to the elevator and made our way to the first floor without saying a word. It wasn't until we placed our orders with the barista that we found our voices.

"This is wrong on so many levels," Mason said, waiting for his drink. Mine had been called, and I was now forcing myself to take a sip of the hot chocolate.

"I can handle it if he doesn't remember me because he's stuck with me. All he has to do is look at himself in the mirror, but for him not to remember you. I'd trade it all away so quickly, Lily. I really would. You're the mother of his child." His drink was called, and he grabbed his cup off the counter while I tried to absorb what Mason just said.

Hearing someone else verbalize my very fear of Ayden not remembering me, or the fact that I was pregnant with our child was nothing short of paralyzing.

"I'd feel worse about it if he remembered me but not you," I whispered, taking a seat.

Mason shook his head in protest. "It all really sucks. Plain and simple. What did the doctor say about it?"

"That it's common and not to be too alarmed."

Mason let out a grunt. "We aren't supposed to be alarmed that Ayden can't remember his fiancée or his identical twin brother. Right." He took a swig of coffee.

I nodded in agreement. "I know there are way bigger things in life to worry about, but I wonder if I should cancel everything in Bermuda..."

I felt guilty for even bringing up the wedding, when we were still trying to get Ayden to recognize his own flesh and blood, but it suddenly felt like Mason was one of the few who I could talk about it with. After all, we were both scratched from Ayden's memory.

Mason shook his head. "Absolutely not. We'll get him there one way or another. Even if he's kicking and screaming down the aisle."

I couldn't help but laugh at the vision.

"Wasn't exactly how I dreamed of our wedding day, but at this point I'd take it." I smiled, feeling slightly better than when we'd gotten on the elevator for our drinks. I appreciated the Rhodes boys and their sense of humor.

Would Ayden still have the same humor I fell in love with?

"Let's get back up there and try to shake some sense into the idiot," Mason teased.

"I'm not sayin', but I'm sayin'," I burbled, feeling immensely better that I wasn't the only one the *idiot* forgot, even though it pained me to the deepest level I'd ever known.

We tried to remain positive and lighthearted on the way back up to see Ayden, the closer we got to his room, the more the feeling slipped away.

Laughter filled the air, and Mason and I traded glances.

Great! Seemed like things were back to normal minus two very important people.

Mason grabbed my hand and pulled me through the door with him as we both turned our attention to Ayden. He was sitting up in bed now, and many of the cords had been removed from his body and head. From here it looked like he only had an IV.

Ayden's gaze fell to our hands, and he looked over at his parents. Their eyes fell to our hands, and something sparked between us all.

"Tori is going to kill me," Mason whispered. "But I've got an idea. Maybe what Ayden needs is a real-life enactment, a history lesson of sorts."

My brow rose in surprise that he'd even consider such a far-out way of dealing with things. I glanced across the room at Brandy who seemed to be following Mason's harebrained idea.

Mason's parents walked over next to Brandy and sat down, while Mason and I walked to the foot of the bed. Every time I was around him, I prayed for a flicker of recognition to flash across his gaze.

I bit my lip and glanced at the floor, ready for Mason to start whatever it was he had planned, but instead, Ayden spoke.

"You're Brandy's friend from college," he said grinning. He pointed at me and wagged his finger.

My heart knocked my ribcage with each pounding pulse as I watched Ayden try to put the pieces of the puzzle—our life—together.

"Uh, yeah. Kind of. That's how it started," I stuttered. My hands became clammy, and I glanced in horror at Brandy. That was it? That was all her brother could remember?

"Not good enough, man," Mason said, under his breath.

Without warning, Mason wrapped his arms around me and pulled me into him. His hands ran up my back as he his lips hovered so close to mine. I think we were both hoping his brother would say something before it happened. Before the kiss.

I shut my eyes, not because I enjoyed it, but because I was scared to death that I was about to kiss Ayden's twin brother. Mason ran his fingers into my hair, and his lips touched to mine. I assumed we were doing the church kiss, but once his lips parted, I knew he was fully committed to this role.

There was no connection. It was like kissing a sibling, but we both persevered until I realized Mason hadn't taken a breath since the entire ordeal began. I slowly released my mouth from his and gently slid one more soft kiss across his lips before turning to face Ayden.

Ayden's eyes were blazing with fury. He gritted his teeth and attempted to disconnect himself from whatever was keeping him in the bed. Mason smacked my butt and Brandy laughed; all the while Ayden's anger boiled over into swift action.

"Who do you think you are?" Ayden demanded, trying to stand up. His eyes flew to meet Mason's, but his equilibrium hadn't quite caught up to his returning memories.

"I'm your brother, trying to speed the process along, for all our sakes." Mason grinned and winked at me.

Ayden centered himself back on the bed, trying to stop the room from spinning as he pulled his stare away from Mason's. Ayden's mom started to rush toward him, but her husband held onto her hand not letting her get very far.

I walked over to Ayden. "Are you doing okay? Do you need me to get a nurse?"

Ayden's gaze remained focused on the ground as he attempted to slide back into the bed.

"I'm fine," he snapped.

"No. You're really not, but that's neither here or there. Let me help you get back into bed."

Ayden waved me away, but I refused to leave. Instead, I straightened out the sheet and thin blanket that Ayden had thrown to the side in his haste. He attempted to lift his legs into bed, and I noticed them shaking. So I quickly wrapped my hands around his ankles and brought them up and over, while he maneuvered his upper body where he wanted it. I swiftly covered him with a sheet and the blanket and didn't look into his eyes. I was too afraid of what I'd see.

"I can't wait to walk that woman down the aisle," Mason almost shouted from the foot of the bed. "She's a real keeper."

I hadn't expected Mason to keep going, but Brandy couldn't keep in her giggle.

"That's enough, Mason," his mom warned.

And I hid my chuckle at how his parents still felt the need to reprimand their thirty-year old children. The Rhodes family dynamics never ceased to amaze me.

Ayden's blue eyes flashed to mine, and I couldn't help but widen my grin when I saw a flicker of recollection that was deeper than being Brandy's friend flash through his eyes. Ayden narrowed his eyes and bit his lip as if he was about to say something and then thought better of it.

I would take that expression any day over the blank one I'd been receiving all morning. Mason apparently didn't think the progress was quite fast enough so he sauntered over and gave me a big kiss on the cheek and then snaked his arm around my waist because he could. I saw another dash of anger run through Ayden's gaze, and it puzzled me. An emotional response was being pulled from him over seeing me and Mason together, but it wasn't enough to put all the pieces together.

Mason let go of my waist and walked over to his brother and smiled. He dipped his mouth next to his ear and whispered something none of us could hear, and before we knew it, Ayden tossed an empty plastic cup at no one in particular, and Brandy's eyes widened in horror.

I didn't think this was how the doctor had imagined Ayden's recovery would go, but he'd never run into the Rhodes brothers before either.

"Settle down there," Mason said, taking a couple steps back.

Mason stood next to me, and I glanced over at his mother, who looked like she wanted to cart Mason out by his ear, and I wouldn't be surprised if that happened within the minute.

"What do you have to say for yourself?" Mason asked.

Ayden's jaw clenched and his eyes flashed to mine. I saw despair sitting right behind his expression, and I realized Ayden was coming back slowly, but he was coming back. I had to commend Mason. He really knew what buttons to push. I'd planned on taking the slow and easy road.

"How are things progressing?" the doctor

asked, wandering into the room. He glanced around at all the various expressions and then focused his eyes on the patient and shook his head. "You tried to get out of bed?"

"I did. I'd like to get out of here, but my head is spinning, and I have a headache," Ayden said, and I wanted to run over and squeeze him, hold him tightly until it was all over.

"Not unusual for that to last for days, sometimes weeks." The doctor slid his electronic tablet out of his coat pocket and started punching things into Ayden's medical chart.

"When can I go home?" Ayden asked.

"Do you even remember where home is?" Mason asked wryly.

Ayden looked like he wanted to deck Mason, but thought better of it.

"It depends upon your progress. Could be as soon as a day to more than a week."

I caught Brandy's eye as she did the math between Ayden coming home, possibly remembering or not remembering who I was and the wedding. Her expression changed to dismay, and I realized we came up with the same result.

Chapter Thirteen

Whether Ayden truly believed or remembered that Mason was his brother, none of us knew. But once Brandy whipped out a tiny mirror from her purse, there was no disputing the fact.

I, on the other hand, provided for lots of wiggle room and no pretending. I was at least on his radar, but I wasn't getting my hopes up. I saw the blank looks and puzzled expressions sneak up on Ayden when he glanced my way.

Mason refused to tell any of us what he whispered to Ayden, but I believe it got Ayden a little more interested in me.

But not enough to remember me or us.

We were all exhausted from the day at the hospital, Ayden included. He had fallen asleep about an hour ago; around the same time we all left his room and said our goodnights. The difference was that while everyone went their separate ways to the homes they shared with loved ones, I stayed firmly anchored at the hospital.

They all thought I left when they did, but I just drove around the block, parked, and went to the espresso stand to get a ham sandwich and decaf latte. Even if Ayden didn't remember me, I certainly couldn't forget him. He was the one who was supposed to be waiting for me at home. I had nothing and no one to go home to so until he chased me away, I'd be by his side.

I finished up my sandwich and went back upstairs. The lights in Ayden's room were off, but there was still the faint glow of the reading light by his bed. I wanted to crawl in bed with him so badly and snuggle next to him.

I swallowed down the worry that getting to do that might not ever happen again. Since Ayden's somewhat acceptance of his brother, my mind whirled with the realization that just because Ayden might—at some moment—remember me, didn't mean that he'd still love me. There was no promise that he'd recall who we were together, how we met, and what we envisioned for our future. There was also no guarantee that because I was carrying his baby he'd remember the excitement we both felt when we found out we were expecting. There was no promise of anything.

I walked around the side of the bed and stood at the window watching the entry to the emergency room. I wondered what our view would be of if they moved him.

Why did I care?

I turned around and scared myself when I saw Ayden's gaze on me. Our eyes connected, and my heart started fluttering with anxiety. I felt like I was crossing a line or a boundary by being in the room with him alone.

"I'm sorry. I was just—"

He shook his head and slowly sat up.

I noticed something resting behind his gaze, but I refused to believe it. I didn't want to get my hopes up. I couldn't afford to indulge in the possibility. Not yet.

"You have nothing to apologize for," he replied. "I'm the one who's sorry, Lily. I'm so, so sorry. I never should've stepped into the ring."

My breath hitched, and I shook my head, afraid to assume that he remembered anything or anyone beyond the fight.

Like me.

"I can't imagine what I put you through..." his voice trailed off as he attempted to slide off the bed, but I took two steps forward and stopped him.

"Do you re..."

I didn't want to ask. I couldn't finish my question. I didn't want to face the rejection.

Again.

The soft glow of the reading light highlighted the blue in Ayden's eyes as he reached his hands out toward me, and I started to let myself believe that maybe, just maybe, he did remember me.

Remember us.

I took his offered hands, and he pulled me into him. I stood between his open knees as he clasped my hands tightly.

"Please say you'll forgive me," he whispered.

I was scared to say anything at all. I was afraid he'd fall back asleep and forget this glimmer of his history.

"You did nothing wrong, Ayden. Absolutely nothing. You were injured. It's not your fault," I whispered.

He pulled me in closer, making the gap between us almost invisible.

"I should've pulled out of the fight. I was selfish."

"You weren't selfish. You were undefeated. You wanted to prove to yourself you are the best. And you did. You won. None of us could have predicted what happened after..." my voice trailed off.

"I don't even remember," he said.

His hands untangled from mine, and he settled his arms around my waist.

Every single cell in my body was igniting with hope and joy at the mere thought of Ayden remembering us, all of us, as he held me. He rested his head on my chest, and I felt the weight of his world blend with mine, and I knew we'd be able to get through whatever was thrown our way.

"I love you, Ayden," I murmured.

"I love you, soon-to-be Mrs. Rhodes."

Hearing those words come from his lips made me ignite with a muted hope that we still had the possibility of a future together. The expectation of becoming his wife was uttered from his lips, not mine. Relief spread through my body, and the surreal world I'd been numbly moving through, collided with an overwhelming amount of sharp emotion. He remembered.

Ayden straightened up and released his arms from my waist. He glanced at the recliner I'd set up for myself and then back at me.

"I know it's not much, but would you like to sleep here? We can put the rails up so neither of us falls out," he offered.

My heart immediately melted into a world of bliss.

Ayden remembered me.

"Do you think it's okay to do that?"

"When have you ever worried about rules?" His brow arched.

He really did remember me!

He scooted back on the bed and rested on his side, patting the empty space next to him.

I was worried about snagging his IV cord, but he maneuvered it out of the way as I crawled next to him. He wrapped his arm around me and placed the IV cord over us as he hugged me into him.

"I was so scared, Ayden," I whispered, feeling his body next to mine. "So scared."

He tightened his hold and buried his head into my neck.

"You don't have to worry any longer. I'm here."

I nodded and felt his strength wrap around me as I settled into the first good night's sleep I'd had since spending the weekend at Mason's.

It wasn't the sunlight or nurses that woke us up. It was the excited chatter of Brandy and Mason as they walked into the room, spotting Ayden and me. I felt the bed shaking back and forth as I tried to open my eyes and blink away the blurry mess in front of me.

"Knock it off," Ayden growled at his brother.

My eyes still hadn't adjusted to the light so I only saw the faint figure of Mason extending his arms to wiggle the hospital bed.

"Seriously, dude. My stomach isn't back to normal yet."

"Sorry," Mason chuckled. "I got kind of excited to see my experiment worked."

"And what experiment was that?" I asked, lowering the bed rail so I could crawl out. Even though I had a great night's sleep, every muscle in my body ached.

Mason's brow quirked up slightly. "I couldn't have been that forgettable."

Brandy's voice rippled. "Or maybe you were."

I placed my hands over my mouth. "Oh, God. That's right." I glanced at Ayden and shook my head. "Your brother tried to cop a feel with your fiancée."

Mason shook his head and walked over to his brother, giving him a hug.

"Oh, please. You know you liked it."

Ayden's eyes narrowed on his brother.

"Why don't you explain to us all whatever possessed you to kiss Lily right in front of Ayden?" Brandy placed her hands on her hip and stared at her brother.

"First of all there's no denying that Lily is unbelievably hot, beautiful, brilliant. The list goes on and on, but my God, woman, your breath was so bad." Mason winced and pretended to wipe his mouth with his sleeve.

"Are you serious? I've been at the hospital all day and night and day without brushing my teeth. It was your brilliant idea to dive right in. Common sense should've told you to swim at your own risk." I crossed my arms in front of me and glared at him. "Besides, you liked it."

"I'll never tell," Mason sneered.

"That's probably a wise idea," Brandy chuckled, rubbing Ayden's shoulder.

"Well, when Lily and I were downstairs getting a coffee." Mason returned to his story.

"You drank caffeine? I thought you were trying to avoid it?" Ayden interrupted, turning to me.

My heart sang with happiness. He was remembering so much, so quickly.

I shook my head. "Nope. Still no caffeine."

"Do you want to hear my brilliance at work or not?" Mason questioned.

"It's probably the only thing that will get you of this mess you put yourself into," Ayden joked.

"So as we were downstairs, it occurred to me that even though you weren't able to immediately recall memories of me or Lily, maybe somehow if I reenacted a scene with Lily, it might pull something out of your subconscious. I was hoping it would speed up the process. In all honesty, it hurt that you didn't remember me, but it destroyed me that you didn't remember Lily. I thought what if all of our memories are like little movies just waiting to be viewed. My hope was that you'd see yourself kissing Lily."

"You did get pretty pissed," Brandy offered.

Ayden pulled his brows together. "I was furious and I couldn't figure out why."

"How did you remember her?" Mason asked.

Hearing his question made my pulse race.

"I'd fallen asleep, and I started dreaming about Lily. I woke up and saw her standing by the window and realized I wasn't dreaming, those were actual memories of us together."

"I'll take total credit," Mason replied grinning.

"Whatever helps you sleep at night," I teased.

He rolled his eyes.

"Does Tori know?" I asked.

"She sure does. I used a whole bottle of mouthwash, and she wanted to know why."

"Aren't you on a roll," I chuckled.

"I almost forgot. Tori gave this to me to give to you." He reached into his back pocket and whipped out a new toothbrush and handed it to me. "And then this." He pulled out travel-size toothpaste, which I snagged from him.

"Please tell her, thank you." I headed to the bathroom and turned on the water and unwrapped the toothbrush, squirting plenty of paste onto the bristles. Just as I started brushing, I heard the doctor come into the room.

Figured.

Ayden relayed the good news about his memory, and the doctor examined him and

135

asked him about his pain level.

"Well, I think if your progress continues, I'd feel comfortable sending you home later this afternoon."

I squeaked excitement with a mouth full of toothpaste and turned around to spit it out. That was the best news ever. I quickly rinsed, leaving most of the grit still in my mouth, and flung myself into the room.

"I would want you to take it easy for the next week. No exercise. Mostly resting and taking life easy."

"He's not very good at sitting still," I told the doctor.

"I gathered that by looking at him, but it's imperative that he doesn't do anything to interrupt his healing process. If he feels up to it, slow walks around the block would be fine. But nothing more."

Brandy traded glances with me.

"He has a trip to Bermuda planned in a couple weeks. Is he allowed to travel?" she asked.

"I advise against all air travel for the first ten days. After that, if his symptoms are gone, then I don't see why a flight to Bermuda would be a problem."

Ayden smiled widely and his eyes connected with mine.

I literally felt like a teenager getting ready for my first prom. I let out a deep breath and couldn't help but smile back. To have come so close to losing Ayden, only to have him wake up and not remember a thing about me, to now seeing him look forward to our wedding did all kinds of crazy things to me. This wasn't only a rollercoaster of emotions; it was an epic upheaval of life itself, and something told me in some form or another this was what living life with Ayden would be, and I was beyond okay with that.

"So how do we know if he gets to go home this afternoon?" I asked.

"The nurses are going to come in and remove the IV fluid he's been receiving, along with the catheter. If he can walk around the corridor without much dizziness, we'll discharge him."

I nodded and glanced at Ayden, who grimaced slightly.

Dizziness hadn't been his friend this morning, but I knew we both wanted him home.

"Any other questions?" the doctor asked.

We all shook our heads and he left the room. Not long after, the nurse appeared and chased us out so she could remove his catheter and IV.

Brandy grabbed my hand in the hallway and jumped up on her toes.

"How did it happen? How did he remember you this morning?" she asked.

"It wasn't this morning, actually." I grinned. "When you all left, I stayed behind and went back up to his room. He started by apologizing..." I pushed down the joyous tears that wanted to take over the moment. I wasn't the crying kind, and no matter my exhaustion level, I wasn't going to start now.

Brandy shook her head. "I can't even tell you

what I was feeling last night. I couldn't sleep. Aaron and I were up all night wondering what we were going to do."

I nodded and smiled. "That's how I started my evening too. I honestly couldn't fathom it. This entire ordeal has felt like one bad dream, and it all started with Viktor."

Viktor.

"Speaking of him, has anyone heard about what happened to him after his buddies drove him away?"

Mason's eyes fell to the floor, and he kicked an imaginary stone as if he was in first grade.

"What?" I almost whispered.

"He was in pretty rough shape, but we took it too easy on him, avoiding the vital areas, at least from what I heard. He went to the ER and got stitched up and only had a few bruised ribs."

I shivered.

"Hopefully, we can put it all behind us."

Mason nodded solemnly. "It didn't bring out a side of me that I'm proud of."

"It wouldn't. We all went through a lot."

Brandy agreed and let out a breath. "How long does it take to pull out a catheter?"

Mason shrugged. "I'll go call our parents and let them know the good news. I know they were as devastated as the rest of us when they left."

"Amazing how life can change so quickly. Now if we can only make it to the wedding."

Brandy laughed. "Honestly, with the way things have been going, I'd say no promises."

"That's kind of the theme I'm sensing."

Chapter Fourteen

Ayden was home, spread out on the couch. I'd snuck in a quick shower after I got him situated the first time. We started with him lying in bed for the first thirty minutes of being back home, but that was all he lasted. So I brought out a ton of pillows and blankets and made him comfortable on the couch. He wasn't very good at following instructions, and I figured it was good I learned how to deal with this trait before we walked down the sandy aisle in Bermuda.

In order to navigate the next many decades with a man who stands when you say sit and sits when you ask him to stand, I now had time to mentally prepare myself for the practice of reverse psychology.

"You probably want me to keep the light on, don't you?" I asked Ayden from the kitchen.

"No. It'd be great if you could switch it off," he replied.

I hid my grin and turned off the overhead canister lights, leaving the soft glow of the lamp in the corner. The doctor had advised against harsh lighting for a few days to help with the headaches. He also wrote down that light meals would help settle Ayden's stomach. I knew if I came right out and told Ayden I was making soup, he'd groan about it, no matter what his stomach told him so here went reverse psychology experiment number two.

"Would you be into tacos tonight?" I asked, glancing over my shoulder before I opened the fridge. "We've got the tortillas, cheese, tomatoes…"

"Maybe that tortilla soup you make, babe. Might be a little better for the moment," Ayden called over from the couch.

Mission accomplished.

"Yeah. That sounds perfect." I smiled and pulled out the tomatoes, onions, and garlic from the fridge. Could it be this easy? How had I never thought of this before?

"Mason and Brandy want to come over tonight. I'm guessing you need to take it easy, but I thought I'd check."

Ayden picked up a catalog and flipped through the first couple pages before tossing it over to the coffee table. I honestly had no idea whether or not he was up for company.

"That'd be fine," he said, reaching for the remote.

The doctor had mentioned that bright lights from a television could set off his headache, but I debated about saying anything in this instance. I didn't want to sound like his mother.

"Okay, I'll let them know. Gabby wanted to visit too. She's been a nervous wreck, and since she wasn't allowed in the—"

"Totally fine," he assured me with a smile.

I grabbed my phone and sent a group text to everyone, inviting them all over for tortilla soup. Within seconds I got their responses and had to laugh. They didn't let the grass grow under their feet.

I poured the ingredients into the pot and placed the lid on top to let it simmer. I glanced over at Ayden, who happened to be watching my every move in the kitchen. I'd been so worried I'd never get to experience a moment like this again. And here I was and here he was, and I wouldn't change anything for the world.

"You're so sexy." Ayden's eyes stayed focused on me, and I shook my head, chuckling.

"I've been crashing at a hospital and feel like I crawled out of a bomb shelter."

"Well, you obviously went into the bomb shelter looking better than most."

I rolled my eyes but couldn't slide the grin off my face as I trundled over to where Ayden was lying.

I took a seat at the end of the sofa and he shook his head, patting right next to him as he scooted toward the back of the cushions.

"I know your tricks," I laughed, eyeing the welcoming space next to his extended body.

"I wouldn't resort to tricks."

"Yeah right."

He sprang up and grabbed my wrists, somehow tumbling me on top of him.

"This is definitely not what the doctor ordered," I blathered, attempting to wrestle my wrists away from his grasp. "You're not supposed to do sudden movements like this."

"Doctors don't know everything." He nestled his whiskered chin into my neck, and I couldn't help but giggle.

"You aren't supposed to do anything that elevates your blood pressure."

"Just looking at you gets my blood pumping."

"You're impossible."

He kissed my throat, sending my entire mind and body into a euphoric place, knowing I almost lost this—these—moments with Ayden Rhodes.

"If your recovery goes backward, then you won't be able to get on the flight to Bermuda, and then we won't be able to get married, and then—"

He stopped my laundry list of "ands" with a long kiss as he slowly released my wrists. My body relaxed into his, and I felt the length of his body pressing into mine, all of him. His kisses twisted and tugged at my resolve to do the right thing, and my self-control slowly started to slip away.

But the wedding.

The flight.

The flight that was needed for the wedding.

I slowly shook my head and reluctantly broke free from his kiss, backing myself away from the determined look on Ayden's face.

"You are quite the manipulator," I teased. "You almost got your way."

"Oh, don't even doubt it for a moment. I'll get my way." He flashed a wicked grin and I shook my head.

"I don't think so. In fact, I think with everything you've been through, the best thing to do is to wait until the big day, actually." I smiled an equally wicked smile and sat back at the end of the couch.

"You wouldn't be that cruel." He sat up.

"Cruel. I wouldn't call it cruel. I'd call it strategic. It'll keep you on track."

"Baby, I'm already on track."

"We'll see about that."

"I barely pulled through. I had a severe head injury and—"

"You had a moderate head injury, and you almost forgot who I was," I teased. "Me... *Me*? of all people. I want to make sure you don't forget who I am again, dangle the carrot so to speak."

"I'm not a rabbit, Lily."

"That is for sure, but I think it will make the moment even more special. Imagine the sexual tension by the time we get to the big day."

The doorbell rang and Ayden just let out a sigh. His fate had been sealed.

"You know, I remember some of the things you whispered to me while I was in the hospital," he offered, as I walked toward the door.

I froze in place.

"Like what?" I called behind me.

"Forever in my debt? And something about taking advantage of me if there wasn't a nurses' station outside in the hall." His brow arched. "I'm sure the girls would love to hear what you were whispering to your comatose fiancé."

"They wouldn't believe it," I challenged, turning back around to get a glimpse of the man behind the threats.

I absolutely loved the challenge of Ayden.

His brow arched. "I can be very convincing. Give me what I want and I might play fair."

"I won't."

A shiver ran up my spine as I readied myself for the challenge ahead.

I pulled open the front door, and Gabby was standing on the porch with Jason slowly making his way up the steps behind.

"I can't believe you guys rode the bike here. It's the middle of fall." I shook my head and motioned for them to come inside.

"How's he doing?" Jason asked softly.

"Better than you can imagine." I twisted my lips in an exasperated expression as I took both their coats and put them in the closet. "His highness is in the family room on the couch."

"He's not in bed?" Gabby questioned.

"Oh, no. He wouldn't hear of it." I smiled, loving every second of the fact that Ayden was not only home, he was who he was before the fight.

Gabby handed me a pastry bag and smiled. "Not sure if he's up for sweets, but I brought over a batch of chocolate chip cookies. They'll keep for a few days if he doesn't want them today."

I opened the bag and sniffed in the wonderful amount of sweetness.

"Even if he doesn't have any, I doubt they'll last through the next twenty-four hours with me around. Thank you."

We all walked into the family room where Ayden was sitting up in a chair.

"You are supposed to be on the couch, lying down." My brow quirked up in exasperation.

I knew it was only a matter of time before he pulled this stunt. It was going to be a long couple of weeks.

"I needed to stretch my back."

Jason walked over and gave Ayden a hug and handshake. "We were worried about you. It's so good to see you up and about."

"It wasn't what I'd planned. That's for sure."

"Life never seems to be," Gabby agreed.

I trundled into the kitchen and placed the cookies on the counter and stirred the soup.

"All life can promise is that some plans are meant to be broken." Gabby lovingly looked at Jason and he smiled.

Gabby folded the blankets and stacked the pillows against the wall before taking a seat on the couch.

"Is Carla watching Katie?" I asked.

Gabby shook her head. "Surprisingly no."

"Yeah, Katie decided she didn't need a babysitter so we left her by herself." Jason rubbed his hands. "We'll see how that goes."

"That's what I'm talking about," Ayden

laughed. "Sink or swim. Let the toddlers fend for themselves."

I shook my head and poured some chips into a bowl and grabbed a bottle of salsa out of the fridge.

"We want her kindergarten stories to be exciting," Gabby agreed.

I walked the chips and dip over and placed it on the coffee table.

"She actually has her very first best friend. The mom lives down the street from us. She's a sweetheart and her little girl is totally adorable. It's her first official "official" play date."

"Official "official"?" I asked.

"The first time we did it, we dropped her off and pretended to leave, but we were there the whole time making sure she didn't need us."

"We'd spy on her through the windows," Jason added.

"That's not creepy or anything," I joked, taking a chip and dipping it into the salsa.

"The other mom completely understood, and once we realized Katie didn't miss us, we decided to give it a go tonight," Gabby said, taking a handful of chips.

"Yeah. We can't stay too long because we need to pick her up by eight."

I smiled and sat back in the rocker. I admired Jason and Gabby's dedication to Katie. I glanced over at Ayden, and from the looks of it, he did too.

I heard the front door open, and Brandy hollered a sweet hello as Aaron let them in.

"We're back in the family room," I called out.

Brandy bounded down the hall and beelined for her brother.

She wrapped her arms around his neck and didn't let go.

"I'm so mad at you. So mad I could beat you to a pulp."

"I think once is enough," Ayden laughed.

"Never again." Brandy shook her head against Ayden's and released her grip. "I mean it."

"You don't have to tell me twice," Ayden replied, his eyes darting to mine.

I wondered if it was true. Had he really given up fighting or did this just scare him off for a little bit? I suppose only time would tell.

I heard a faint knock on the front door, and then Mason pushed his way through the front.

"We don't need to knock," I heard him telling Tori.

Mason glanced at me and then his brother. Ayden stood up and they both hugged one another. Tori smiled and slid her hands into her jean pockets as she looked on. I could tell she really loved Mason.

Mason gave him one last squeeze and took a step back, spotting the chips. "Nice. I'm starved."

"Since everyone is here, I say we play a fun little game," Ayden said, his eyes fastening on mine.

He wouldn't.

"Let's play *Never Have I Ever*."

I threw him a dirty look. "Where have you even learned about that game?"

Ayden ignored me and glanced around the group who seemed completely mystified; some finally giving hesitant nods to satisfy Ayden's prodding eyes.

"Okay, then. Everyone know how it works?" Brandy asked, excited for any game that people might participate in. A few shakes of the head prompted Brandy to continue. "So each person will come up with something like, "Never have I ever eaten a grasshopper or never have I ever had a threesome" and then—"

"Whoa. How does it go from eating a grasshopper to a threesome?" Jason laughed.

"Only in Brandy's mind does it make sense, and only in her mind will it ever." Mason shook his head.

"Anyway, after the person says their statement, everyone who hasn't done it, keeps all ten fingers up in the air. Anyone who has done it, has to put down a finger," Brandy said.

"Isn't it usually done with sipping a beer?" I asked.

Brandy raised her brow. "I assumed not everyone was into beer sipping at the moment so fingers will do."

I smiled and rolled my eyes. "Point taken."

"Alright, so it begins." Ayden flashed his dazzling smile and his eyes locked on mine. "Never have I ever, and I mean EVER tried to grope or take advantage of a person in a coma."

All heads turned to me, and Gabby started giggling so hard she fell off the couch. Jason attempted to pick her up as Brandy started laughing as Gabby kept all ten fingers in the air.

"I mean it was just like a big misunderstanding...like...I don't know...it just seemed...I thought that...Well if he maybe heard or felt some sort. It's just that I couldn't believe he didn't remember me."

"I'm in shock," Mason laughed. "And to think what we shared."

Tori hit him upside the head, and I sunk deeper into the chair as I caught Ayden beaming about his accomplishment.

"Just wait. There's more where that came from," Ayden assured us.

And I believed it, but two could play this game.

Chapter Fifteen

"Let the partying begin," Gabby yelled into the dead microphone. She tapped it twice and handed it over to Brandy who blew on it a couple times and gave it back to her. It was like watching Tweedledee and Tweedledum blast into the twenty-first century, and I giggled as Emily patted my shoulders.

"Are you laughing at your friends?" she teased.

I smiled and sat back in the chair, sipping my soda water with orange juice.

"Let's show Lily what she's going to be missing. Wild nights of clubbing, singing karaoke, and—" Brandy stopped and tilted her head at Gabby. "What else will she be missing?"

"Beats me," Gabby snickered, and hit the microphone against her hip to make it work.

"Guys, we heard you without it." I smiled.

"You're that loud."

Tori threw her head back with laughter, and Emily stood up and climbed on the stage with them.

We were at a small karaoke bar, and all the tables were full since it was a rainy Saturday night.

Emily walked over to the machine and scrolled through the songs. A wicked grin spread along her mouth as she picked the next number and walked over to Gabby and Brandy with another microphone.

I looked at the screen behind them and laughed even harder. I couldn't wait to see Gabby and Brandy try to sing this song. In fact, this was my perfect ammo for whatever might come at us over the years. I slid out my phone and began recording.

"FYI, girls, the microphones don't turn on until the music starts." Emily smiled and held her microphone tightly, trying not to laugh at Gabby and Brandy. They'd only had a couple shots, but they were goners and it was pretty hysterical.

As the countdown on the screen went from 5-4-3-2-1, I just grinned and sat back in the chair.

"This should be entertaining," Tori whispered.

"This should be what gets us kicked out of here. No one will forgive us for this. I can't believe Emily chose this song."

And the music began.

I slid down in my seat as the trumpet to "My Humps" by The Black Eyed Peas started, and Emily prepared herself to belt out will.i.am's part of the duet.

Gabby and Brandy looked at each other and started giggling, and then they both stood up straight as Fergie's lyrics were about to start...Their big moment to shine.

And shine they did as they sang about their humps, junk in their trunks, and lady lumps. That would've been great enough to record, but it was like a gift from above when they started bouncing their butts to the beat of the music. Next thing I knew, they were covering the stage with dance moves the world had never dared before.

And there was a reason for this.

As I sat recording, I felt almost evil as the crowd roared to life around us, and Gabby and Brandy continued to belt out the lyrics surprisingly well. Tori stood up and started clapping as Emily sang her part of the song. This was priceless.

I watched my two best friends eat up every second of their fame as the song ended, and they took a bow with Emily following suit. After all, it was her impeccable taste that drove the house wild. All three trundled off the stage and wandered to our table while the crowd kept clapping and began chanting, "Encore".

I stopped recording and slid my phone back in my purse.

"That was the most amazing thing I've ever seen," I snorted. "Where did you learn those moves? I've never seen you whip those out when we've gone out before."

Gabby shook her head. "I have no idea where they came from. The song just brought it out of me."

The server came by, and Gabby and Brandy ordered another drink as did Emily. Tori was still sipping her cocktail.

"So what do you think the boys are doing?" Tori asked, plastering on a wry grin.

"I don't know. But it has me suspicious," Gabby replied. "Jason wouldn't tell me one thing. Not one single thing."

"Ditto," Brandy seconded.

"Me either." I glanced at the next act about to start their song and almost felt sorry for them. I wouldn't want to follow Brandy and Gabby's number.

"Are you thinking strippers?" Brandy's eyes were wide.

"Do you think they would when they've got all this at their fingertips?" Gabby motioned to us all.

"I don't know. None of them ever struck me as the stripper type," I chortled.

"Or we wouldn't be marrying them," Brandy said, folding her arms in front of her. "But do you think they have strippers?"

I laughed.

"Well, we were told to stay away from Ayden's house until what was it...two o'clock in the morning?" Gabby asked. "Wasn't that what it was?"

Tori nodded. "Sure was."

"You think they might have strippers coming

to the house?" I asked. "Yuck."

"I don't think they have strippers at all," Brandy stated again, but her voice went up in a question.

"I did tell them we were taking you to a male strip club," Gabby said. "But I was pretty sure they knew I was kidding."

"Were you?" I asked.

She shrugged and smiled.

"So the verdict is still out on the strippers with the guys. What else do you think they're up to?" I asked.

"Drinking. Lots of it."

"Ayden's not supposed to drink yet," I said.

"Well, I'm sure he won't then," Emily said smiling.

Appetizers that we ordered before the singing triplets got on stage arrived, and we all started chowing on mozzarella sticks and fried zucchini. It was a good thing I planned for a forgiving wedding dress.

"I so admire you," Emily prompted. "Most brides are going crazy with worry about fitting into their dress." She beamed and popped in a zucchini spear.

"You're so persistent, and I have absolutely no idea what you're talking about." I grinned, taking a bite of the melted cheese scrumptiousness. "Delicious."

"I think they had a car service reserved, maybe for dinner," Gabby said. "I saw a receipt reserving one for tonight in Jason's jeans."

"Ooooh. Interesting..." I took another bite.

"You don't think they'd ever do something like really stupid..." Tori began.

"Ha," I barked. "Yeah. I'm pretty sure that stupid could enter into the picture when this group of guys gets together, but not the kind of stupid you're referring to. They're a really solid group of men."

Tori was so sweet, and she'd only begun dating Mason a few months ago so I understood her worry. Her boyfriend's twin brother was about to get married, and they were all at a bachelor party. Between videos that had gone viral of bachelor parties gone wrong and elusive social media posts on the topic, it was no wonder she was worried. But I had total faith in the Rhodes men.

"You know, I saw online this one stripper who came to the house, and she got completely naked. Like completely naked." Brandy's eyebrow rose as she conveyed her findings.

I reached over and squeezed her hand, chuckling. "I think that's how it works nowadays."

"No way," Emily said. "I think it's topless only."

"Is that better, though, really?" Brandy questioned.

"I don't think our guys are even getting one of those services," Gabby said. "We should have faith in them."

"I have complete faith," I said, nodding. "Complete faith."

"Me too," Brandy mumbled.

"Me three," Tori confirmed.

"Well, I don't have faith in men at all so I say we go spy," Emily announced.

I shook my head, but my gaze connected with hers and saw the actual worry lurking behind her eyes. I glanced over at Gabby who noticed Emily's expression as well.

Maybe it was about time we showed Emily what real men were all about.

"You know what? Let's go find the guys. See what they're up to. I bet they'd love if we crashed their party," I said, glancing at the group.

Brandy looked puzzled, but Gabby had already zeroed in on my plan. Emily already had her fair share of bad luck in the marriage and dating department so now it was our duty to show her good men really did exist in the world.

And they did.

Gabby nodded and clapped her hands in excitement. "I can't wait to spy. I even have other shoes in the limo."

"Seriously? Who packs two pairs of shoes?" I asked.

"Always be prepared."

I smiled as Brandy waved over the server for our check.

"So let's do presents in the limo on the ride to Ayden's," Brandy said.

"Sounds good to me."

I could only imagine what kind of bachelorette gifts I had to look forward to...pink and purple battery powered things that shouldn't be pink or purple or have glitter on them for that matter.

My stomach clenched at the thought. I hoped I had lots of nice lingerie on the horizon, nothing more creative.

"Alright, ladies," Brandy said, standing up. "Operation...What should we call it?"

"I have no idea." Emily shrugged.

"Operation *Wedding Singer*," Gabby suggested.

"I love that movie." I stood up from the table and glanced at the couple on stage singing. They looked cute together and were having a lot of fun.

"I do too," Emily agreed.

"Okay. Operation *Wedding Singer* has commenced," Brandy announced. "Let's pile into the limo and decide how best to breach the property without them knowing."

"We could arrive to an empty house," Emily pointed out.

"True, but then we could make ourselves comfy," Tori said. "One thing I know is that they were planning on eating a lot. Mason bought out Costco."

"Curious," I muttered.

We walked out to the waiting limo and piled in.

"I hope this doesn't backfire," Emily muttered, buckling in.

My stomach clenched. I knew Ayden was never into strip clubs or strippers, but things could, I guess, go instantly wrong on a drunken bachelor's night.

But Ayden wasn't drinking.

Yet everyone else was.

That would be awful to show up at the house to convince Emily that not all men were the same and find our guys ogling some naked woman.

Nope. I had full confidence that we wouldn't find a woman or women at the house.

Then why did my stomach stay knotted?

The limo started and pulled onto the road as the girls poured themselves champagne.

"Okay. My present first." Gabby slid a large wrapped box across the floor.

It moved like it was heavy and that had me worried. I glanced at her and she was nearly beaming.

I tugged on the silver ribbon and ripped the ivory paper off the taped box. I opened the flaps on the box and was completely relieved and excited to see what was inside: a beautiful ivory negligee balanced on two handmade photo albums covered in white satin and bordered with red bows.

"Something for the honeymoon and a couple things for after," Gabby said excitedly.

"It's so beautiful," I said, lifting up the nightgown.

"It's nice and loose," Gabby pointed out.

"Why, yes, it is," I giggled, lifting out the photo albums next. "These are gorgeous. Did you make them?"

She nodded.

"They are so pretty." I felt the softness of the cover as I opened up one of the albums. She'd created an entire album geared for our Bermuda wedding just waiting for pictures to complete it.

"This is so awesome. I can't believe in less than a week, I'll have photos to put in here." I opened the card and read the beautiful words Gabby had written, and I felt so blessed to have such a great group of friends by my side.

I handed the gifts to Emily to pass around, and she handed me a gift to open in return. I felt bad that Emily wasn't coming to the wedding, but she'd decided to stay at Gabby's Goodies so Gabby didn't have to shut the bakery down.

The ivory gift bag from Emily was stuffed with silver tissue paper that I quickly dug out to reveal a two-piece lingerie pink teddy that looked extra roomy. The chiffon was beaded along the edges, and there was a matching sheer bathrobe at the bottom of the bag.

"This is gorgeous," I told Emily. "Thank you so much. I absolutely love it, and I'll be so styling in Bermuda and at home. Ayden won't know what to do with me out of flannel."

"It should give him some good ideas," Emily almost cackled.

"I'm making him wait until the wedding night. You know, depending on what we find tonight, maybe I'll play dirty and strut around in these the next couple days."

Gabby nodded and handed me another package.

Next, I opened the present from Brandy. The present was wrapped with so much wrapping paper, I wasn't sure I'd ever get to what was inside.

"Hope you love it," Brandy gushed.

"I'll love anything."

I finally got underneath the wrap and was shocked to see a Tiffany box. I opened the lid and tucked inside was a light teal passport cover and two engraved champagne flutes with Mr. and Mrs. Rhodes scripted on each.

"These are so beautiful," I said, raising one of the flutes into the air. "Wow. I'm totally being spoiled." I caressed the passport cover and grinned." This is so soft."

"Mine next," Tori said, pushing a box into my empty hand. "This is actually from Mason too."

It was a small box, but knowing it was from my almost brother-in-law helped to relieve any worry about it being the elusive gag gift.

I pulled on the gold ribbon and carefully unwrapped the small rectangular box.

"Mason picked it out when we were out last weekend," she said, smiling with pride.

I opened the box.

"This is too much." I shook my head, unable to believe what was inside.

"I told him you'd say that, but he told me to tell you anyone who was willing to put up with his brother for the rest of her life deserved a reward."

I shook my head and chuckled as I lifted out a solitary diamond bracelet looped in a platinum chain. Even in the dull light inside the car, it glittered and sparkled in every direction.

"He thought it could be your something new too," Tori offered.

"This is beautiful. He really didn't have to do

this."

"We both wanted to. You've been through a lot, and you haven't even walked down the aisle yet," Tori said coyly.

"She's got a point," Brandy added. "I'd take it and run. My brother's so lucky you're still getting married to him."

I smiled and shook my head.

The driver rolled down the partition between us.

"Ladies, we'll be arriving at the destination in less than five minutes. Any specific instructions on where you'd like me to park?" he asked.

"Just on the road so no one can see us," Gabby instructed.

"Easy enough." He rolled the glass back up, and I got butterflies in my stomach. It felt like we were about to toilet paper a house or something, and I lived here.

We repacked all the gifts, and the girls polished off the champagne as we pulled onto the shoulder of the road. I glanced at Emily, and she seemed as intrigued as the rest of us to find out what was going on at the bachelor party.

I didn't know why I felt it was my mission to show Emily there was another kind of man out there, but I did. Tori flung open the door, and we all crawled outside, each holding one of the presents. The driver got back inside after realizing we let ourselves out of the car. Who knew we were so excited to see our guys?

We quietly closed the door and walked along the edge of the road, careful not to fall in the mud from the November rains. All of us sneakily marched down the driveway, giggling and tiptoeing along the tree line until we saw the glowing lights of the house. Music was blaring and my heart stilled.

Maybe this was a really bad idea.

I exchanged looks with Gabby, but we knew there was no turning back. We snaked along the driveway, not seeing shadows or figures of anyone inside in the front of the house. A light in one of the upstairs bedrooms flicked on, and for absolutely no reason, my pulse started racing.

There was nothing to worry about. Maybe one of the guys had too much and was going to lie down. I guided us along the side of the house, over the bark, and into some unexpected mud.

"Shoot. I forgot to change my shoes," Gabby muttered.

We all shushed Gabby and continued on through the heavily landscaped area. Between limbs snapping back and spraying us, and rhododendrons wiping their wet leaves along our pants, we were a damp, muddy mess by the time we reached the back of the house.

I stopped and turned around, facing everyone. Gabby looked eager, Brandy looked terrified, Emily looked content, and Tori looked confused.

"Ready?"

They all nodded.

"I'll sneak up to the window first."

I was low and slow as I made my way to the family room window, dodging shrubs and patio furniture. The music was even louder on this side of the house, and hollering from the guys inside made my insides twist.

This was a bad idea.

When I got up to the window, I peered into the family room and pure shock shot through my body. I never would've guessed.

Chapter Sixteen

I looked at the eager shadows behind me, waiting for my response. I motioned at them to hurry over to see exactly what I was witnessing. They all placed the packages on the patio and scampered over. Gabby was the first out of the gate, followed by Tori and Brandy. Emily seemed the most reluctant to see what they were up to, and she didn't even have a guy inside.

Glee filled my entire body as I watched the men inside cheering at the video game on the big screen. Jason, Aaron and Derek were all laughing and shouting as they played some military game. I looked around the room trying to spot Mason or Ayden, and I found neither of them. My mind flashed to the bedroom light turning on. Maybe Mason drank too much and Ayden was playing nurse.

"See? What did I tell you, Emily? It does exist.

Male decency does exist in this world," I whispered quietly.

"Indeed it does," Ayden said from behind.

Gabby let out a frightened yelp and I nervously laughed.

Slowly turning around to see Ayden standing with his brother behind him made it hard to concentrate. It had been weeks since I'd been with Ayden and seeing his smug grin didn't help matters. He was so attractive and seeing what I saw made him even hotter. Ayden had his arms folded on his chest and was shaking his head. I felt my cheeks turn red, and my gaze fell to the patio as I let out a deep breath.

I'd been caught.

"So what are you ladies doing here in the middle of the night?" Ayden asked.

"What does it look like?" Brandy asked, narrowing her eyes at her brother.

By now the other guys had joined us on the patio, and I was ready to crawl under one of the boulders that lined the river.

"It's not the brightest idea to be traipsing around in the dark near a water source," Mason told us.

"So says the cautious brother," Brandy said.

"Is there such a thing between these two?" Tori asked.

"Not that I know of." I brought my gaze up to Ayden's and the butterflies returned. I hoped this feeling never vanished.

I glanced over at all my presents that the girls had set down to commence operation *Wedding*

Singer and wiggled my brows at Ayden who got the message.

He wandered over to the presents with Mason right behind. They picked them all up and Ayden noticed the lingerie.

"Well, this is worth the interruption any night," Ayden said, stopping right next to me. "Do you have other plans for the night or did you plan on hanging out?"

"I think they should hang out," Jason shouted, rubbing Gabby's shoulders.

"I second that," Aaron said.

Tori's brow arched as she waited for Mason to throw in his two cents about wanting the girls to stick around. He swept a kiss across her cheek as he balanced the packages on his way inside, and that was enough for her.

"We've got plenty of food and game controllers." Ayden was already in the house.

I turned around to the girls and shrugged. "What do you think?"

"I say yes." Tori smiled.

"Sounds like a good idea to me," Gabby agreed, craning her neck to give Jason a kiss on the cheek.

"Even though I'll be surrounded by couples still in the honeymoon phase, I think spending the rest of the night in sounds wonderful," Emily said.

I caught her glance at Derek and I wondered...

"Derek, this is Emily," Gabby began. "Emily meet Derek, Ayden's trainer."

"Ex-trainer," Derek corrected.

Gabby smiled. "Emily works with me at the bakery."

Derek flashed a smile and nodded. "Nice to meet you."

"You too," Emily replied.

She looked a little intrigued, but she was hard to read. I think Derek sensed that as well and decided not to come on too strong or at all so he went back inside.

We made our way into the family room, and I wandered over to the fridge to get a coconut soda water. Ayden had the fire going, and the space felt warm and toasty compared to hanging out on the patio. I hadn't realized it, but my fingers and toes were icicles.

"I'll let our driver know he can go home," Emily said, grabbing her cell phone out of her purse.

"I totally forgot about that. Thank you! That could have been expensive," I laughed.

Ayden got all the extra guests settled, and I wondered how in the world I lucked out with him. Sure, he stepped into a ring now and then, but he was tenderhearted the rest of the time. I knew Ayden wouldn't be up to anything too weird at his bachelor party, and I also knew he wouldn't be upset if he found us spying because he didn't have anything to hide. I took a sip of the crisp, bubbly water and grinned as Ayden sauntered into the kitchen, grabbing a carrot stick on the way over.

"I knew you were going to show up tonight."

"You did not."

"I did. Mason and I placed a bet, and obviously, I won."

"Well, Emily didn't believe men could be well behaved at a bachelor party, and I felt it was my mission to show her otherwise."

Ayden didn't look like he was buying it.

"It's true. You can go ask her."

"Nah," he whispered, sliding his arms around my waist. "So about that lingerie."

I giggled as he ran his whiskers along my throat, tormenting me.

"It will be perfect for the warm Bermuda weather."

"I know you're not going to make me wait until our honeymoon."

I laughed. "I've made you wait this long. Why in the world do you think I'd stop now?"

"Because you're not that cruel."

I rested my hands on chest as he pulled his whiskers from my skin and looked me in the eye.

"What?" I whispered.

"Are you that mean?" he asked.

"I am. I really am."

I couldn't tell him how much it was killing me to wait, or he'd use that to his advantage, and my resolve wouldn't be able to last a minute.

"I guess the guests of honor shouldn't hide out in the kitchen," he whispered.

"Doesn't look like we're missed though," I said perplexed, as everyone was chatting away and back to playing video games.

"They wouldn't miss us if we snuck off." He tried again.

"I bet at least one person would."

He exhaled a deep sigh and slid his hand to the small of my back, gently leading us to the family room. They'd left us two places on the couch, which we took over. I curled my legs under me and rested my head on Ayden's shoulder.

"I can't wait to show you some footage of Emily, Gabby, and Brandy singing their hearts out,"

"To what?" Jason asked, completely intrigued.

Gabby giggled. "None of your business."

"Why don't you guess?" Brandy hiccupped.

"Dinner catching up with you?" Aaron asked, amused.

"No," she said exasperated, but another hiccup snuck out and we all laughed.

"So we're walking down the aisle in a matter of days," I began. "And Gabby's walking down the aisle in December..."

Brandy glanced at Aaron awkwardly. "Yeah? What are you getting at?"

"I was wondering when you guys are going to get married? Still thinking of summer?" I asked.

Aaron's gaze fell to the floor before connecting with Brandy's, and my pulse raced. This wasn't quite the reaction I thought I'd get. I expected to hear none of your business or, yeah, next summer.

"We...we haven't really had time to talk about it," Brandy said, her eyes avoiding mine.

"Really?" Gabby was suddenly interested. "I find that hard to believe."

"It's true," Aaron replied. "Since we got back from Paris, I've been playing catch up and Brandy's been busy with—"

"No need to make excuses," Emily assured them both. "When you get around to it, you'll figure it all out."

Ayden squeezed me confirming my sense of things. Brandy hadn't complained about one single thing with Aaron. In fact, since they'd returned from Paris, I'd say things were stronger than ever, but now I wasn't so sure.

It definitely felt like they were hiding something from us, something big, and it bothered me. I glanced around the room, and Jason and Derek were already back playing, and Gabby was snacking on potato chips. Now was definitely not the time or the place to bring it up.

"And I thought we sucked at hiding things," Ayden whispered so low I almost didn't hear it.

I nodded slowly in agreement and watched Brandy and Aaron remain a little distant as the night went on. Maybe this had been building, and I missed it because I'd been so busy with my own whirlwind life of baby, wedding, and fight.

Not to mention what happened after the fight.

A shiver ran through me and Ayden squeezed me harder.

"Are you okay? Too cold? I can get a blanket?" he asked.

"No. I'm just perfect, but I'm crashing quickly."

"Even though no one knows a thing, I'm sure they'd all be understanding if you made it up to bed," Ayden offered, and I shook my head.

Instead of leaving the guests, I fell asleep on them right in Ayden's arms. It wasn't until I vaguely remember being carried down the hall that I realized I'd even been out. I heard goodnights and saw the reflection of lights flick on upstairs as everyone found a place to crash for the evening.

My head lolled back into Ayden, and I felt him glide me into the sheets.

"I could take advantage of you right now," he murmured.

I smiled and held my finger to his lips. "You wouldn't dare."

He grinned and shook his head as he pulled the covers up to my chin.

"I'm going to take a quick shower. Love you," he whispered, giving me a kiss before heading into the bathroom. Maybe I'd surprise him with some sexy time after all.

And that was the last thing I remembered until morning; that and the odd sensation something wasn't right between Aaron and Brandy.

Chapter Seventeen

Brandy and I were in Seattle walking along the sidewalk. The holiday decorations were already making their way onto light poles and in storefronts. I was bundled in a goose down jacket, an oversized sweater, and leggings. The upper half of me was plenty warm and the lower half thought I'd jumped into the Pacific.

I glanced inside a small boutique and noticed several necklaces with matching earrings that looked intriguing and like the perfect gift for Ayden's mom, but I was grateful to have Brandy by my side in case I veered off the path.

We stepped inside, and the jingle of the bell notified the salesperson customers had appeared as I beelined to the necklaces hanging on the plastic forms.

"Anything I can help you find?" a woman asked. She was around fifty with a pleasant smile and short haircut.

"Just browsing," I replied. "Thank you."

"If you need any help, please let me know."

"Thanks." I turned my attention to a beautiful malachite and pearl beaded necklace. The contrasting green and ivory was stunning, and I totally saw Brandy's mom in it.

"Do you think your mom would like this one?"

Brandy took a step closer and examined the necklace. "I think she would love it. The necklace is so her. Stunning, really." She flipped the price tag over and looked a little stunned. "You don't have to spend that much on my mom."

"Well, this is kind of a big event, and I want her to have something she'll always treasure."

"This necklace would accomplish that," Brandy laughed. "She'll be thrilled to acquire another daughter with exquisite taste."

We walked toward the saleswoman, and I explained I would like to purchase the necklace. She quickly came onto the floor to retrieve and wrap up the gift.

"How's my brother doing?" Brandy asked. "Any problems with his memory or headaches?"

"No. I've asked, and he promises his headaches have gone away, and he doesn't seem to be having any issues with memory. Granted, he could be a good faker. Kind of like you." I winked at her.

Her brow furrowed as I handed the saleswoman my debit card.

"Me?" Brandy asked.

I didn't answer until we went outside. The cold air chilled my bones again, and I couldn't wait to land in Bermuda.

"I can tell you're hiding something." I glanced at Brandy.

"I'm not hiding anything."

"I think both you and Aaron are hiding something."

"Why would you say that?"

"Both Ayden and I can tell."

"I need a swimsuit," Brandy said, pointing over at Nordstrom.

"You're avoiding my questions."

"I'm not ignoring your questions. I answered them. We aren't hiding anything."

The crosswalk light changed, and we made our way over to Nordstrom. I probably should be looking for a swimsuit too, but I wasn't going to fall for her techniques. I invented them. Avoidance was my signature move until Ayden.

The door we used landed us in the makeup department, and I glanced around the endless sea of glass counters staffed with women and men pushing the latest and greatest beauty products. Another department I should probably hang out in before the trip.

"Brandy, I love you to death. I do. But I'm telling you that I know you're not being honest with me, and it hurts my feelings."

She stopped abruptly in the purse department and spun around to stare at me.

"I could say the same thing, but I'm not."

"I think that's because we know my secret ought to make itself known fairly soon. There's no secret there. We just haven't announced it."

Brandy wouldn't make eye contact with me. Instead, she stared in the direction of the escalator. It felt like she was casting me away, and it felt off, unlike anything Brandy would ever do.

"Is everything okay between you and Aaron?" I pressed.

"Of course. He's amazing. Ever since Paris…"

I smiled and her gaze came back to mine.

"He's sensational."

"Would you please just tell me so we don't spend the rest of the day with me begging you to tell me, and you denying there is anything to tell."

Brandy's jaw tensed. "I'm getting a little stiff. Do you mind if we find a seat?"

I saw a seating area by the escalator with four velvet chairs on an animal print rug and motioned for her to follow me over. We both took a seat and she stretched out her leg.

"Are you in pain?" I asked.

She shook off the question with a wave of her hand, and I knew the answer was yes.

"I'll tell you, but I don't want to do it here, and I'd rather have Aaron with me." She had a faraway look in her eyes and it unnerved me.

"It must be serious."

"It's complex."

I sat back in the chair and looked around at all the busy shoppers. It seemed like the world always scurried on by barely stopping to allow even the slowest members to catch up.

"So at our dinner tonight, you'll have Aaron

tell me what's going on?"

"He's not going to be happy about it, but yeah, I'll have him fill you in."

She stood up and stretched. "All better. Now let's do some shopping."

"Right. It'll be so easy to focus when I'm dying to know what my best friend is hiding from me."

I followed Brandy to the escalators. Sportswear and swimsuits were up a floor. Truthfully, I hadn't even thought about swimming and fitting in a suit. It was probably a good idea to not assume I could still fit in the ones I had at home. Maybe the visual of me in a suit would be distracting enough to keep me occupied until dinner.

Racks of yoga pants, leggings, sports bras, and tube tops occupied the space and made me extremely aware of my ever-changing body. It was the body I couldn't keep up with. I ignored the last thought and stood on my toes, finally spotting a tiny section of swimwear.

"It probably isn't the best season to buy a swimsuit," I muttered.

"Beggars can't be choosers."

"How does that apply?" I chuckled.

Two racks of suits backed against the wall. There were several string bikinis, purple flowered two-pieces, skimpy monokinis, and a few one pieces that appeared to be shaming themselves so we wouldn't have to do it for them.

Brandy picked up a cute sherbet orange two-piece. The bottom was high-waisted with stripes and the top was polka dots.

"That is super cute," I gushed, my hand landing on a one-piece.

I pulled it off the rack and examined it. The world was full of beautiful and sexy one-piece suits. How in the world did I find the one rack in town that made me feel like I was on the high school swim team?

Brandy eyed it suspiciously. "That's an interesting choice."

The royal blue stripe running down the center did nothing for the imagination. It did nothing for life itself. I pushed the suit back into the rack, hoping the other suits would eat it alive as I skimmed across the other fabrics.

"What about this?" I asked, pulling out an ivory one-piece with shells twisted on the straps and a rope that tied around the waist.

"That's cute. Is it lined?"

I looked in the crotch. "No, but it seems like thick material."

Brandy's boisterous laugh turned some heads in the department. "You want to trust important bits to thick fabric? Let me paint this visual. You're feeling good about life. Your long, wet hair is cascading down your back. You're taking a few steps out of the water, the warm breeze kissing your skin."

"Doesn't sound all bad."

"As you continue to emerge from the crystal clear water, more eyes turn toward you. Men are smiling, and women are blushing on your behalf. You glance down at your body and you see everything. And by everything, I mean down to nipple color."

Laughter erupted from my gut. It wasn't a small burst of laughter. It was the feel good, change-your-day kind of laughter as I heard Brandy relay her own personal experience exchanged with the "you" pronoun.

"And then their eyes slip south." Brandy continued. "And it only gets worse."

"So it sounds like I should put this suit back."

"Swim at your own risk. That's all I'm saying," Brandy teased. "Why not this one?"

She pulled out a cute two-piece, teal fabric with white piping.

Flashing a grateful smile, I shook my head. "Maybe if we can find it up a size. That's my old size."

She slid the suit back in and began checking tags.

"How about this?" Her brows shot up in excitement.

"It looks pretty tiny."

"Nah. The top might be a little tiny, but the bottoms have full coverage. See?" She twirled the red suit around and pointed at the back.

I thought about everyone who was coming to the wedding. Did it really matter if someone saw me in a two-piece with a belly that no longer sucked in? No. And I certainly didn't care if some stranger saw me.

I snatched the suit out of her hands and carried on looking through the racks. I found a black suit with a top that zipped in the front and a pale pink suit with a floral design.

One of the sales associates led us to our dressing rooms. Brandy still only had the one suit to try on. I assumed she was pretty confident in her choice. I, on the other hand, had absolutely no idea what I was getting myself into.

I hung up my goose down jacket and stripped out of my leggings and top, tossing them on the seat.

I decided to start with the zipper suit. I pulled up the bottoms and glanced in the mirror. I looked like I was exploding marshmallow out on all sides with my white underwear gushing out. I didn't have a good feeling about the rest of the day. I quickly slid out of my bra and slipped into the top, zipping it up before shoving my white underwear underneath the black bottoms so I could somewhat visualize how this should look. Pushing in the last piece of fabric by my thigh, I looked in the mirror and turned around.

It wasn't that bad. In fact, it was kind of cute. A piece of underwear fell out under my butt, and I tucked it back in. This wasn't a definite no, but it wasn't a definite yes either.

I unzipped the top and pulled off the bottoms and put them back on the tiny hanger. I looked between the pale pink suit and the red one, deciding which one to try on next.

"How's it going?" I hollered to Brandy.

"Great."

"Great," I mimicked back in a snotty tone, and she snickered.

I pulled on the pink suit and didn't even need

to bother with the top. This was a definite no. The triangle portion of the suit turned into a deformed hexagon as my thighs ate the fabric and my belly guided the way.

I exhaled dramatically. And reached for the red suit. Did I really want to call this much attention to myself?

To be different, I started with the top and tied the string around my neck and fastened the clasp around my back.

I glanced in the mirror and chuckled at the reflection of myself in a sultry red bikini top and a white pair of granny panties that were beyond loose. I wasn't quite busting out of the top. There would be a point in the future that would happen, but I doubted it would be while we were in Bermuda. I turned to the side, blocking out my white underwear, and bounced. Somehow, things were staying in place.

I pulled the red bottoms off the hanger and slid them up my legs. The bottoms offered so much coverage I barely had to stuff my underwear underneath the bikini bottoms. It was a sign.

"Found it," I exclaimed.

Brandy's door slammed shut, and her voice was right outside my door. "Which one?"

"The red one."

"Can I see?"

I opened the door slowly and peeked around the hall. Seeing no one but Brandy, I opened the door all the way.

Brandy's mouth dropped open. "Wow. You're

a stunner."

I twirled around once and then quickly shut the door on her.

I changed out of the red suit and tugged my leggings back on and pulled my top over my head. That's all it took and a meltdown commenced. It suddenly felt like I'd been thrown in a sauna. I stared at the goose down jacket and didn't even want to touch the thing. The heat was internal. It was rolling out of my skin. I glanced in the mirror and saw the tiny beads of sweat dotting my hairline.

"Crap."

"What's up?" Brandy asked, as I swung open the door. "Oooh."

"Can you hold my jacket? I think if I even touched the goose down I would literally melt."

"Totally."

I handed Brandy my jacket and picked up my purse and the bag containing the necklace. All I wanted was to get outside and let the cold air wrap around every crevice. But I had a cashier and an escalator in my way.

"Mission accomplished," Brandy said gleefully, making our way to the cashier.

I paid for my item and glanced at the receipt. It was almost time to meet up with Aaron and everyone for dinner. It was our last group dinner before we headed off to Bermuda. We were going to go out a couple days before everyone else.

"Who knew bathing suit shopping was such a time sink? Looks like I'll be getting my answers before we know it."

Brandy stiffened and nodded. She handed the cashier her debit card and waited to push in her pin.

She looked over at me as she waited for the receipt to print and let out a big breath. "I just don't want anything to take away from your big day."

"It won't. Promise."

Brandy grabbed the receipt and her bag, and we began our trek to the outside world where I'd hopefully be able to cool off before we met everyone for dinner.

"You know how sometimes you think you want to know something and then you find out what that something was and you almost wished you didn't know?" She asked.

"Yeah."

"Well, I only hope that's not what's about to happen here."

Chapter Eighteen

Brandy and I stood in the lobby of the Italian restaurant in downtown Seattle. The rustic décor and dim lighting created the perfect place to defrost. The moment we'd hit the sidewalk outside Nordstrom, I instantly cooled off. It felt like an Arctic blast was barreling through Seattle, but it was too early for that.

We walked over to the oversized stone fireplace and warmed up as the hostess grabbed ten menus for our large group.

"It's freezing out there," the hostess said. "I almost froze to death walking from the bus stop."

"It's brutal outside," I agreed. The hostess gestured for us to follow her behind two red velvet curtains that were pulled back. Two tables had been pushed together to seat all ten of us.

"And to think you're ditching me for Bermuda early," Brandy pouted, pretending to scowl.

"Bermuda?" the hostess asked. "That sounds

amazing."

"I'm pretty excited," I confessed, taking a seat in the middle of the long table.

"She's getting married there," Brandy informed her.

"Wow. That's going to be so cool. I've never been anywhere tropical. Maybe after college." She grinned.

"It does seem like a lot of fun happens once a person graduates," I promised her.

"I'm hoping so. Your server will be over in a moment, and I'll bring your other guests back. Is there anything I can start you with?"

"A decaf tea would be great. Thanks." I glanced around the room that overlooked the bustling sidewalk. There were two sections in this restaurant, and I'd hoped we'd get this one facing the street. The other room was a little more private, but it felt like a cave sometimes, and after my earlier meltdown, I didn't want to feel stuffy or overheat in front of my potential in-laws.

I placed the bag containing the present by my feet so I didn't accidentally blurt out something to Ayden's mom. That was a nasty habit of mine. I'd get so excited about the gift that I'd want to share it immediately, which was why I procrastinated when it came time to shop for birthdays and Christmas.

"Doesn't it smell amazing?" Brandy sniffed in and shut her eyes.

I wasn't sure which of us was actually expecting by the look of ecstasy on her face.

"It does. It's always good to go to eat plates of pasta before a beach vacation."

She opened her eyes. "At least you have an excuse."

"I have no idea what you're talking about."

My phone buzzed and I slid it out of my purse. It was a text from Ayden.

"Ayden's gonna be late. He's trying to finish something up at the office. Having so much time off for his shenanigans really made things pile up, and now we're headed out of town."

"I hadn't even thought about that," Brandy said, opening up the menu. "Should we do the family style option?"

"I think so. How about I put you in charge of that?"

"My kind of project."

The hostess led Ayden's mom and dad through the restaurant, and I hopped out of my chair to give them each a hug

"You look amazing," his mom said, taking my hand in hers. "This wedding thing really suits you."

"I can't stop dreaming about it," I confessed. "But your daughter pulled me into the swimsuit department at Nordies today, and that almost blew me out of the water."

"I'm sure you looked fabulous. I'm the one who should be worried being surrounded by you young ladies on a beach all week."

She took a seat across from Brandy and glanced across the table at my drink and smiled.

"Where's Ayden?" his mom questioned.

"He's going to be late. He's trying to finish up at the office."

"I'm sure his mishap put him behind." She frowned and slipped her napkin in her lap as Jason, Katie, and Gabby walked to the table.

"It is like Antarctica out there." Gabby shivered. "Can we come with you tomorrow?"

"Go for it." I smiled and noticed Brandy hadn't stopped staring at the menu as she tried to pick items to complete our family dinner.

"Is it that tough?" I asked her, ribbing her arm.

"It is. I can't decide between eggplant or chicken parm."

"With the men we have at the table, my gut says chicken."

She folded her menu up and placed it next to her plate. "Then chicken it is."

Gabby folded her arms around Brandy and then myself before taking a seat next to Brandy's mom and dad. Jason plunked Katie in between Gabby and himself. They all ordered their drinks, and Brandy placed the long order for us all.

Aaron and Mason strode in, and Mason slid a gentle kiss across Brandy's cheek, and she grabbed his hand and squeezed it.

"Where's Ayden?" Mason asked, taking a seat next to Jason.

"He's going to be late. He's at work."

"Ahh."

The server delivered bread and took drink orders from the latest arrivals as Brandy began detailing our swimsuit expedition.

"Do you think it's fair to expect us to step into

a swimsuit in the middle of winter?" Gabby reasoned. "I'm as pale as a ghost, and I've even been indulging in the products I sell."

"It would be unfair for some of us, if you didn't," Jason laughed.

Gabby beamed and pulled some crayons and a coloring book out from her purse and placed them in front of Katie, who immediately began coloring.

"I was thinking of saving this until we arrived in Bermuda, but with my luck I wouldn't be allowed to pack it on the plane or they'd lose my luggage," Ayden's mom said, and we all turned to see her tugging two small boxes out of her purse. "I'd wait for my son to arrive, but I think I'd lose it if he were here so it's best to do it without him, especially since we're in public."

She slipped the small boxes toward Brandy and I. Brandy nervously glanced at me and then at her mom as she took the ivory box from her mother's hand. I took the lightweight box, and my pulse accelerated as all eyes were on us.

"My great-grandmother had two daughters, and she gave each of them a locket necklace. My mother and her sister wore them until their passing." Brandy's mom glanced at the table and her eyes met mine. "You're already like a daughter to us, Lily. I've always been so proud of Brandy's impeccable taste in friends. And Gabby that goes for you too."

"Thank you," Gabby said, wrapping her arm around Katie.

"But when my son told me he wanted to

marry you, I couldn't have been happier to know you'd soon officially be family, and I knew I wanted you to have the other locket. Okay, enough of my speech. Open it up, both of you. I thought when it came time to wear the something old, this would qualify." She smiled and her eyes went to her daughter as she opened the box first.

Brandy removed the lid to reveal a beautiful silver locket with a round stone in the middle of filigree.

"Go ahead," Brandy's mom prompted. "Open yours too."

"It's beautiful," Brandy replied, picking up the long chain.

My hands were shaking as I lifted the lid and saw the matching necklace. While the locket itself was around an inch long, the actual locket was very delicate. I couldn't believe Ayden's mom was willing to give me something of such great sentimental value. It meant so much to me. I lifted the tiny chain from the box and examined the locket closely.

"I'm in shock," I whispered. "This is too kind of you. I can't accept this."

"I'd be heartbroken if you didn't." His mom's smile was genuine as her eyes stayed on mine. "You're part of our family, Lily. You always will be. You took such good care of our knucklehead son, and for that, we're forever grateful."

Brandy unclasped the chain, and Aaron helped to fasten it around her neck. It looked lovely the way the locket laid against her chest.

Brandy motioned for me to turn, and I complied as Brandy fastened the necklace around my neck too. My palm pressed against the locket, and I swore I felt a comforting energy surround me.

"Thank you so much. I'll treasure it forever." And maybe if I have a daughter she'll get to wear it someday.

"Thank you," I said again. Brandy hugged me and placed her head on my shoulder.

"Now, I couldn't forget my other daughter, Gabby. How does that work? Let's see...Aaron will marry Brandy and since Aaron's your brother, that makes you a sister-in-law to Brandy, too, and that's close enough to inheriting another daughter, right?"

"It's so wonderful to be gaining children left and right without the tuition bills," Brandy's mom chuckled, pulling out yet another box from her purse. "I couldn't leave you out either."

Gabby started shaking her head. "You didn't have to do anything."

"I know, but I wanted to. Unfortunately, there's no long and involved story with this gift, but it's just as special."

Gabby took the small box from Brandy's mom and thanked her just as the appetizers were delivered. I noticed an odd trade of glances between Aaron and Brandy, and my stomach tightened. What were they hiding?

Once the server left the table, Gabby opened the box, revealing a beautiful silver cuff bracelet.

"That was my mom's bracelet. A funny story about that bracelet was she thought it was too "show-offy" as she put it. I, on the other hand, love it."

"It's gorgeous," Gabby replied. "Absolutely amazing."

"Glad you like it."

"I love it."

Mason shoveled a few fried ravioli on his plate, along with some olive tapenade. "Guys get the short end of the stick, I see."

His dad's boisterous laugh filled the air. "What do you mean? We get to marry these lovely women."

"I guess that's good enough," Mason retorted. "But my woman is going to be really sad she missed this meal."

"Where is she?" I asked.

"She's on the dance committee and they're planning the Christmas dance," he answered.

"They're actually allowed to have a Christmas dance?" Brandy asked.

"Perks of a small school on an even smaller island."

As we all enjoyed the amazing appetizers, I glanced at Brandy who was, no doubt, hoping I'd forget my earlier request.

Which I hadn't.

"Gonna let me in now that we're being fed?" I whispered.

She let out a deep exhale and glanced at Aaron. "Might as well. Everyone at the table knows except you."

My blood froze at the admission and my appetite took a nosedive.

"I can't take it anymore. I'm horrible at hiding things and Lily won't stop pestering me. We need to tell her what's going on."

Brandy's mother gave a sideways glance to her husband, who'd stopped eating, and Gabby glanced at Jason.

I glanced at Katie, who seemed equally as oblivious as I was, and waited for someone to begin.

"Shouldn't we wait until Ayden gets here?" Mason asked nervously.

Mason was never nervous.

"Nope."

"Maybe we should only tell Lily and wait until we're sure Ayden's out of the woods," Ayden's mom replied.

What was going on here?

"Would someone please just tell me?"

Aaron scowled and wiped his mouth with a napkin before slapping it down on the table.

"Viktor went to the police," Aaron began.

My heart started hammering in my chest. "So?"

"He's attempting to press charges against us all."

My blood boiled. "What? It was self-defense."

"Yes...and...no," Brandy's mother responded.

"Viktor almost killed Ayden. How is that not self-defense."

"Ayden wasn't the one who threw the punches after the fact."

"*After the fact*, Ayden was left to lose consciousness, and if it hadn't been for all of you,

Viktor would've continued to pummel him. This makes no sense."

"Well, we probably didn't need to all pounce on Viktor as we did."

My heart was thudding inside. "Like hell."

"That's my daughter-in-law," Ayden's dad muttered. "Love her fire already."

"We're hoping the prosecutor sees the situation clearly," Ayden's mom continued. "But as of now there are potential assault and battery charges."

I couldn't believe it. We'd gotten through the nightmare of the event and were finally getting to focus on our future, and then this horror of a human being wanted to act as if he was the victim in all this?

"What about Ayden? He's not pressing charges."

"Not yet, but we may need to go down that path. Only time will tell," Ayden's mom responded. "We're in a wait-and-see situation, which was why we didn't want to tell you before your wedding."

"We hoped it would all blow over," Mason jumped in.

"Is that a chance? A real possibility?" I questioned.

"It is," Ayden's mom acknowledged.

Ayden didn't need protecting anymore than I did. But he'd been through so much. If there was the slightest possibility this whole fiasco could blow over, maybe we didn't need to tell him. I didn't want anything to interfere with his recovery or our wedding.

"Wow. That wasn't what I expected to hear. I don't do well with things being hidden from me, and I know Ayden's just as bad... But maybe we shouldn't." I stopped myself.

I looked at Brandy and saw something more resting behind her stare. Aaron's gaze flew to the entrance, and I saw Ayden making his way over to the table.

Even though I thought about hiding it from him, it didn't take long for Ayden to figure out something was very wrong as his eyes went from one worried expression to the next.

"What? What did I miss?" Ayden asked.

I felt guilty for wanting to keep it away from Ayden, but we'd been through so much. I didn't want something to trigger amnesia or make his headaches come back. I didn't even know if stress could do that, but I didn't want to chance it.

"We didn't want you to wind up reliving everything again so soon. We hoped it would either go away or wouldn't pop up until after the wedding," Aaron began.

"Why would it matter? What's going on?" Ayden asked.

My eyes connected with Ayden's, and my gaze fell to the window behind him, shocked at what I saw.

"Ayden, was it snowing when you came inside?" I asked.

All the heads at the table turned to face the window as the snowflakes fell slowly to the ground.

He shook his head and glanced behind him. "Whoa. Did anyone hear we were going to get snow?"

I shook my head and reached for my phone. Every once in a blue moon, we'd get snow in November, but not this early in November. I looked at my weather app as if that would tell me, "No, it's not really snowing outside," and couldn't believe my eyes.

"Guys, we have a National Weather Advisory. We're getting a snowstorm," I announced.

"What time does your plane leave tomorrow?" Gabby asked.

"At night. Like ten o'clock."

"Whatever snow we might get will be gone by then," she stated

"I don't know. The weatherman didn't even predict this," Ayden's mom replied. "We were just supposed to have cold temps, which made me all the more excited to get out of town."

I glanced at Ayden as he bent down to give me a hug, and I knew this was a sign from above to keep this tiny revelation from him for the moment. We needed to focus on the future and the wedding and getting out of town.

"We'll be fine," he assured me.

We both glanced out the window again as the snow quickly turned to a white sheet, and I couldn't do anything but laugh.

Because we both knew how the city of Seattle handled snow. It shut down like we were in the middle of an apocalyptic event.

Every.
Time.

Chapter Nineteen

"Do you realize in less than seventy-two hours you're going to be my wife?" Ayden murmured next to my ear. He'd just come inside from putting the last of the luggage in the car. Within hours we were going to be on our way to Bermuda. My wedding dress hung on the front door, and I'd tucked Ayden's ring in my purse, along with both of our passports. So far everything was going according to plan. Except for the once-every-hundred-year blizzard that was laughing at us from the great beyond.

I hadn't heard from my mom since I'd called her from the hospital, and truthfully, that wasn't a surprise, and I was okay with the idea of them not showing up. At this point in my life, I couldn't imagine my parents showing a sudden interest in me.

Ayden's mom had provided a wonderful amount of support the moment we'd gotten back from Paris. She helped with contracts, picking out flowers, and going with me to choose my dress. All things I hoped when I was a little girl I'd be doing with my own mother, I'd done with Ayden's mom. And then of all things to be given a gift that was of such incredible sentimental value, I knew I'd found my place in life.

"What I really can't believe is that we're having a snowpocalypse, and it's not even Thanksgiving. Then I'd follow that up with I can't believe in less than seventy hours I'll be a Rhodes. A real Rhodes. If we can get there."

"Not even a blizzard is going to stop that process. There's no escaping us now."

"I'd never want to."

"I'll go lock the windows upstairs, and then I guess we should take off," he said, sounding as amazed as I felt. We'd finally made it to this moment. "I think we do have enough time for one little—"

"Nope. Not gonna happen. We need every second on that roadway to make it in time."

Ayden climbed the stairs and groaned. "This is crazy."

"But you're kind of intrigued by not getting any, aren't you?" I hollered after him.

"Only marginally."

We were going to Bermuda before the others. I wanted to make sure we had all the details finalized before our guests arrived, and we both wanted some time alone before the frenzy started. Although with the weather, it already felt like the frenzy had started.

My phone buzzed, and it was Ayden's mom wondering if we'd gotten to the airport yet. No, but we probably should have...

I quickly texted that we were about to leave and received another text back that made me chuckle.

Did you remember to pack wedding dress, garters, sandals, rings (both of them) curling iron, straightener, aspirin, baby powder, swimsuit, hairbrush, and something old, something blue and something new and something borrowed? See you soon and lots of love to you and our son. Drive careful.

The garters! I forgot the garters. I texted quickly back.

Thank you! I totally forgot the garters. See you soon and love to you.

I jogged down the hall into the master bedroom.

"I almost forgot the garters," I shouted.

"Where are they? I can go get them."

"I got it. They're in our bedroom."

I rustled around in the second dresser drawer until I found the two garters I'd decorated with beads and tiny flowers. It was Gabby's idea and I loved it. I glanced toward the river and took a deep breath in. We'd made it. We were almost to our wedding day. The blizzard had laid a thick, white blanket of snow with only the river trail etched along the bank.

Perfection!

"We should probably get going," Ayden said, walking into the room.

We were taking a red-eye flight to JFK and then a morning flight to Bermuda. Hopefully, everyone was heeding the Mayor's advice and staying off the roads, but if we weren't, I'd imagine others weren't either.

"I am officially psyched. I can't believe it's here," I almost squealed.

"About time," he laughed, ushering me down the hall.

I shoved the garters in my purse, and Ayden unhooked my garment bag, containing my wedding dress, from the front door.

"Alright. Let's hit it." He turned on the alarm, and we both exited our home into the brisk November air.

"I can't believe I'll be cooking the turkey as Mrs. Rhodes." He grabbed my elbow as I slipped on the porch.

"I can't believe we'll be eating a turkey you cook as Mrs. Rhodes."

"Hey now." I playfully pushed him as we made our way to the car, snow crunching underfoot. He hung up the dress in the back seat, and I climbed into the front seat. It was freezing outside. Only yesterday I was trying on a swimsuit, and today I was bundled up like I was headed for a ski trip.

Just as he opened the front door and crawled in, another flurry hit. He closed his door quickly, but still let a crazy amount of snow into the car.

"Crap. I hope this doesn't delay the flight."

"It's Seattle," he assured me.

"What does that even mean?" I teased.

We pulled out of the driveway and onto the main road to get us to the airport. With the snow, a forty-minute commute would probably be a two-hour drive, but we had plenty of time before our flight took off so I tried to play it cool.

My phone vibrated, and I glanced down, expecting it to be Ayden's mom again, but my heart stopped when I looked down and saw a text from my mom.

I sighed.

"What? What's wrong? Do we need to go back home?"

I shook my head.

"My mom just texted that she and my dad won't be coming to the wedding."

"You're kidding." It wasn't a question. We already figured it out, so why another text was sent, I had no clue.

"This is the kind of mind twisting I've always told you about. I really don't get it. I think we already latched onto the idea they wouldn't be coming. Why wait until the last minute to remind me I'm not that important to them?"

Truthfully, the thought of them being there made me cringe, and I'd gotten used to the idea of them not coming. I had imagined how the entire event would play out. Jason was even walking me down the aisle for crying out loud. I guess one part of me was relieved to make it official they weren't coming, but I'd rather have heard months ago.

"I'm so sorry, babe. I honestly can't believe it. I was actually thinking they might change their mind, and I was going to sic my dad on them. He can talk to a tree stump and be perfectly happy."

I giggled and shook my head in shock. "I honestly figured I wouldn't hear from them until after the wedding."

Ayden slid his hand to my leg and rubbed it slowly.

"Did I ever tell you about the one time I planned to spend Christmas with my parents when I was at boarding school?"

"I didn't know you were even at boarding school," Ayden said.

"It was short lived when I was in junior high. Anyway, we'd planned for me to come home for the holidays, but after I'd flown home, they weren't at the airport. They'd forgotten that they'd told me I could come home in December so I sat at the airport for hours while they were with Ivy and Heath at some mountain resort. A stranger at the airport finally realized I'd been stranded there and somehow tracked down my parents. They sent a car for me after hours at the airport. How in the world can you forget your youngest child is coming for Christmas?"

Ayden grimaced and shook his head.

"It was like I was always an afterthought." I let out a deep breath.

"They're the ones missing out. Not you."

I nodded and bit my lip. "I suppose I should

write them back about how sorry I am to hear that."

But I couldn't bring myself to do it. Not this time. This time I let my fingers and heart do the talking.

Not a surprise. Thanks for letting me know.

"Whoa." I whistled. "I can't believe I just sent that."

"What? What did you send?"

I read him my text and his eyes widened. "I'm impressed. That took some balls."

I giggled and furrowed my brows. "Or an extraordinary amount of hormones flowing through the veins."

He laughed. "Well, either way it should make you feel good for once."

"True."

He was right. No matter what my parents did, I always attempted to keep the peace and never spoke my mind. It might be a small gesture, but I was thrilled I finally said what I thought.

I kept staring at my phone wondering what my mom thought about it. My stomach started twisting in knots as I thought about how to fix it. But fix what? I didn't do anything wrong.

"Do you think she thought I thought she was actually coming?"

"I don't really know. This is their pattern. How many times have they said they'd come visit you just since we started dating."

He was right.

"I don't want to deal with the drama that can come with pointing out the obvious to them. I'm not used to saying much of anything beyond yes, no, please, and thank you. It's always been the elephant in the room."

"Hon, I'd say it's more than an elephant in the room. You finally hit your limit with them. You asked them several times if they were coming. We all know money isn't an issue and neither is travelling. They have the one and do the other all the time. Everyone has a limit and you hit yours."

"I still feel like crap about it."

"And that is why I love you. You're a fabulous human being. Speaking of fabulous humans, what do you think that was all about with Brandy and Aaron? Has she mentioned anything to you?"

I froze.

"Not really."

And truthfully, I knew Brandy was still hiding something from me, which I pressed her about once we were leaving the restaurant. I asked her about the trading of glances between herself and Aaron when her mom brought up the wedding, and she ignored my question completely.

I drew in a deep breath, hating the idea that I was hiding something from Ayden, but I would focus on Brandy's relationship since I didn't want to relay or fib about the other revelation they exposed last night.

"I assumed things were going well, but it certainly didn't feel like it last night. When your mom gave us both the presents and talked about

Brandy's wedding, I saw Aaron stiffen and Brandy refused to look in her mom's eyes."

"I know. I felt like they were hiding something from us, too." He was quiet for a minute. "Especially from me."

We'd hit the snow "rush hour" near the city and were constantly bobbing back and forth in the sparse traffic as unskilled drivers kept slamming on their brakes.

"I wonder at what point people realize they aren't supposed to do that?" I asked.

"About the time they're in the ditch," Ayden laughed, as we slowly drove by one such SUV that was being pulled out by State Patrol.

"Probably shouldn't jinx ourselves."

"Good call."

It felt like I was on the high seas, and we yet were only going fifteen miles per hour on a freeway not on the Bering Sea. I swallowed down the nausea and stayed focused straight ahead on the snowflake confetti.

"I know this sounds horrible, but try not to let my sister's situation bother you while we're in Bermuda. This is our moment."

"Well, I'll try not to."

"I hope it's nothing serious," Ayden added. "Aaron has seemed like he's been in heaven, especially recently."

"Oh, no. What if he found someone else?"

"There's not a soul out there more perfect than Brandy for him." Ayden frowned.

"Preaching to the converted on that one. Oh my word though. I would just be sick. I can't even think about it. What if she's keeping it from us until after we get married so she doesn't detract from our happiness? That would be so Brandy."

Ayden's scowl deepened. "I refuse to believe it. I think we're getting ahead of ourselves, and it will all sort itself out."

"Do you think you can ask Aaron? See if you can get anything out of him?"

"Sure. If that will make you feel better, I can try. But I'll be honest, if I find something out that will devastate you, I won't tell you until after the wedding."

Sounded familiar!

"Please." I rolled my eyes. "You're talking to a woman whose fiancé didn't remember her weeks before the big day. I can handle whatever it is."

Ayden turned off onto the airport exit, and my excitement level went through the roof. We were about to fly across the country and tie the knot.

"You know what's cool about this whole thing?" I asked, as he turned into the parking garage.

"I can think of many things."

"That we're all getting married. You, me, and baby Rhodes will be at the ceremony."

Chapter Twenty

I looked down into the azure water and saw all the way to the bottom. Ayden's arm was wrapped around me as we stood on the wooden platform that hovered over the crystal clear water shimmering deep below the earth's surface. Spectacular crystal formations surrounded us, and our tour guide flipped us jokes mixed with history while the group we were with ogled at the beautiful formations.

Colored lights bounced off the ivory crystals providing a dazzling display of underground magic as we treaded deeper into the caverns. And to think, I didn't even know the caves existed until we spotted the signs from our scooter.

"And don't lean too far over the railing or your camera might end up with the others down below," the guide continued. I peeked over the railing and saw necklaces, watches, loose change, a couple cell phones, and a camera sunk deep into the sand. "We only do a scoop once a week, and all the change goes to our retirement funds."

The group chuckled, and we were led deeper into the caverns. I glanced behind me, noticing just how far away we were from the entrance, and I wondered how much deeper we'd go. I wasn't looking forward to the million steps back up to the surface, but it was worth every step to be down here with Ayden. It felt like one of those once-in-a-lifetime experiences. I felt Ayden's eyes on me and blushed, giving him a sideways glance. It felt good to still be noticed and, by the look in his expression, desired.

I turned my attention back to the cavern in front of us that sparkled with green lights bouncing off the shimmering crystals that dripped from the cave's ceiling. The idea that something this beautiful could be hidden felt truly enchanting, and I wondered how many hidden worlds existed on our earth yet to be discovered.

"Maybe we should lead expeditions into the great unknowns of the world," I whispered to Ayden.

"I thought that was what parenthood was," he teased.

I had a sneaking suspicion he was right.

Ayden tightened his embrace, and we followed the group into the last cavern. This cave had even more formations hanging and twisting from above and jetting up from below. The air was moist and stagnant, and I had an urge to flee, but I focused on the wood railing in front of me and steadied my breathing. There was something about being so far in that made me feel vulnerable. I glanced at Ayden who caught my gaze.

"You doing okay?" he whispered.

"I think I've hit my limit."

He squeezed me and slid his hand away from my waist to give me space and air. The guide was finishing up his spiel and collecting tips. I glanced around the group as they began to disperse and tapped Ayden.

"Ready?" I asked.

Ayden slipped a bill into our guide's hand and thanked him for a wonderful time before following me back along the wooden platforms. When we reached the steps leading out, I felt the fresh air hit my bones and was grateful to have made it without any embarrassing situations.

We scaled all nine thousand steps—well, that might have been an exaggeration, maybe a couple hundred—and made it to the dazzling blue skies and bright sunshine.

I looked around the patio and saw a beautiful garden down the steps.

"That was something magical a person doesn't see everyday," Ayden said.

"It's pretty incredible. This whole trip has been pretty incredible."

"And we haven't even gotten hitched yet."

"Hitched?" I chuckled.

I leaned my head on his arm as we wandered

through the gardens.

"It's funny coming from somewhere that is cold and wet that somewhere like this exists at the same time with flowers blooming and sunshine pouring over us."

I glanced at the purple flowering vines that intertwined the wrought iron fence and the red and white poinsettias that edged the path.

"Maybe we should move."

"And give up feeling the constant mist on our skin ten months out of the year?" I asked.

"It would be pretty tough to give up." He sounded hesitant. "We should probably head back soon. Our guests are going to start arriving."

"And before we know it, we'll be at our rehearsal dinner."

He pulled me under the shade of a large palm tree and rested his hands on my hips.

"Lily, thank you for putting up with me. All of me."

"Why wouldn't I?"

"Why would you is more to the point."

I shook my head. "You're an amazing man. Protective and fiercely loyal with the heart of a saint."

"Don't let that get out," he murmured.

"Well, maybe saint is the wrong word. How about the heart of a man who deeply loves his fiancée?"

He grinned. "Probably more accurate."

Ayden looked around the gardens and not a soul had followed us out here. His eyes fell to my mouth, and his lip curled slightly in admiration.

"What?"

"Waiting this long has been torture," he murmured.

Ayden's gaze hungrily searched mine. The dynamics had shifted somewhere along the way of us waiting. He knew he had the power over me to do things I wouldn't normally do. And I realized he'd had the power to push me one step beyond, but he'd respected my wishes while we waited for our honeymoon. No matter how I wanted to believe that I was the one calling the shots, it wasn't true, and I enjoyed stumbling upon that fact as he pressed his lips to mine.

Ayden's mouth was soft, hinting of peppermint. I giggled internally realizing he'd been planning this moment, and nothing but sweet desire drifted through my body for the man I was about to marry.

I let out a soft gasp of anticipation as his hands slid down my back, bringing me in closer. It didn't matter that we were in public in the middle of a garden where people could watch and whistle. All that mattered was that I was in Ayden's arms.

My mind submerged into the blissful realization that I no longer had to be in charge, my heart was no longer afraid to be shattered. Ayden's kisses intensified, and my arms slipped around his neck, tightening my hold on him.

We were both losing our self-control, and the moment Ayden took a step backward with me in tow and leaned against the palm tree, I knew we were in trouble. I ran my fingers through his hair with an eagerness I hadn't predicted. The idea of waiting until tomorrow seemed extreme as his lips gently tugged at mine before he brought his head back up.

I licked my lips, and his smile deepened in satisfaction.

"I was beginning to worry..." his voice trailed off.

"Worry?"

"Your resolute determination against..." He scowled playfully. "Giving me what I wanted...had me worried."

"And what exactly do you want?"

"All of you."

His hands worked their way around back to my hips, and I took a step back.

Satisfaction coursed through his gaze, and all I could do was grin. He knew how close he was to making me unravel.

"You said something about the guests earlier," I mumbled, lost in a daze and left to wonder why I'd resisted him for so long. "Why do I suddenly feel like the shoe is on the other foot?"

"Because you're perceptive," he replied, pleased at the power he'd regained.

I sighed and drew my finger along his abdomen in wonderment, feeling the hardness underneath.

"You healed up well."

"The ice packs and antibiotic ointment did the trick," he laughed. "Trying to change the subject, I see."

"What subject?"

"The subject of us. In our suite." He looked at his phone. "In twenty minutes. Naked."

My heart flittered with fulfillment, but even with all my growth as a human, I couldn't resist torturing my future husband. I took a step forward and snuck my fingers under his shirt and then along the waistband of his board shorts, getting dangerously low to an area that could drop him to his knees.

His gaze hardened as his eyes locked on mine, and my fingers sank deeper before slipping away. I sucked on my lip and flashed him my widest and most innocent expression before turning around and walking away.

Even with my moment of almost weakness, I managed to get back to the hotel, change, and wiggle my hips just enough to leave Ayden groaning as we left the hotel room to meet everyone on the beach.

By some miracle of God, we'd all made it out of the storm of the century to arrive in Bermuda where we found ourselves wandering beaches and Crystal Caves.

I was so excited. The texts had started coming in that they'd all arrived at the hotel and would meet us downstairs at rehearsal time. It felt as if the world had suddenly been flung into fast-forward with no signs of stopping.

"Are you ready?" Ayden whispered, while we waited for the elevator. "There's no turning back soon."

I laughed and shook my head, leaning against him just as the elevator opened up.

"No, playing dirty," I glanced up at him as we stepped into the elevator.

"I never would," he insisted, slowly following behind.

I pushed the lobby button and stood a few feet away from Ayden. There was something electrifying about being in small spaces with him, and he was using it to his advantage.

"I don't bite."

"Yes, you do." I smiled and his mouth broke into a daring grin.

"Maybe sometimes."

Without another floor passing, he stopped the elevator and wound his arm around my waist while swooping me into him. His mouth scattered along my neck, and my pulse raced as his other hand ran up my bare leg, the sundress working too much in his favor. The elevator buzzed, and a woman's voice broke over the elevator music asking if we needed assistance. I giggled at the rude interruption as Ayden released me, and he reengaged the elevator after apologizing to the mystery voice.

The plan had been to meet everyone on the beach, but as the doors glided open, we were greeted with Brandy and Gabby's smiling faces.

"We heard the elevator buzz and we knew it had to be you," Brandy informed us.

"You did not."

"And she's got rosy cheeks," Gabby pointed

out.

"Please," I said. "We were rushed. We just got back from the Crystal Caves."

"I don't buy it," Gabby said. I gave her a hug and she jumped in place. "Can you believe it? I can't believe it."

I shook my head and gave Brandy a hug.

Ayden had walked over to where Mason and the others were congregating by the automatic doors that led out to the beach. It was funny to watch Katie, Jason, and Aaron taking turns hopping out of the way of the door's sensors.

"We've got one shot to memorize what to do for tomorrow," Ayden's voice instructed his guys. "Let's not blow it, or I'll never hear the end of it."

"Blow it," Katie repeated.

"I'm just glad you're doing the big deed first," Aaron joked. "I can watch and learn."

"Ready?" Ayden called over.

I nodded as we all walked to the guys and headed toward to the beach where we'd meet up with Jenny, our event coordinator, and learn exactly what we needed to do for the big day.

Brandy gave me a quick squeeze as we headed outside. The balmy breeze swept through the air carrying pure anticipation of tomorrow. I looked toward the sandy beach and saw where we'd be saying our vows, and my soul became filled with promise.

This time tomorrow I'd be walking down the aisle!

Chapter Twenty-One

Ayden and I held hands on the elevated platform and gazed into one another's eyes as Jenny instructed who did what and when. Aaron and Mason stood behind Ayden, and Gabby and Brandy were giggling behind me.

Jenny announced us as a pretend Mr. and Mrs. Rhodes and instructed us to walk back down the aisle. We were like giddy high schoolers and I loved every second.

"Can I get a kiss first?" Ayden asked, but he didn't wait for my response. He slid a quick kiss along my lips and grinned. "There's more where that came from."

I rolled my eyes and giggled.

We walked down the aisle and turned around to see Ayden's mom and dad stand up from the front row and walk down next, followed by the groomsmen and bridesmaids. My nerves ignited at the thought of doing this for real tomorrow in front of our friends and family. We were so close. There was only one dinner and a night's sleep in the way.

Ayden's mom squeezed me tightly.

"We are so lucky to gain a daughter," she whispered. "One who loves our son as deeply as we do."

She took a step back and wiped away an escaping tear as her husband squeezed her tightly.

"Come on, now," he chuckled. "The waterworks can't start until tomorrow."

"Alright, alright." She reached over and gave my hand one last squeeze.

Katie let out quite an exasperated groan and sat down on the sand as we congregated and chatted too much for her liking. In order to avoid a possible meltdown with Katie, Jenny led us a little ways down the beach where our other guests were already waiting with drinks in hand and appetizers circulating.

The hotel had done a beautiful job. Candles flickered in the sand near the water, and several arrangements framed the entrance to a canopy that had been erected for our dinner. It was a beautiful night. The weather was calm, the breeze light, and the temperature a pleasant seventy-two degrees. All poignant reminders of how lucky we were to be so far away from Seattle at this particular moment.

Jenny took us to our seats and gathered the guests inside the canopy. Everything was going seamlessly, and it was as if all the cares in the world had never existed. I looked around the table where Brandy, Aaron, Gabby, Jason, Mason, Tori, Ayden's parents, aunts, uncles, and four cousins had settled in. Seeing everyone's smiling faces as they chatted with one another made tonight the casual and fun-loving night I'd wished for.

I wasn't a stuffy kind of person, and I was thrilled that the resort had created a relaxed rehearsal dinner. Three long driftwood tables had been put together to make one giant table where ivory candles flickered on top of shiny green anthurium leaves that were used like placemats, and ivory orchids towered over the appetizer plates.

Ayden's hand was on my knee, and I swore the pull we always shared was only intensifying. Ayden's eyes gleamed, and he leaned over, placing his mouth near my ear.

"Do you remember the first time I kissed you?"

My smile widened, and my body warmed at the thought.

"I even remember the first time I hoped you'd kiss me, and the first time I fantasized about kissing you," I whispered back.

It felt as if the world had fallen away, and it was just us two sitting on the beach, remembering how we first fell in love.

"When was that?" His eyes glinted with amusement.

"The night you showed up to my place to tell me about Brandy and Gabby's plan to find my high school boyfriend, right after I'd had that disastrous date."

"You wanted me to kiss you that night?" his voice lowered.

"I prayed you would."

"And what about this fantasy you mentioned?"

"Same night," I confessed, giggling.

"Really." He was intrigued. "A woman who knows what she wants."

"Yep. I thought about my hands running underneath your sweater."

"You even remembered that I was in a sweater?" he asked.

"Absolutely."

He threw his head back, and his fabulous laughter wrapped around me. "And to think I drew it out so long."

Brandy caught my gaze. "Okay, you two lovebirds. What's so funny?"

"Just reminiscing." I flashed a grin and she rolled her eyes.

"Already, I sense too much information on the way," Brandy said wryly.

"You asked. No secrets, remember?" My brow arched, and Brandy's cheeks reddened as she glanced at Aaron for help.

So they *were* hiding something from us.

I glanced around the table and noticed everyone completely immersed in their own conversations, the sign of a healthy dinner party, and also, the sign of the perfect time to pounce on Brandy. I wanted answers.

"Is there anything you're not telling me?" I

whispered, leaning slightly against the table.

"I could ask the same," she replied.

I looked at her quizzically and let out a slight miffed sound.

"When we both know what I'm hiding, I wouldn't really say it qualifies as hiding..."

She wrinkled her nose and glanced at Aaron, who was busy talking to one of Ayden's uncles about photography.

So it really *did* have to do with Aaron.

"I have to be honest." I glanced over at Ayden who'd jumped into a conversation between Jason and Ayden's dad. "It's making it hard for me to concentrate on all my festivities. Today Ayden planned a tour for us at the crystal caves and do you want to know what popped into my mind?"

"What?"

"What could Brandy and Aaron be hiding from us?" I answered.

"I didn't mean to detract from your day," she said softly, and my chest constricted. Please let their relationship be okay. "Aaron and I just decided that—"

Oh, no. Here it came. As if food would be my friend during this time, I forked a few pieces of bruschetta on to my plate and took a bite.

"That life is too short, and when everything happened to Ayden, it made things crystal clear," she continued. "It brought things into perspective."

"What things?" I could barely speak. I needed backup, but Ayden was deep in conversation, and Gabby had excused herself to go to the restroom.

"Sometimes no matter how much you want to plan, life can do a one-eighty."

"True."

"Between my accident, Paris, and Ayden's..." she stopped herself and glanced at Aaron, but he was still deep in conversation. "Basically, Aaron and I decided that we knew what we wanted out of life."

"And it wasn't the same thing?"

Brandy's eyes widened, and she shook her head. "What? Why wouldn't it be the same thing?"

I scowled unsure of why I thought it wouldn't be.

She leaned closer and whispered. "We got married."

My fork slipped out of my hand and clanged against my plate. All eyes turned toward me and I grimaced at my clumsiness.

"Sorry," I said, beaming.

And to think I was worried they were going to randomly break up!

Shame on me and shame on this cynical world we live in!

Everyone went back to chatting and eating, and Ayden placed his hand on my shoulder.

"You okay?"

"Yep. More than okay."

He kissed my cheek and turned to answer a question his brother tossed in his direction.

Brandy's eyes were fastened on mine and I shook my head.

What a stinker! A conniving stinker!

"When did you?" I tried to speak as cryptically as possible.

"The day before the bachelor/bachelorette party."

"You're kidding."

"Nope." The moment the secret was released between us, her beautiful smile appeared, the one that been missing recently, and now she was radiant.

"I'm so-so-so happy for you," I whispered the word happy.

"Thank you," she mouthed.

"Does anyone know?" I asked, my voice low.

She shook her head.

"I thought?" I angled my head.

"Our wedding is still planned for June. Officially. I told my mom the date this morning on the plane."

"Officially," I muttered.

"Officially." She winked, and it felt like the weight of the world had been lifted.

Of course I wanted details and to hear the why and when and how of everything, but the specifics would have to wait until later or until tomorrow. And here I thought Ayden and I were going to be the first to walk down the aisle.

"It makes sense," I teased, a little louder now.

"What does?" Brandy asked.

"That you'd beat me to the punch. Your competitive streak is insane."

"What can I say? I was raised by a lawyer."

Gabby came back to the table and crawled

onto the bench.

"What did I miss?" she asked.

"A ton. So much you won't even believe it."

"Really?"

"Yep," Brandy seconded.

I took another bite of the bruschetta, and Brandy sipped on her martini as we both let Gabby hang a little longer than necessary.

"Come on, tell me."

"It's a secret," I whispered.

"It really isn't a secret." Gabby stared at my stomach.

"Not that. It's about Brandy."

"She's pre—" Gabby started to ask.

I shook my head. "Getting closer, but no."

Gabby looked between Brandy and me, her eyes squinting as she settled her gaze on me.

"Are you gonna tell me or what?"

I leaned toward Gabby and whispered, "They got married."

Gabby gasped, and all heads swung to stare at her.

"You girls are certainly active down there," Ayden's uncle joked. "Sounds like one big revelation after the next."

"Just active imaginations."

As the conch chowder was served and Ayden had a moment's peace, I leaned closer.

"Brandy and Aaron got married. That's what they've been hiding from us," I whispered.

Ayden's eyes grew huge.

"My own sister didn't tell me?" He seemed genuinely shocked and a little impressed.

"No one knows and they're still forging ahead with their summer wedding. We can't tell a soul."

"I thought they said they didn't know when they were getting married."

"I think they were just caught off guard."

"And my parents don't know?"

"Leave it to Brandy to get it done quicker."

"Give Lily a ginger beer," Ayden's dad told the server.

I glanced at Ayden in horror. How would I get out of drinking beer without looking rude to my future father-in-law?

"It's not real beer. It's kind of like ginger ale only stronger and more carbonated," Ayden informed me.

"Thank you," I called across the table.

"It's my new favorite drink," his dad replied.

"Speaking of favorites, this is the best soup. Ever," Gabby said, slurping up the chowder. I glanced down and saw the red bean soup I'd mentioned a day earlier to Jenny. I mouthed a thank you to her for remembering my shellfish dilemma. The spiciness of the soup lit up my taste buds. We all quietly enjoyed our chowder and soup. The server delivered the ginger beer, which I took a giant gulp of and was pleasantly surprised. It had a bite to it that I wasn't expecting.

The evening went by quickly with lively discussion and a few impromptu seated dance moves to entertain. By the time dessert arrived, I couldn't believe it was our moment to announce the big news. As the servers delivered mango &

pawpaw mousse to each person, my anxiety level rose through the canopy. Even though most knew our secret, Ayden's parents didn't. Or if they did, they certainly didn't let on. As everyone made moaning sounds over the delicious dessert, Ayden wrapped his arm around me and squeezed.

"Ready?" he whispered.

"Ready."

He dinged his glass a few times interrupting everyone's euphoric mousse experience.

Once all eyes were on us, we both stood up.

"If you'd all follow us out to the beach, we have a little announcement we want to make."

Gabby and Brandy couldn't hold in their smiles as they clutched their fiancé's hands and got in line behind us. Ayden's dad came over to us and narrowed his eyes.

"Getting married tonight instead?"

I shook my head. "Nope."

I motioned for everyone to follow us as we walked slowly down the beach.

Candles guided our way until we hit a heart, which was shaped by countless candles. We were far enough away no one could tell what was piled inside the heart until Gabby and Brandy walked up next to the flames and spotted the pink gift bags.

Brandy let out a gleeful yelp and hugged her mom, who looked clueless.

Ayden hugged me and kissed the top of my head before he picked me up and lifted me over the candles and set me down inside the giant heart where all the pink bags were scattered. I began picking up each bag, reading the labels and handing them out accordingly.

"Don't even think about opening them up," Ayden warned.

Katie took the bag from Jason and began tossing it around. My stomach tightened at the thought of the contents spilling out, ruining the surprise so I handed the bags out quicker.

"Okay, mom. If you could open your bag first."

Ayden's mom couldn't keep the grin off her face as she opened the bag and pulled out the tiniest pair of pink saltwater sandals available.

His mom yelped, and tears began running down her face as the realization hit her that she was about to be a grandma.

"Inside each bag, you'll find a marker and a different sized pair of saltwater sandals. Each pair of sandals comes with a blank tag for a different stage of our daughter's life. You've all shaped our lives somehow and touched us in ways that made it possible for us to deeply love and for that we can never thank you enough. Our hope is that over the week, you'll come up with a bit of advice for our daughter for us to read to her as the years go by. We've got eighteen pairs of sandals so not one year goes by without some sort of sage advice. We're also hoping you'll pack them in your own suitcase so we don't have to bring them back ourselves."

The group chuckled as they dabbed away tears, and I felt completely full of happiness.

"The pressure," Jason said, rubbing his jaw as

Katie opened up the bag she snatched from Jason.

"And hopefully, her feet don't grow past a size nine because that's the biggest size we bought," I added.

"You're not worried about big feet then from Ayden's side, I gather?" Aaron teased, as everyone laughed so hard they cried.

Ayden's mom and dad gave us a huge group hug, and I was so happy to have finally revealed our secret. And I knew I needed to tell Ayden about his friends before the wedding. It wasn't fair to keep him in the dark about what they faced when we all got back home.

Chapter Twenty-Two

I woke up alone and that was how we planned it. He had his room the night before, and I had mine. Extending my arms toward the ceiling, my body arched into an unbelievable stretch.

Today was the day!

The night before, I'd told Ayden about what was going on with Viktor, and he unsurprisingly took it all in stride, which was one of the many reasons I was marrying this man. Nothing ever ruffled his feathers.

I reached over for my phone and turned off the alarm before it rang its shrill morning reminder. I had set the alarm in case I didn't wake up, but not only did I wake up on my own, I woke up early. I stood up from the bed and wandered toward the balcony and opened up the double doors. The warm air swathed my bare shoulders, and I took a deep breath in of the salty sea air and let it out slowly. It was hard to resist traipsing down the hall to Ayden's room, but I was trying to abide by as many traditional rules as possible...aside from some of the biggies.

It was so peaceful outside at this time of morning. The ocean waves rolled into the beach, and birds hopped from one tree to the next. A few hotel workers wandered the paths and a couple of gardeners freshened up the flowerbeds. The island air exuded calm, and I was determined to embrace the vibe—until I turned back around and saw my wedding dress hanging on the closet door.

I didn't have time to be calm.

I was getting married!

I jumped up and fist pumped myself before grabbing the remote and turning on some music to get me even more excited.

I felt like a little wind-up doll as I walked to the hotel phone. My body was zinging with anticipation and excitement. I placed my room service order, hopped in the shower, blow-dried my hair, changed into my "Mrs..." yoga outfit, checked my email for our latest proofs on an ad set to drop in three weeks, answered the door for my eggs benedict on wheels, ate breakfast, watched a few minutes of cable news, steamed my veil, laid out my jewelry, and shoes, and finally called Brandy and Gabby to wake them up.

I grabbed my phone and despite my best efforts to stop myself, I unzipped my "Mrs..." hoodie and pulled up more pregnancy cleavage as I readied myself for a selfie. I grinned into the lens and clicked the phone.

Miss me?

Within seconds Ayden texted back.

I think you have it in for me.

I unzipped my hoodie a tad more and took another shot, sending it over to Ayden. This time I pouted my lips.

Wish you were here

.

He texted back.

So do I...

I chuckled and left him hanging as Brandy sent me a text.

Will be there in a few minutes. Grabbing a bagel and lox. Need anything?

I texted back.

I had over-hard eggs benedict.

Ayden texted.
And the image almost dropped me to my knees. My cheeks warmed as I zoomed into view this beautiful specimen of a man. The bruising to his ribs had diminished, and seeing his stomach

literally made mine flutter.

I had to turn it up a notch so I unzipped my hoodie completely and took a shot of my lace bra and my best version of a sultry pose and sent him the shot with the caption.

Bet you're wishing you could...

A text returned.

Could what?

I glanced at the sender and nearly died. I'd sent it to Brandy. How in the world did that work?

I texted back.

Nothing. Wrong person.

Determined to give Ayden a piece of his own medicine. I re-sent the photo and this time changed the caption.

Sorry had to finish.

He texted immediately.

Finish what?

I giggled and wrote back to Ayden.

You'll never know...

Ayden sent a picture of himself on the balcony, again shirtless, and pouting into the screen. I couldn't stop laughing as I texted back.

You are one sexy beast. See you soon, Mr. Rhodes.

His last text landed seconds later.

Not soon enough.

A knock at my door hurled through the room, and I shoved down my embarrassment. It wasn't the first time we'd all swapped texts inadvertently, and I was sure it wouldn't be the last. I swung open the door to Gabby holding up Brandy's phone in one hand and her dress in the other while wiggling her brows. They were both dressed in the matching pink bridesmaid sweats I'd bought for them, and they promised they'd schlep around the resort wearing them.

"Feeling extra frisky this morning?" Gabby teased.

"Not anymore than usual," I explained.

"Gross." Brandy swatted at me, while grasping her dress in the other hand. "He's my brother."

I pointed at my belly and furrowed my brows. "You do know how these things happen, right?"

Brandy rubbed my belly. "Hahaha. Yes. I've got a firm grip on the birds and bees."

"Have you thought about names?" Gabby asked. "Maybe Gabriella or Gabrielle Brandy Rhodes..."

"I don't think so, my dear. That little princess is going to be named Brandy Gabriella. Isn't that so?" Brandy's eyes darted to mine.

"Not quite so."

"Well, there's got to be some sort of shout-out." Gabby sat on the bed and turned down the volume on the television.

I shook my head. "We can't decide. Thankfully, we have months to toss around ideas, but I'll be sure to pass onto Ayden your thoughts. I kind of like the idea of bringing back some oldies but goodies."

"Like what?" Brandy asked, spinning in the swivel chair.

"Violet, Agnes, Ethel, Myrtle, Tillie…"

Brandy's forehead creased slightly. "All cute names."

Gabby nodded. "Yeah. All cute names."

"I'm sensing a but…"

"Well, you don't want to prematurely age your daughter. Ethel is super cute, but I'm not sure I can imagine a ton of first graders hollering for an Ethel."

"I like the idea of being different, but you think Ethel is too much?" I questioned.

"I think anything you call your little Rhodes will be perfect," Gabby added her two cents. "You could start a fad, and Ethels could be everywhere by 2020."

"Agnes isn't far behind," Brandy mumbled.

I folded my arms and pretended to glare at Brandy. "What would you name your niece?"

"How about Lula or Hattie."

"Those are actually really cute," I said.

"What do you mean actually?" Brandy glanced at my veil. "You already got the wrinkles out?"

"I meant actually because those are still quaint names but extra cute, and yes, I got the wrinkles out. I've got this flat lavender nail polish I thought we could do on our nails." I walked over to the dresser and slid it toward Brandy. "Does that meet your demands?"

"Cute. I'll go first."

"How do you want our hair?" Gabby asked.

"I thought we could all do loose braids." I opened my suitcase and searched for the jeweled pins I bought. "And then maybe slide one of these in? Just a thought."

"Love it," Gabby said, snatching a pin out of my hand.

"So cute," Brandy said, in complete agreement.

"Thank goodness." I sat on the bed next to Gabby and stretched out my legs.

"It's so refreshing to see how well your wedding is coming together, and you don't seem stressed at all," Gabby propped herself on her elbows and glanced toward the beach.

"I was a tad nuts a couple months ago, but I think having the distance and being forced to rely on someone else helps. Not to mention what Ayden and I went through put things in perspective."

"I bet. I have to confess. I'm so grateful for Carla's help. She's a great stepmom, but she is such a perfectionist. Sometimes the conversations wear me out, and we haven't even gotten to the event yet."

"So tell me whose idea were those green dresses? Yours or Carla's?" Brandy's brow quirked slightly.

"You don't like them either?" Gabby chortled.

"I didn't say that. I was only curious."

Gabby let out a deep breath and smiled. "Anyway, whether it's the final menus or flower selection, I sometimes envy your method."

"Your wedding is going to be off the charts," I assured her. "And every little thing will have been worth it. I already know it's going to be absolutely magical. Anything Carla touches is magnificent, and you're nothing short of glorious so it's a winning combination. And you have hundreds of guests coming. Can you imagine trying to shuttle hundreds of Carla's friends?"

Gabby shivered at the thought. "I love how it's your big day, and you're having to reassure me that mine's going to come out okay."

"That's why we're the perfect fit."

"The perfect fit," Brandy added, finishing the last coat of paint on her nails. "Next?"

Gabby reached for the polish and began dabbing the color on her nails when someone knocked at the door.

"So Gabby and I wanted you to have a little extra pampering." Brandy got up from the chair and glanced at me as I began to squirm.

"What did you two plan?" I straightened my posture and waited for Brandy to open the door.

"Round one is a pregnancy massage while Gabby and I go take care of some last minute details down at the reception area. And when we come back, hair and makeup will be up to get us all shined up for the big event." Brandy let the masseuse into the room and pointed at me.

"You two didn't have to do this." I gave Gabby a huge hug, as the masseuse set up her portable table, complete with a hole for my belly. "But I appreciate it so much. I'm feeling like the Energizer bunny right now."

Brandy hugged me next and rocked me back and forth. "Enjoy every second of the ninety minutes."

"You guys went all out," I gushed.

"I'm fancy like that," Brandy teased.

"You have made me feel like a princess, and I didn't even know this was something I wanted."

"Needed." Brandy winked, and I exhaled deeply, feeling the stress I didn't know I had slowly releasing from my body.

"See you in a bit," Brandy called from the door with Gabby right behind.

I followed the masseuse's instruction crawling under the sheet she held up for me and closed my eyes as she began working on arms, and sleep slowly drifted over me as I dreamed about walking down the aisle to marry the man of my dreams.

Chapter Twenty-Three

"You're so fancy," Brandy joked, poking and prodding at Gabby.

"That's me. Miss. Fancy." Gabby rolled her eyes. Sometimes too much of a good thing was wearing, and Brandy always knew how to push Gabby's buttons. It was a fun spectacle and a guilty pleasure.

Brandy turned her attention to me, and Gabby breathed a sigh of relief.

"You are the most beautiful bride. Ever," Brandy gushed.

"Without a doubt," Gabby agreed.

"Thanks to the hair and makeup team you two hired."

The balmy breeze brushed against my bare shoulders, and my dress shimmered in the wind. I glanced at the mirror the hotel had placed in my open-to-the-beach bridal room, and I took in a deep breath. The stylist took my idea one step farther and wrapped a loose braid around the crown of my head, leaving the rest of my hair long and flowing down my back. I loved it.

"You think?" I asked, suddenly shy about what Ayden might think. I'd hidden the dress from him since I'd picked it out with his mom, and now he was about to see it and me for the first time.

"We know," they both shouted. "You're angelic."

I looked in the mirror and smiled as excitement pulsed through my veins.

"I'm. Getting. Married." The smile was permanently etched onto my face.

I was sure of it.

Now, hopefully, I wouldn't look like the Joker in all of the wedding photos.

"Thanks for not making us wear a conch shell," Gabby said smiling.

Brandy furrowed her brows.

"Why would she make us wear a conch shell?" Brandy asked.

"Long story. But be grateful your BFF didn't blow it for you, or you'd have one on top of your head."

Brandy shuddered, and Katie laughed as she tugged on Gabby's finger before pointing to a rogue crab the size of a sand dollar that had crept up the steps and into our suite.

Gabby jumped up and let out a half-scream as Brandy knelt down to help the little fellow back outside, and Katie began twirling in place to make her dress float. I hoped we all made it down the aisle in one piece.

I looked in the mirror again just as Jenny, the

event planner, popped in to our little hut.

"That is one of the prettiest dresses I've seen for a beach wedding," Jenny said, as if it were fact.

I glanced at myself again and noticed just how feminine the wedding dress turned out to be. It was actually pretty spectacular for being so simple, if I did say so myself. The chiffon draped delicately from the empire waist, and small silver thread wove throughout the fabric. With every movement, I felt like a princess, but I also felt like me. The dress was comfortable, bordering on casual, yet elegant. I glanced at Brandy and Gabby. Theirs looked equally as beautiful.

"You women look gorgeous," Jenny said.

"Yes, they do," I seconded.

"We're ready when you are. Say the word and we'll begin."

"Word," Katie yelled.

"Yeah. Word it is," I laughed as a fit of butterflies flapped in my belly.

"Then word it shall be."

"Is Ayden all ready?" I asked.

"He is. And he looks extremely handsome." Jenny patted my hand in a comforting gesture. She signaled over to her assistant, and the music began like clockwork.

My world sped into a flurry of activity the moment we uttered it was go time. I wanted to savor every second of what I was about to do, but I already felt like I was losing important moments to the goblin of time. The photographer began clicking away toward the crowd and aisle, and Katie was chasing after the crab that was now clawing its way back through the sand.

I peeked through the greenery that the resort had used around our hut for privacy. It wasn't a big wedding by any means. Only family and a few really good friends of ours and Ayden's parents had been invited, but it felt perfectly charming and right for us.

My heart fluttered as I heard the music begin, and I glanced nervously over at Brandy and Gabby.

This was it!

Really it!

"You look amazing," Brandy whispered.

I went from being as cool as a cucumber to a shaky, hot muddle of chaos. Gabby took a sip of champagne and I playfully scowled at her.

"Would you like some?" she joked.

"Very funny," I hissed.

Ayden's parents walked down the aisle, and an amazing flood of exhilaration ran through my body, but that word wasn't even enough to describe what I was feeling inside.

The music changed to the "Rhythm Of Love" by the Plain White T's, and I saw the man of my dreams slowly walk down the sandy aisle. My heart hammered in my chest as the lyrics filled the air. They couldn't be more fitting for how we arrived at this wonderful moment. If I could burst with happiness now would be the time. I spied on Ayden through the leaves as he stepped up to the altar and folded his hands in front of him. He looked down the aisle, and it almost felt as if he was looking at me, but I knew that wasn't possible.

He was so damn good looking dressed in a pale grey suit. His chiseled features were set in a serious expression. I could tell he was nervous too, and I delighted in that.

Brandy gave me a quick air kiss on the cheek and a hug as she gripped her small bouquet of white orchids dripping in pearls as Aaron led her out of the hut.

"You look beautiful," Aaron whispered over his shoulder, and my heart filled with joy as I watched him wait to escort her down the aisle once the song switched to John Legend's "All of Me". As the lyrics washed over me, my mind spun to the many special moments I'd cherished with Ayden.

The moment we tackled each other in the snow and got caught kissing by ski patrol.

The moment we found out we were pregnant.

The moment he got down on one knee in Paris and asked me to marry him.

The moment he punched Austin for calling me a name.

The moment he hired me at his company.

The moment he asked me to move in.

The moments we share over dinner.

The moments we share on the way to the office.

The moments he tells me I'm beautiful.

The moments he shows me I'm beautiful.

The moment I thought I'd lose him.

The moment he remembered me.

The first time I saw him step into the ring.

The last time I saw him step into the ring.

Jason walked into the hut and smiled at me. "You look gorgeous."

He gave a quick kiss to Gabby as Mason led her out of the hut. They waited at the end of the aisle a few more seconds before walking, and my pulse accelerated.

This was it!

"You ready?" he asked.

I watched Mason and Gabby begin their walk, and I nodded, dabbing the tear that escaped when the last few thoughts of being with Ayden flooded my mind. Mason and Gabby made it down to where Ayden stood stoically waiting for his bride.

And I was that bride.

Katie who was not only our flower girl, but also our ring bearer began trucking down the aisle with such style at a speed like no other, and the guests laughed while she took a seat at Ayden's feet, throwing petals at Gabby.

As the song faded, I took in a deep breath and closed my eyes asking God to bless our new family before making my way down the aisle.

Jason looped his arm through mine, and I picked up my bouquet filled with orchids, pearls, and miniature lavender roses.

"Thank you for walking me down the aisle, Jason."

"The pleasure is all mine." He cupped his hand over mine, and I nodded at Jenny who instructed the cellist to begin Bach's "Prelude Cello Suite

No. 1 in G Major" and my walk on the clouds began.

When Jason led me to the aisle, we paused, and I watched everyone stand and turn. My heart raced with excitement and fear. Not fear that I was about to get married.

No. I was a simpleton.

I was afraid I might trip or forget my vows.

I raised my head and looked down the aisle at Ayden. His mouth parted slightly as he took me in. His expression told me that we'd conquer the world together, and I knew I was ready to walk down the aisle. I let out a deep breath, and took my first step to becoming Mrs. Ayden Rhodes.

As I clutched my floral arrangement between my fingers, I felt Ayden's eyes on me while I floated down the aisle. It felt like the world stopped turning when I saw Ayden take a step down and reach his hand out to meet Jason and me. The music fell silent, and my pulse calmed to an almost bearable rate.

"Who gives this beautiful woman away to this fine fellow?" Ayden's father asked.

I smiled and the guests snickered as Ayden's father began to officiate our wedding.

"I do. Jason Baines, friend and brother in spirit."

Ayden bowed his head slightly and took my hand from Jason's. Jason placed a quick kiss on my cheek and took a seat in the front row. That simple move was all it took for Katie to bolt right to him. The guests chuckled and paradise shrouded our area of the beach. Something going on here was special, intimate, and perfect.

Ayden and I stepped back onto the platform and turned to face one another, my hands still in his as Ayden's father began.

"Love is complicated. Love is brutal. Love is uplifting. Love soars with the eagles and slithers with the snakes. Love sees things that no one else does. Love understands what no one else can. Love doesn't conquer, love overcomes."

Ayden squeezed my hand.

"Love defines lives. Love helps two people choose how to live. Love doesn't make life easy, but it makes life worth living. Love seizes those small forgettable moments and creates a sensation so deep—so profound—that life becomes extraordinary. Love doesn't predict the future. Love doesn't promise a future because love is beyond promise. Love is one step better than promises. Love is potential."

Ayden's gaze steadied on mine, and I took a deep breath in, trying to push down the lump that was already forming.

"Do you have your vows?" Ayden's father asked.

We both nodded and I began.

"Love is beyond reason. Love can be waiting for a person right in front of them, and they don't see it until the time is right. Ayden, the time is right."

The guests twittered and Ayden's lips curled into a glorious grin.

"You've seen me at my worst and have lifted me to my best. I couldn't ask for anyone more loyal, protective, kind-hearted, and fun loving. You're full of life, a life I'm blessed to be part of. You broke down my walls and made me realize what it meant to truly love someone unconditionally. And you're patient, which God knew I needed. I love you, Ayden Rhodes, and I can't wait to spend the rest of our lives together in or out of the ring, jumping out of planes, diving into the deep blue sea, heli-skiing, or watching movies at home. Sharing my life with you is heaven on earth, and I look forward to my own version of paradise."

Ayden took a step forward and leaned down, kissing me.

"Not how it works, son," Ayden's dad laughed, along with the rest of the guests.

Ayden's lips fell from mine and he took a step back. I detected a slight smirk and my heart filled with glee.

"Lily, something I don't think you understand—truly understand—is that I've been in love with you from the moment I first laid eyes on you. My brother and the rest of my family can attest to it."

"It's true," Mason whispered.

I blushed but basked in the glory as Ayden continued.

"People roll their eyes when it comes to love at first sight, but I think they're missing the point, and that point is that finding someone you connect with offers hope. It offers promise so the idea of love at first sight is really offering a promise to explore the idea of love. Being near you spoke to my heart. It showed me what I'd be missing if I couldn't have you. I'd miss out on your jokes, your feistiness, your glorious laughter, your sultry voice. I'd miss out on the chance to get to know a person who offers me great promise. Promise to become a better man for the woman I love. I knew I wanted to spend the rest of my life with you, Lily. You make me smile when I don't feel like smiling, and when I can't smile, you smile for me. I can't imagine my life without you in it. I want to be in the weeds with you as much as I want to soar with you. You've made my life extraordinary, Lily. And for that I thank you."

The tears I vowed to not shed were slipping down my face. Brandy stuffed tissue in my hand and I dabbed the joyful tears away. I glanced at Ayden's dad, who was also swiping at a few strays as well, and I knew I was in good company.

This time I leaned over and stood on my toes, sweeping a kiss across Ayden's mouth.

"I give up," Ayden's dad teased.

I came back down and stood in place.

"Do we have the rings?"

Gabby walked over to Katie and took the pillow from her and stood back behind me.

"Repeat after me, Lily. I, Lily, take thee Ayden, to be my husband, to have and to hold, from this moment forward..."

I, Lily, take thee Ayden, to be my husband, to have and to hold, from this moment forward..." I paused and waited for more.

"For better—for worse, for richer—for poorer, in sickness and in health, to love and to cherish till death do us part and even after that."

The guests chuckled.

"For better—for worse, for richer—for poorer, in sickness and in health, to love and to cherish till death do us part and even after that."

"The ring?" Ayden's dad asked.

Gabby handed me Ayden's platinum band and I slid it on his finger.

"Like a glove," he whispered and I giggled.

"I, Ayden, take thee Lily, to be my wife, to have and to hold, from this day forward for better—for worse, for richer—for poorer, in sickness and in health, to love and to cherish till death do us part and even after that." Ayden squeezed my hands and took the ring from Gabby. He slid the diamond and ruby band up my finger, and I wanted nothing more than to be kissed by my husband.

"I now pronounce you, husband and wife. You may kiss the bride."

I wrapped my arms around Ayden's neck, and our lips met in our first kiss as husband and wife as the excitement and realization zipped through my body at an unstoppable speed.

Ayden slowly released his embrace, and I unwrapped my arms from his neck as the guests cheered. I turned to my two best friends and whispered, "You're next," as U2's "Beautiful Day" led us down the aisle to a party and a life that was just getting started.

Chapter Twenty-Four

The reception was like one big beach party. Hanging lanterns stretched across the sand, and short and tall tables dotted the beach where friends and family congregated. I looked over at my husband, who was drinking a beer and standing next to Mason, chatting away. He was leaning on one of the taller bar tables that had been draped with burlap. Orchids hung along the rough fabric, and seashells mounded in the center of the table created the perfect centerpiece with the candles flickering in the night's breeze. Appetizers were being passed and soon the buffet would open. We decided to change up the order of events, and Jenny informed me now was the moment to grab Ayden for our first untraditional tradition.

I made my way across the beach, sinking into the soft sand and shaking the granules off my foot with each step toward Ayden.

"Ready?" I whispered, sneaking up on him.

Ayden set his beer on the table and spun around. His molten gaze secured mine, and I liquefied on the spot. His eyes were so arresting that it wouldn't take much for me to forget we had a beach full of guests and follow him to the suite never to return.

"Absolutely, Mrs. Rhodes. Whatever you say." He bent down and gave me a long kiss. My short veil shrouded us from the guests as his kisses deepened, and my stomach stirred with a pull that told me to leave the reception far behind.

"Really?" Mason interrupted.

My giggles ruined our kiss, and Ayden released me, smacking his brother's arm. "You just wait."

"Yeah. You just wait," Tori goaded.

Ayden slid his hand around mine, and we wobbled our way over to the cake table. Jenny handed me a microphone and the music softened. I flashed a dimpled grin and felt Ayden's embrace as I began

"Because in life, I don't think we should ever have to wait for cake, we're cutting the wedding cake now."

"My kind of wedding," Brandy seconded.

"Since I think cake is one of the most important aspects of this whole event, feel free to grab a slice whenever you like."

Katie jumped up and down, clutching onto Gabby's small arrangement of orchids, and shouted, "cake," to the world as if it were the most exciting thing in Bermuda. And maybe it was.

Ayden and I stepped toward the three-tiered cake, and I glanced at Ayden and whispered, "It's so beautiful. I feel bad for cutting it."

"It's beckoning us," Ayden assured me as we both stood holding the knife as the photographer snapped away.

Even though the wedding cake was three tiers, the form itself was narrow. The base was ivory, and tiny aqua fondant ribbons draped each layer, and centering each bow was an edible pearl. The flavors varied by tier with banana-blueberry chiffon on the bottom, raspberry champagne in the middle, and strawberry vanilla on the top. Fondant seashells were scattered the table, each containing a fortune.

Ayden steadied my hand and gripped it tighter as we sliced through the first layer.

Our friends and family cheered behind us as the chant began. Ayden promised there would be no cake in the face and I believed him, but there was a certain glint in his eye that told another story.

We toppled the slice onto a plate and held it, each of us gently taking a piece, readying to feed it to the other.

I didn't know what came over me, but a charge of adrenaline coursed through my veins and rather than feed him gently, I smashed the cake on his mouth. When his gaze met mine, I realized he, too, had planned the same, but I beat him to the punch.

Shaking his head, he dipped his finger in the

frosting and dotted the tip of my nose, beaming.

"I knew you couldn't be trusted," he murmured.

"I don't know what came over me," I giggled.

"That was totally premeditated."

"I swear. It wasn't."

"Sure it wasn't." He dabbed the crumbs with a napkin and then wiped away the frosting from my nose.

"I saw it in your eyes and I knew I had to act," I countered.

"I'm a complete gentleman. You're mistaken. I would never do that to my bride."

He grinned wryly and kissed me.

"Come on," Ayden's uncle shouted. "That was too tame for the Rhodes clan."

I hugged Ayden and closed my eyes as Jenny began cutting small pieces in case anyone besides the bride wanted cake before dinner.

The music was turned up again, and the mingling commenced as Ayden and I snuck away for a few moments of peace.

"How does it feel to be Mrs. Rhodes?"

"Pretty incredible, and if I let myself think about it too hard, I'd say surreal."

"Surreal?"

I nodded. "To come from what we faced a few weeks ago to this? Yeah, I'd say a bit surreal."

Ayden drew me into an embrace and rested his chin on the top of my head.

"Mason was just telling me that the prosecutor didn't find enough evidence to support Viktor's claims. My mom talked to someone at the prosecutor's office this morning, who told her it was considered an instance of self-defense since the victim couldn't defend himself, and they had to step in."

"Oh, thank goodness." I exhaled. "That's the best wedding gift ever."

"It is."

"Should I have even bothered to tell you? Would you've rather I kept it from you."

"I think you know the answer to that, or you wouldn't have told me. No secrets, remember?"

"Brandy and Gabby wondered if we had any names picked out for our daughter?"

His squeeze tightened. "And what did you tell them?"

"Ethel," I whispered.

"Ethel?" Ayden's laugh drifted into the air as he shook his head. "That's awesome."

"I thought it would throw them off for a little while."

"Indeed." His arms fell away from my waist, and he took a step back. "I guess we should go back."

"I guess. Can't we sneak off to where the magic happens?" I wiggled my brows.

"I think the magic already did."

I grabbed his hand and squeezed it. "Thank you for being the man you are."

"I couldn't imagine being anything but."

Jenny waved us over to the buffet line. Dinner was served. We both reached for plates and began piling on the delicious food. There were spicy chicken kabobs, grilled vegetables, and rice pilaf. And that was just this table. The next table had a beautiful rib roast on display, along with mashed potatoes and green beans. I piled my plate high and waited for Ayden before we walked over to our table and took a seat.

"I just realized I haven't eaten anything since eggs benedict this morning."

"You fit in eggs benedict?" Ayden asked, cutting through the prime rib.

"I did and a massage and hair and makeup."

"Sounds like a nice day."

"A pretty incredible day."

One of Ayden's uncles took a seat, along with Mason and his parents.

"I've been meaning to ask. I noticed a hint of a shiner on your cheek there," his uncle stated, pointing at Ayden. Pretty much all hints of Ayden's escapade in the parking lot had vanished, but if you looked closely, rosiness rested under his skin.

Tori took a seat next to Mason and took a sip of water.

"A little scuffle," Ayden said. "A lesson learned."

"Something I've never told you about your nephew," Ayden's dad began. "He's a fighter. Does it as a hobby."

Ayden turned his head toward his dad. "And just how long did you know?"

His dad laughed and tossed the napkin on the table. "I think I caught your very first fight. Mason was slinking around the garage, evading my questions about his plans for the night so I got curious. I followed him, parked, and went inside."

"You're kidding," Mason said.

"I never would've guessed," Ayden told his dad.

"So you lost the fight that gave you that?" his uncle asked.

"No. I'm undefeated. This happened in the lot after the fight."

"You should've seen the other guy," Mason chuckled and looked around at us all. "Wait. Was that inappropriate? Too soon for jokes?"

"Only your kind," Tori whispered, trying to keep the smile off her lips.

"I've learned my lesson, though," Ayden announced. "I'm done. Might as well get out while a person's ahead."

"Smart move, son," Ayden's dad agreed.

"Smart," Ayden's uncle echoed.

Unlike most brides, I was determined to enjoy my dinner and savored each and every bite until it was announced that the first dance was about to take place.

Ayden clutched my hand and led me out to the dance floor that hovered over the beach. The lanterns bobbed gently in the wind, the flame flickering as Ayden wrapped his arms around me and began to move with me without music.

"I love you, Mrs. Rhodes."

"I love you, Mr. Rhodes."

And our very first dance began as the "First Day of My Life" by Bright Eyes came echoing through the air. I rested my head on his chest as we swayed back and forth to the beautiful acoustic melody.

"I'll take care of you from this day forward," Ayden whispered, pressing his lips to the top of my head. "I'll be there for you. I promise."

"I promise more." I raised my head from Ayden's chest, and our eyes locked as we continued to dance. Between the smell of the salt air and the faint murmur of our friends and family commenting on how blissful we looked, I felt like were in our own version of heaven on earth.

"Did you mean that about being there for me if I jump out of a plane?" he asked.

I chuckled and nodded. "Yeah. But I'll be there with you jumping out of it."

"You'd jump out of a plane?" he asked, his blue eyes wide. "That kind of makes me worried."

"No. Kidding. Imagine how it makes me feel. My track record's been a little better, might I add."

"Such a low blow," he chuckled. "So we can both scratch off jumping out of a plane?"

"Maybe until after the kids are grown."

"Good call," he chuckled.

"Kids, huh? As in multiples?" His brow arched.

"Yeah. What the heck? Lily Rhodes against love of all kind gets married and wants lots of kids to make our life exhausting and...actually, I'm not sure what comes after exhausting."

"At least you've gotten good practice with me," he teased.

His embrace tightened as our song slowly

wound down, and more couples began to spread on to the dance floor as the next song, "Stand by Me" by Ben E King, came on.

"Can this be any more perfect?" I asked, the waves crashing in the background.

"Not if we planned it."

"We kind of did."

My eyes scanned the crowd that had grown, and it was almost impossible not to get teary eyed as I saw my two best friends dancing with the loves of their lives, and Ayden's parents holding onto each other even tighter than Ayden held me.

Ayden's one hand slipped from my waist, and I twirled into the crowd before he pulled me back into him.

Gabby and Jason cheered, and I sunk deeper into Ayden's arms as the song changed to the son and mother dance. As Ayden let me go, I smiled and took a deep breath in, taking in the best moment of my life.

Ayden's dad asked for my hand, and I appreciated the gesture. I'd done a good job of pushing out certain moments, like being walked down the aisle by my father or the first dance, but sometimes it was nice to be remembered along the way. Not all parents were created equal, but if I had to choose some, these two were at the top of their form.

"Ayden is one lucky man and we are the luckiest parents. We couldn't have handpicked anyone better to join our family."

"Thank you so much. I feel like the luckiest

girl."

I looked over at Ayden, and his eyes were on me as he danced with his mom. My heart fluttered as if it were the first time I let myself realize that I'd fallen for Ayden. His dad somehow danced his way next to his son and traded me away for his wife. The bouncier "Home" by Edward Sharpe and the Magnetic Zeros pumped through the air, and Katie started jumping all around the dance floor, followed by Gabby and Brandy right behind, bobbing their heads and twisting their hips as Katie grabbed their hands.

"You should go," Ayden whispered, gently pushing me to them.

Katie let go of Gabby's hand and grabbed mine as Gabby wrapped her arm around my waist. With every twist and turn, Katie squealed into the night air a joyous sound that was infectious. Every single guest began grabbing one another's hand and circled us four girls as we danced our hearts out until the bouquet toss.

The music quieted, and the unmarried gals congregated on the floor. Jenny handed me the replica bouquet, and Ayden asked if the crowd of single ladies was ready. They roared to life, and the music began as I tossed my bouquet behind me. I turned quickly to watch Gabby diving toward the bouquet, as Brandy almost snatched it away from her right before Tori jumped toward the sky with such gusto, we all dropped our jaws. The moment her fingers wrapped around the stems, I knew it was a done deal.

Mason was next.

More photos were taken as I hugged Tori, and Ayden pushed Mason over to Tori where a few more photos were snapped. I glanced at the chair Jenny had now placed on the floor, and Ayden motioned me over with his finger. They began playing Bach's "Funeral March", and I scowled playfully, plunking in the chair where Ayden lifted my dress over my knees.

Slowly his hands worked up my leg, and his fingers wrapped around the garter. He flashed a devilish grin and, without warning, ran his chin along my knee until his teeth firmly gripped the garter. A fit of giggles erupted from my belly as all the men started cheering. I tipped my head back as Ayden lifted my leg and worked the garter over my knee. The moment it was over my foot, I stood up and gave Ayden a deep, passionate kiss before he made some guy's night lucky.

As all the unmarried men were called to the floor, I scanned the crowd. There were a lot of men out there. I spotted Aaron in the front and Jason strategically to the side. Mason was all the way in the back, even though Tori was trying to persuade him to move to the front. The music changed, and Ayden turned his back on the men as the countdown began.

Within seconds, I saw the white garter fly into the air as if it were finding its forever home with some unsuspecting soul. As the garter came closer, I watched all the men dive bomb away from the dance floor, leaving Mason alone staring up toward the sky as the garter landed in his hands.

The guests broke into applause as Mason's eyes looked dazed and confused as to what just happened. Tori came bounding onto the floor and jumped into his arms as a smile broke immediately onto his lips.

Life couldn't get any better than this.

Until he whispered those magical words, "Should we go upstairs?"

I looked around the dance floor that was now lively with couples displaying their drinking moves, and I knew no one would miss us if we snuck away. I waved over to Gabby, who pulled Brandy my way as Ayden went to say goodnight to a few family members and friends.

"Thank you for everything," I whispered, flinging my arms around the girls. "You made today perfect."

"You're beautiful inside and out, Lily. My brother's a lucky guy."

I took a step back and Gabby dabbed away a joyful tear. "I'm just so happy this is how tonight turned out."

I knew exactly what she meant, but all I could do was nod as Ayden snaked his arm around my waist.

"See you on the beach tomorrow—"

"Or the next day," I interrupted.

Brandy and Gabby hugged each other and watched as we walked across the beach toward our hotel.

As we made our way to the elevator, a few

hotel guests uttered "congratulations" and I beamed proudly as Ayden held my hand. We rode the elevator up to our floor, and my heart skipped a beat. The wait had been worth it.

"Never again," Ayden whispered.

"I don't know what you're referring to."

"Waiting like this."

Ayden and I stopped in front of our door.

"I love you, Mrs. Rhodes, but I'm going to be honest. There might come a day in the near future, I won't be able to carry you across the threshold. I think it's important we do it while we can."

He slid the key card into the lock and pushed the door open with his foot. Scooping me into his arms, he carried me into the hotel room and I chuckled, nestling my head in his neck.

Ayden's face softened from the thunderous expression he'd worn as he set me down, and his gaze traveled from my messy, braided hair to my breasts and down to my hips. A slight arch of his mouth drew me closer, and my pulse accelerated.

My body trembled in Ayden's arms, and he could resist no longer. He cupped my chin in his hands, and his gaze steadied on mine.

"I'll never forget this moment for as long as we both shall live."

"And after," I whispered.

"And after," he repeated.

My body ached with longing as our lips remained so close, but he refused to let them touch. It was as if the last few weeks of pent-up desire was an addictive game, and the longer we held out, the more we needed one another. Yet we both refused to be the one to give in.

He ran his fingers slowly over my bare shoulders and down to the top of my strapless gown. "You are the most beautiful bride."

My cheeks flushed at the admiration I saw in his eyes. He brushed the seam of my mouth with his tongue, and I shuddered, parting my lips, begging him to kiss me deeply.

The desire was so spectacular it drilled into every part of my body with such an intensity my body burned for him. I leaned into him and brushed my lips against his, and in return, he pressed his mouth to mine. His kiss heated my entire body as my eyes closed, and his hands slid along my waist. His mouth released from mine as he slowly worked his tongue down my jaw to my throat sending a shockwave of longing through me.

His hands ran up my spine, slowly tugging on the zipper of my dress. I felt the tightness ease as the zipper sank lower, and the gown dropped to the floor. My breath caught as I watched his gaze canvas my body as if it were the first time he saw me naked. He quickly threw his jacket on the bed. I slowly unbuttoned his shirt and slid it off his shoulders. My tongue tasted his shoulders, chest, and stomach before I began unbuttoning his pants.

He sucked in a deep breath as my hands fumbled with his pants, grazing him, as I slipped his boxers down. His hands slipped around my wrists, and he pulled me to the bed with him. The calmness we both tried to exude quickly slipping away as our bodies tangled with one another.

He caught my lip softly between his teeth as his fingers ran through my hair. Ayden slipped his mouth lower as his hands slid my lace panties to the side. I sucked in a deep breath as his hands slid down between my thighs. I clutched my nails into his shoulders, his fingers controlling my every whim.

"Ayden, please," I almost whimpered, the playfulness trading for pure want and profound desire.

"Please what?"

I opened my eyes. His gaze was steadied on mine as he drove his finger deeper, commanding something from me that we both needed.

"Deeper," I moaned, his lips curling into the expression I adored.

He moved his body over mine, kissing me along the way. His mouth traced along my throat as he moved into me, filling me with a sensation that immediately heated me all the way through.

His body rocked harder into mine, and my craving only intensified. An almost helpless noise escaped my lips as my mind and body succumbed to the pleasure flowing through my limbs.

Ayden drove himself into me, and my fingers clutched into him. Tilting my hips slightly as his eyes locked on mine brought an explosion of sensation to us both. His body tensed and breathing quickened as we shared the overpowering awareness running between our bodies. The pleasure surged through my body in endless waves as I watched Ayden's strong body thrust into me and spin my love into a utopian existence for only us to share. I succumbed to every part of Ayden as my body arched, and he held me in his embrace. I licked my lips, feeling the sensation of where his mouth rested only seconds before.

"Amazing," I whispered.

He propped himself on his elbows, tucking a smile behind his gaze.

"I guess you were right," he confessed.

"About what in particular?" He slid his finger along my jaw as his gaze stayed fastened to mine. His mere touch made me lightheaded as I imagined the world I'd been blessed with, the man I'd been blessed with.

"About waiting."

"Pretty spectacular."

"But nothing I want to practice often."

"I don't think I could ever hold out again. It was pure torture."

"Torture?" His brow arched.

I nodded and he rolled off, admiring me as he stood up and tugged on the sheet, wrapping it around him.

"Do you know you always make me feel amazing?" I asked.

"How so?"

I shrugged, still staying in bed. "Not sure. I guess it's the little things."

He walked to the hotel door and slid the chain. Turning off the lights, he made his way back to the bed and crawled in beside me.

"Get enough little things and they add up to the big things." He ran his hand along the length of my body, and a wave of shivers ran through me.

"I love you, Ayden. I loved you even before my mind caught up to my heart, and I never want you to leave my side."

"I love you, Lily Rhodes."

"I'm right here, and I always will be," he murmured, as we drifted to sleep like an old, married couple.

Chapter Twenty-Five

Lying on the beach, feeling dynamite in my red swimsuit, I heard some teenager behind me whisper, "Is she pregnant or just fat?"

I sat up in my chaise and turned to face the troublemakers.

"The answer is yes, I'm pregnant, and see that guy out there on the paddleboard? He's my husband and he's an ex-fighter. Undefeated, actually."

"Sorry, lady. We were only kidding."

I narrowed my eyes at these two and realized they were older than I thought, probably just out of high school, maybe in college already.

"And do tell me what part is the funny part if I didn't happen to be pregnant? Do you think that's very kind? Did your parents forget to teach you manners on the way to Bermuda?"

"No ma'am," they replied.

"Word to the wise. Even if you're positive a

woman is pregnant and might even give birth in front of you, keep your mouth shut. You wouldn't like it if I pointed out your undeveloped bodies to the world. Oops. Just did."

"Hey, girl," Gabby said, running up behind me from the water. "Trying to pick up men already?"

"Boys," I corrected. "They couldn't handle a woman on their best day."

The two guys stood up and apologized once more before trudging down the beach. I dusted my hands off and leaned back on my chaise. Tori was in the chaise in front of me and turned around, giving me a thumbs up sign.

"What was that all about?" Gabby asked.

"Just trying to teach our youth some lessons to live by."

"Youth? They're like in college."

"And just think how much we've learned since then, I thought I'd speed up the process." I slathered more suntan lotion on my belly and chest and slid my sunglasses on.

She chuckled and shook her head. "Why do I think there's more to that story."

"Because there always is. So how was the water?"

"I think you should at least get in to your ankles."

"We'll see."

"Do you know what I just realized?"

"What's that?"

"With our weddings so close together, we'll be able to throw anniversary parties together. Can you imagine what our twentieth will look like?"

A shiver ran through me. "Our daughter will be in college," I almost whispered.

"Crazy, isn't?"

"It is."

"Can I confess something?" Gabby asked, sliding into the chaise next to me.

"Please do."

"I almost envy Brandy's method of getting the deed done."

"Are you serious?" I asked.

"Kind of. On one hand, I can't wait to have a big wedding. On the other, I'm dreading the headache."

I reached over and grabbed her hand. "With Carla in charge, there will be no headache, and Brandy and I will be there every step of the way."

My eyes connected with Gabby's and a huge grin was plastered on her face. "I. Can't. Believe. I'm. Getting. Married."

I let out a squeal of delight. "You know the feeling of excitement you have right now?"

She nodded.

"It doesn't even come close to the level of excitement on the big day. I'm still on a high."

"Speaking of which." Gabby spotted the server and signaled she was ready for a drink. "I'm absolutely parched."

"I'm sure something with rum is in order."

"Absolutely." She ordered her drink and I ordered a tea. "By the way, you look stunning in that suit."

I furrowed my brows and let out a sigh. "Thanks. I needed to hear that."

"It's the truth."

And I believed it. After all, that was what friends were for: telling the truth and shaping our view of the world.

Brandy bounded up with a plate full of nachos. "This is the best breakfast ever."

"Rum for a breakfast drink and nachos for breakfast," I joked. "How are we ever going to function in the real world again."

"I was wondering the very same thing," Brandy said, finding a spot to sit at the end of my chaise.

"Do you realize what a whirlwind the last couple of years have been?" Gabby sighed. "Especially the last year."

I rubbed my belly again. "And something tells me the fun is only beginning."

Brandy crunched on a cheesy chip and glanced out toward the water. "We've got something pretty special."

"We do," Gabby agreed.

Tori stole a chip from Brandy's plate.

"I was wondering..." I stopped myself.

"What?" Gabby prompted.

"Nah."

"Come on. Don't leave us hanging," Brandy demanded.

Tori lifted her head up and looked perplexed.

"Moi? Leave you hanging?" I teased. "What if we set up Emily?"

My eyes widened in anticipation.

"As well as that worked for you with Austin?" Brandy shook her head.

"I'm not touching that with a ten-foot pole. No. Way. No. How," Gabby echoed.

"And look at where that amazing plan led," I pointed out. "I married the man of my dreams and I'm with child."

"With child?" Gabby snorted. "The Madame is with child. Let her rest."

I grinned. "Seriously, guys. I think Emily could use a little GBL magic."

"What in the world is GBL magic?" Tori furrowed her brow. "Oh, I get it. Gabby, Brandy, Lily,"

"The teacher strikes again."

Tori began rubbing the sunblock on her fair skin. "It's the heat. I don't function like others in the sunlight. I prefer darkness."

"A vamp," Gabby cooed and Tori giggled.

"Seriously, I don't know about this idea. I learned my lesson." Gabby shook her head. "Look at what a creep Austin turned out to be, and we've all run out of brothers."

A hearty laughed escaped and my sunglasses fell to the sand.

"You're missing the point. We're on a white, sandy beach in the middle of the Caribbean. Not because you chose the right person for me, but because you let me stumble around the idea of love on my own terms. All I'm saying is that I think we need to be on the lookout. If we spot someone hot and with a good heart—"

"Maybe we should reverse the order on that," Gabby interjected.

"Tomatooo...Tamatoh."

"I get where you're coming from, and even though I retired from the matchmaking process, maybe I'll keep an eye out."

Brandy raised her shoulders. "Couldn't hurt."

Our waiter brought our drinks over and I sipped on my tea.

"Exactly. A little GBL magic couldn't hurt," Brandy agreed. "But this goes no further than us. We don't want the guys to get wind of it."

"Let the fun begin," Gabby gushed, sliding her legs onto the chaise. Brandy stood up and found a trashcan for her empty nacho plate and slogged back to the chaise next to me.

"This is a tough life," Brandy said, dropping onto her chaise.

"Isn't it?" I agreed.

"I wouldn't want it any other way," Gabby said.

"Me neither," Tori whispered, her eyes closing.

My head lolled to the side as my body relaxed, and I watched Ayden paddle past the boundaries toward the open sea.

Of course he did.

Why wouldn't he?

Mason was paddling right behind him as was Aaron and Jason, and I shook my head.

There was no taming these men.

And I'd never dream of it.

THE END
(Almost)

BEYOND the MISTLETOE ~ Available Now

and ISLAND COUNTY SERIES ~ Available Now

Note From Karice

I hope you enjoyed the sixth book in the Beyond Love Series. As a special thank you to all the loyal readers of this series and to commemorate the series end, I'll be releasing a holiday Beyond Love book, "Beyond the Mistletoe". In addition to reading about Gabby, Lily, and Brandy, we'll get to experience Emily's journey to her Happily Ever After, and I'll also be including a special bonus novella of Gabby's wedding for my newsletter subscribers.

Don't forget you can follow all your favorite characters in the Island County Series, which is a crossover series. Haven't read how Mason and Tori got together? Check it out in "Finding Love in Forgotten Cove"! Again, thank you all for reading my stories. I hope they provide you with as much happiness as they give me.

~Karice

P.S. Keep reading for a glimpse of Mason and Tori from Island County!

AND

Emily and Derek from Beyond the Mistletoe!

Finding Love
in
Forgotten Cove

Karice Bolton

Island County Series

The last of the students shuffled out of the room, and I leaned against my desk wondering what in the world I'd signed up for. The silence wrapped around me and so did the dawning realization that I'd be stuck on the island all summer. It seemed like a good idea a few weeks ago, but once I arrived, I started having immediate doubts. Maybe teaching tenth grade summer school wasn't the best idea to keep busy. I had more than enough to occupy myself with managing my dad's affairs and getting his house ready to sell, but it was too late now. I'd signed a contract, and I needed to make the best of the situation. It was very clear none of the students wanted to be here and I didn't blame them. Who would want to spend a summer indoors on the island? I needed to come up with a plan to get them interested and keep myself focused along the way.

Easier said than done.

I looked around the dull and dingy classroom and eyed the yellowed Shakespeare poster that been on the wall since I'd attended school here, and I didn't need to count the years to know that had been a very long time ago. The beige walls were spotty from years of touch-up paint, and the only improvement I'd noticed was that the individual scarred wooden desks had been replaced with long, plastic tables. This space was dismal. I totally grasped why the kids wouldn't want to be stuck inside this room all summer while their friends got to run around the island.

I'd always loved summers on the island, but that was before my family splintered apart with never the hope of coming back together again.

I kept in a sigh and began organizing the students' papers in a folder. So much of this place had stayed the same. It was like going back in time and the only thing that had managed to age during the process was me. Not a very amusing thought since there were moments I still felt like a teenager inside.

A breeze swept through an open window in the classroom lifting up one of the loose papers from the desk. I reached over and snatched the sheet out of the air and plunked it back down, anchoring it with my empty coffee mug. The sound of a metal ladder clanging along the side of the brick building caught my attention, and I glanced out the window to see the most well-defined stomach peeking out from under some guy's shirt as he climbed up the ladder. My eyes were glued to his abdomen as he reached up to work on whatever it was he was doing, and it appeared I really had been flung back into high school.

I needed to get out more.

Instead of turning my attention away, however, I kept staring at this small gift from above and trundled over to the window as he worked his way up the ladder. Complete disappointment washed over me when his shirt fell to cover his stomach, but I still stood at complete attention hoping for one last glimpse. It wasn't until I heard a woman clearing her throat behind me that I realized how close I'd gotten to the window and the man outside it. I had no idea what had come over me.

I spun around, and my eyes met with the woman who'd hired me and two other female teachers who I'd seen around the campus.

Such was my luck.

As the embarrassment slowly permeated every ounce of my body, I noticed all of the women displayed a sort of knowing smile, but none of them said a word so I stood in place, cheeks flaming. My mind raced in every different direction to come up with a clever comeback, and of course, nothing of the sort came to mind.

"I was just checking to see what all of that ruckus was about outside," I stuttered, knowing my fair complexion gave me away. One of the many gifts about being a redhead—I lit up like a Christmas tree. "You know...in case he was in danger or the ladder wasn't steady. I thought I should get a closer look. It sounded pretty dire."

"Indeed. I can understand that," Rosa replied, still grinning. She was the principal and the woman behind getting me onboard for summer school. Her dark hair was trimmed short, and despite the warmth of summer, she wore a cream linen suit. Most teaching positions went to locals, but she had known my father and understood my situation and for that I was grateful. "We wanted to stop by and see how your first day went. You didn't run screaming out the doors, which I take as a good sign."

I laughed and shook my head. "Nope. Not gonna run. I'm hoping I can get the students interested in history before the summer is over. I only had a couple of texters, and I can't say I blame them. The weather is beautiful, and I couldn't imagine being stuck in school all summer at that age." I smiled and heard the clank of the ladder again as it got moved along the building, but I stayed put, staring directly in front of me. I wasn't going to fall for that trap twice, but I noticed one of the teachers looked out the window, and it was difficult not to follow her gaze.

"As the summer goes on, their attention span gets worse," the other teacher said, stepping out from behind Rosa. She reached out her hand and I shook it. "I'm Samantha. If you need anything, I'm only two doors down."

"Thanks. I appreciate that." I nodded. "What's your subject?"

"This summer I'm teaching biology," Samantha replied.

The other teacher ripped her gaze away from the peep show outside and brought her eyes to mine. "I'm Tessa and I'm four doors down, across the hall. I teach math."

Tessa was in a pair of black capri leggings and an oversized pink shirt. Her hair was in a bouncy ponytail, and her smile made me feel as if I'd known her for years. Samantha, not so much. Samantha followed Rosa's lead and wore a white tailored suit, and I had the distinct feeling it would only be to my detriment if I asked her for any help or advice. I sensed she was a woman with an agenda and any questions would be a sign of weakness.

"Well, I hope to be able to get the kids outside," I started.

"Off school property? That's always a hassle and never worth the headache," Samantha spouted.

Tessa opened her mouth as if she was going to object, but shut it quickly, locking eyes with me.

"Stop by the office on the way out, and Martha will get you all the necessary paperwork you need ahead of time if you decide to do that. I think any method that encourages the students to learn is a plus," Rosa replied, giving me a wry smile.

Samantha looked agitated and flashed me a cold stare, and it was hard not to chuckle as Tessa rolled her eyes at Samantha's agitation. The island dynamics were already at play.

"Well, thank you very much. I appreciate the opportunity to teach this summer," I said, hoping to tidy up the classroom quickly and get to the house that had so much left to do. Every second I devoted to the home was a second closer to getting off the island.

"Don't forget, we have an opening for full-time status this fall," Rosa reminded me.

My stomach clenched at the thought of having to stay around any longer than the end of August. It wasn't that I didn't have good memories being back here, but there were also plenty of sad ones, and I doubted I was ready to relive any of them, good or bad. The sooner I could get off the island, the better.

"I appreciate the offer, but I think this assignment fits me perfectly."

Rosa nodded, and I smiled as I watched all three women walk out. Only a few seconds passed before Tessa reappeared.

"Just ignore Samantha. That's what we all do. She knows Rosa is going to be retiring in a few years and has decided to make it her mission to be the next principal. Not gonna happen if you ask me, which you didn't." Her grin widened, and I noticed what a pretty plum color her lips were naturally. In order to get anyone to see mine, I had to paint several coats of gloss on top and hope that I didn't lick it all off before the morning was over.

"I figured something had to be going on." I glanced out the window without even thinking and saw that the ladder had been moved but was still in view.

"It's always a treat when he shows up," Tessa chuckled.

"How often does he show up?" I asked.

"Not often enough."

I laughed and reached up to close the window as the mystery man began stepping down the ladder. My fingers fumbled as I dropped the blinds right before his face appeared in the window. I could shut the window later.

"You won't be disappointed," Tessa explained, wiping my board down for me.

I wondered if she knew I hadn't closed the window yet.

"With what?"

"The whole package," she mused.

"Package?" I asked, trying to act as if I had no idea what she was referring to.

"The guy outside. He's the complete package. One hundred and ten percent perfection."

I shook my head. "Doubtful. No man ever is and if they are, it's only a mirage. I've sworn off men completely—no matter what kind of package appears."

Tessa threw up her hands and shrugged her shoulders. "I'm tellin' ya. He's really got it going on. And he's a twin."

I couldn't help but chuckle at her latest revelation. As if being a twin was a benefit. My chest tightened, and I dropped my gaze to the desk, pushing away the guilt that flooded through me.

"Does he work at the school?" I asked.

She shook her head, her ponytail extra springy with the excitement of relaying the bits of gossip. This was one of the many things I remembered about living on the island. Word always traveled fast about a person. "He works for some construction company on the mainland."

"Aww... I see." I smiled as her words hit me. I'd forgotten how most of the islanders referred to Seattle and the general vicinity as the mainland. It was an entirely different world over here. The pace was slower and the smiles kinder. Maybe being here was what I needed for the summer, a way to escape the reality that had so stubbornly presented itself time and again back in New York.

"But I'll tell you this, whenever the construction contract is up for renewal, all of our moods change as we wait to hear who's won the bid. It happens every two years, and I can tell you it's a real mood shifter around here. But I wouldn't be surprised if he wasn't the main reason so many of us sign up to teach summer school." She winked.

"It's not for the betterment of the students?" I teased.

"Well that too. But he's a strong second. And most of the repairs and maintenance around the campus are done in the summer. I always make sure my classroom is in tip-top shape before summer school ends and fall quarter begins." She was almost beaming and I couldn't help but laugh. Being around Tessa was a definite mood lifter.

"I can't imagine why," I replied, still smiling. "But his workout regimen certainly seems to be working well for him." I couldn't believe those words tumbled out. I would absolutely die if the man on the ladder knew I was in here even having a discussion like this. I wasn't easily impressed, and I never really talked about men or the fact that I noticed them to anyone. It wasn't my style and within a matter of hours on my job here, I got caught red-handed ogling over some stranger's six-pack. Not my finest hour and certainly not the gossip I wanted circulating around the island. There was already enough misinformation running rampant about my family here. I needed to stay buttoned up and not let myself make any mistakes. It was the least I could do to honor my father's memory.

Tessa was on her way out the door. "If you don't have any plans tonight, I'll be over at Mudflat Tavern around seven, munching on..."

"The famous fresh-cut french fries with chili and cheese sauce?" I interrupted.

"How'd you know?" she asked, turning around to face me.

"I grew up here and that was the only reason we ever went to Mudflat," I said grinning, as the memories filled me with unexpected comfort. Even though there was a tavern in the name, it was a family restaurant, one that my family frequented quite a lot.

There was outside seating on a deck that overlooked the Sound. The restaurant even had a pier for boats to dock and pick up orders to go. I remembered one of the times I'd been there, I was running my hand along the old wooden deck railing when a splinter rammed right under my skin. It wasn't a typical splinter. In fact, it looked more like a knitting needle once my father managed to get it out of my palm. When it happened, I didn't say a word, but my dad knew immediately because I stopped moving, and my already pale face had competed with Casper to take home the award for most ghostly appearance. That was right before I fainted from the pain. Needless to say I got free cheese fries for life. Not that I would hold them to it after all these years... but I never trusted wood railings after that.

"So you understand their addictive quality?"

"Absolutely do and I'll have to take you up on the offer next time. I've got some things I need to take care of tonight."

"Totally. The offer is always there." She flashed a grin and walked out of the classroom, leaving me alone with the ache of memories I'd never intended to visit today. I wanted to believe that being back here was going to be good for me, but as each day ticked by I wasn't sure.

I pushed the folder with the students' papers into my bag. My desk was as empty as it was when I entered this morning. I'd definitely need to bring in some fresh flowers or something to liven it up a bit.

The sound of the ladder jiggling had stopped so I snuck over to the window and before I had a chance to lift the blinds and close the window, a husky laugh washed over me from behind. I turned around to see the man, who'd been hanging outside my window, right in front of me, grinning as if he held a secret I wasn't privy to.

And Tessa was right. He was the full, complete, impossibly perfect package. Every amazing ounce of him looked delicious. His gaze met mine, and all I could do was turn right back around to secure the window and hide my embarrassment for the second time in less than ten minutes.

"You know, we have feelings too," he said bemused.

Oh, dear Lord.

As I worked the window shut, I flipped the locks in place and brought the blinds down once again before turning to face the music and the man. I let out a silent sigh and slid the smile off my lips. I didn't need his head to get any bigger than it already was.

"I have no idea what you're talking about," I said, walking over to my desk.

"Oh, but I think you do." He flashed an even wider grin, and my heart nearly stopped on the spot. I wanted to be swallowed up in the ground and transported all the way back to upstate New York. So I did what any normal human would do when faced with an overly cocky man, I grabbed my bag and walked past him.

"Don't flatter yourself," I muttered.

"I wouldn't dream of it. By the sound of it though, the teachers around here do enough of that for me. But don't listen to anything they tell you." He winked, and I couldn't help myself from stopping right where I was, which happened to be in the doorway, while I wondered how much he'd actually heard perched outside my window.

We both stood in silence for a few moments. His vibrant, blue eyes held an intensity that was intriguing as he let the words sink in. He definitely had the upper hand, but I would change that. The smile swept all the way through his expression, and it was impossible not to be a little interested in the man on the ladder, who was now smirking in front of me. His dark blond hair and olive skin tone was a disastrous combination for someone trying to stay uninterested. His broad shoulders filled out his shirt and the slouchy jeans he was wearing made my eyes want to do another dip, but I refused to give in.

He knew he was good-looking. There was no way a person could be that attractive and not know it, but there was also something absolutely adorable lurking behind his gaze. He was trouble, and I certainly wasn't looking for trouble this summer. I'd left enough of it behind to last a lifetime.

He leaned along the doorway and stretched his arms slightly, but I refused to fall for it. I did not look down. I kept my gaze securely fastened on his. I was less than a foot away from him, and I felt every bit of that closeness. To say I felt electricity zipping between us would be a great disservice to the storm I felt brewing inside of me, and I wholly blamed the man in front of me for knowing how to make a woman swoon. It had to be a learned technique otherwise all the teachers here wouldn't be under his spell. I was just annoyed with myself for falling for it or him or whatever this was swelling inside of me.

"So my real reason for popping in on you was to see if there was anything around the classroom that you needed fixed before summer school gets totally underway? I always like to get these rooms started first if there is a task that needs to be completed."

I looked around the room and the only thing that could help this space was a complete overhaul, and I knew that wasn't in the budget so I shook my head. "I hope to get the kids outside as much as possible."

He tapped his fingers on the door and gave a slight nod. "Brave woman. Okay, well if you need to add anything to my list, I'm usually here on Fridays, but I wanted to get a jumpstart for the summer."

"Thanks." I said, attempting to get by him.

"So where do you plan on taking the students?" he asked.

I was surprised by his question, but even more thrilled that I'd made it all the way into the hallway. Distance from this man definitely worked in my favor.

"I'm not sure yet. There are so many amazing beaches close to the school that it'll be hard to pick. Or I could take the students to one of the piers, and we could take a class on wooden boatbuilding. Although, I think getting that to fit into the history lessons might be challenging. I could definitely work it into the maritime history of the island, but only time will tell, which I don't have much of. It's probably going to be a very rough go of it. Getting the kids interested during summer school seems almost impossible."

He'd moved into the hallway with me, and he grinned as his eyes fastened on something behind me. I turned to follow his gaze and saw a huge poster of a pelican. Each classroom was referred to as a seabird. I happened to be in the "pelican" classroom.

"So are you a pelican or a pelican't?" he asked, his eyes twinkled with a mischief that made me want to know more about him.

"Excuse me?" I asked, not sure I heard him correctly.

"Are you a pelican or a pelican't? You strike me as a pelican." His brow rose, and I couldn't help but burst into laughter at the most horribly wonderful pun ever heard by mankind. "But you were starting to sound like a pelican't."

"I suppose I'm in the former group."

He folded his arms and his smile deepened. "And which group would that be?"

"I'm not going to say it." I smiled, glancing at the noble pelican on the poster. I liked it even more now.

"You're not going to say which group you fall into?" he asked.

"Nope."

"Well, I'm a pelican. Always have been a

pelican. Pelican'ts drive me nuts, but until I hear you say it, I guess I won't know which group you truly fall into."

Tessa poked her head out of her classroom and gave me the thumbs-up sign and I wanted to shoo her away. Everything about this encounter was so awkward and he was eating it up.

And I loved every second of it.

My cheeks were almost hurting from the amount of smiling that started when I first saw part of this man balanced outside the window, and it took everything in my power not to give into temptation and hand him what he wanted. But I was doing it for my own sanity. I couldn't afford to start any relationships in the near or distant future.

"I guess you'll just have to wait to see which group I fall into."

"I don't think I caught your name," he said. "And it's not listed on the door yet."

"Victoria." I didn't dare ask for his.

He flashed a knowing grin, which worried me slightly, but I shook it off.

"Well, it was nice to meet you, Victoria. I hope I get the pleasure of standing on a ladder right outside your window next week, and just maybe you'll sign up for summer school next year."

My cheeks reddened again, and I let out a completely unattractive chortle-laugh and shook my head. "You heard that?"

"I heard it all." He smiled and walked into my classroom, leaving me to wonder what in the world I'd gotten myself into.

BEYOND THE MISTLETOE

CHAPTER ONE

Christmas Eve
Six Years Ago

The Christmas music crooned in the background as I put the final touches on a watercolor painting I'd been working on. The door to my studio banged open with a thud and in strode my sexy husband of seven years. I couldn't help but admire how attractive he was. Everything about him was neat and orderly. His blond hair was trimmed close against his head, and there wasn't even a hint of a five o'clock shadow. His finely tailored suit hugged his extremely fit body. He liked order, which was the exact opposite of me. Maybe that was why we fit so well together. Who knew I'd fall for a straight-laced accountant? I smiled at him and felt the usual rush of love for Paul. My eyes dipped back down to my watercolor painting before I filled him in on our dinner plans. I didn't want him to see the gift I'd been working on for him so I moved my water bowl slightly to the left.

"The ham should be ready in twenty minutes or so. I put extra glaze on it, just how you like it." I swirled the tip of my paintbrush in water and took in a deep breath of happiness. I adored everything to do with the holidays.

"I don't love you any longer."

My paintbrush fell out of my fingers as my gaze flashed to my husband's. His stare was icy and determined.

"What?" I whispered, certain I'd misunderstood.

"You heard me," he replied, completely detached and impatient.

I glanced around the studio he'd built for me. The space was filled with Christmas decorations he'd hung to surprise me only a few weeks ago. A small tree stood in the corner with its blinking, white lights, and a nativity scene sat on the desk near the door. Garlands framed every window. I looked down at the watercolor painting I'd been

working on, the painting that was going under the tree for him in the morning. The scene was based on last summer's trip to Ireland, the rolling hills, and the couple in the distance admiring the rugged beauty of the landscape represented one of our many adventures together.

Together.

He didn't like being together?

No. This didn't make sense.

I didn't understand.

My gaze locked on his. "Is there someone else?"

He shook his head. "No, Emily. There is no one else. But there is the thought of someone else someday."

His words were like knives viciously stabbing my soul. I never saw this coming. There was never a hint. This man—my husband of seven years—showered me with affection. He woke me up with chai lattes from Starbucks and breakfasts in bed. I'd surprise him with his favorite meals at dinnertime and weekend getaways. We were a happy couple. We'd dated since college and waited a sensible amount of time before getting married.

And we were happy.

Weren't we?

I slumped onto the stool behind me. My hands trembled as I stared at the man I no longer knew.

"Paul, whatever you think the problem is, I know we can fix it. I thought you were happy. Is it your job? Do you want me to go back to work?"

He didn't answer. Instead, Paul walked over to the stereo and turned off the Christmas music. He didn't turn back around to face me as he slid his hands underneath his suit jacket and into the back pockets of his slacks. He let out a long, exaggerated sigh.

As if even having this conversation was too much effort.

"Don't make this harder than it needs to be. You always make things difficult." Not even a hint of emotion straddled his voice as his words slapped me with every syllable.

"I'm not trying to be difficult." My voice trembled despite my best effort to sound in control. "I just don't understand. I thought what we had was good, amazing actually. Usually, a person gets some sort of clue that there's a problem. We don't fight. You shower me with affection as I do with you. I love spending time with you, and I thought the feeling was mutual." I licked my lips and forced myself to swallow. A lump in the back of my throat grew by the second, but I would not cry. I would get to the bottom of this. "I love you."

This was all a bad dream. He would come to his senses.

I slid off the stool and wiped my hands over my smock that had been splashed and spotted

with brilliant colors over the years. Taking in a deep breath, I untied it and tugged it off, walking to where he stood.

"Paul, what's going on?" I whispered, touching his shoulder lightly.

He turned around slowly, and his gaze locked on mine His blue eyes that had once reflected genuine love for me, now canvased over my body as if he'd despised me for merely existing.

"I haven't loved you for a very long time." Paul's eyes fell from mine. "Not the way a man needs to love his partner."

The room got smaller by the minute. All four walls squeezed in on me. I couldn't bear the weight of his words, but then things slowly started to click.

Our prenuptial agreement.

We'd made it to seven years this past November, which entitled him to one-quarter of my savings. The one caveat my attorney advised me against, but Paul insisted on. I was the one who came into our relationship with a substantial amount of money I'd socked away, but I never thought that factored into anything. We'd always lived somewhat frugally and money never seemed to be an issue. Apparently, I was wrong.

My hand recoiled from his shoulder as if I'd been burned.

And on many levels I had.

Every part of me had been singed with deceit.

Did he ever love me? Had everything been a lie? Was I the only one who'd been in love?

"Our families are coming over tomorrow for Christmas. What do we tell them?" My words were only a whisper to the stranger in front of me.

"Nothing. Absolutely nothing. We'll have a nice Christmas like we'd planned, and I'll be out of the house by the end of the year. There's no point in ruining anyone else's holiday."

"Just mine. You wanted to make sure I knew before morning? Couldn't you have waited?" The anger built at an unstoppable rate.

"I've waited long enough."

He spun on his heels and walked out of the studio. Loneliness surged through my body, and bit-by-bit, the walls sprang up around my heart.

If I was going to get through the next twenty-four hours, I needed to get good at pretending.

And I became an expert.

I never did shed a tear that night, not one. Granted in the days, weeks, and months to come, I shed more liquid sorrow than anyone ever should, but in that one bitter haze of confusion, all I felt was anger toward the man who played the biggest trick on me in my thirty-plus years of existence. The betrayal ran deep.

He tricked me into believing he loved me.

CHAPTER TWO

Present Day

"I don't know how I got so lucky. You're everything I've ever wanted and more." I glanced at the gorgeous specimen sitting on the couch.

His brown eyes caught the sun's last bit of light before nightfall, and I couldn't help myself as I chuckled aloud. He was just too cute, and he was all mine. Life had a way of turning around.

"It's not every single day someone comes across a partner who completes them in every possible way. Do you know how hard it has been to find someone who likes going on hikes, enjoys tasting all my experimental recipes, and not to mention, worships the ground I walk on? I'd almost given up hope, Bodie."

Bodie grunted, and my insides lit up with happiness. I smiled to myself and inhaled the sweetness from the last batch of cookies I'd pulled out of the oven.

I knew perfection was unrealistic in relationships, but I felt we were teetering on the brink of it.

Placing a few cookies on a plate, I walked over to the couch and took a seat next to him. His brown eyes took me in before falling to the gingerbread cookies, and I noticed just how long his dark lashes were. He greedily snatched up a cookie off the plate and finished it in an instant. Gazing at me for more, I nuzzled into his neck and gave in.

Bing Crosby singing White Christmas played in the background, and I truly felt in my element. It might have taken six years, but maybe there was a glimmer of hope that I'd learn to love the holidays again.

"My only complaint is that you drool during your sleep, and your whiskers are really pokey." I scratched Bodie's chin, and he sat up straighter, his eyes focused on the last gingerbread man. "But I know that's not your fault."

My hands fell from Bodie's chin, and he immediately pawed me for more pets and the last cookie.

"Now if only I could bring you to Gabby's wedding as my date, I'd be all set."

I glanced around my cozy family room and let out a sigh. I had a lot of decorating left to do. The Christmas tree was still at a slight tilt, but I was just thrilled I got the nine-foot tree anchored in the stand all by myself. As long as we didn't have an earthquake, the tree should make it through the holidays without crushing Bodie or me. I still had our stockings to hang, and dancing Santas to arrange near the fireplace, but I was getting this place more ready for the season than it had been in years.

The front door opened and a huge gust of icy wind funneled down the hallway as Gabby stepped inside and hollered a cheerful greeting.

"Knock, knock," Gabby sang out. "It's freezing out there."

"Maybe I can convince Gabby tonight that you're my plus one," I whispered to Bodie. His tail wagged, and I was certain as long as he could have some cake, he'd be an excellent date.

"Hopefully your wedding dress will be lined with fleece," I teased, standing up from the couch. "I can't believe how cold it's been this fall."

Bodie looked at me longingly, and I scratched his ear before dashing off to take Gabby's jacket.

"I definitely need to thaw out." She smiled and shivered.

"Do you think it will actually snow?" I asked, giving Gabby a big hug before taking her jacket to hang up. The already packed closet made squeezing in another puffy jacket challenging but doable.

"If not down here, it will definitely snow up by the lodge." She grinned and took in a deep breath. "Do I smell gingerbread?"

I nodded.

Even though the girl owned a bakery, she could never get enough sweets, but who was I to talk? I worked at her bakery and still baked treats for Bodie and myself.

"Would you like one?" I caught her eyeing the rack of gingerbread cookies.

"Absolutely."

Gabby was not even two weeks away from walking down the aisle with Jason. They were a great couple, deeply in love, and their relationship was almost as perfect as mine was with Bodie. Their love was one of those that made a person realize that sometimes fate needed to step in and clobber someone upside the head a few times to steer a person in the right direction, and that's exactly what happened to them both. Those two were stubborn to begin with, and now they were stubbornly in love. It made me realize what love in my life should have been. I'd settled and hadn't even realized it.

She helped herself to the cookies, and I poured us each a glass of milk before we took a seat at the breakfast bar. I dusted a few crumbs off the granite and grabbed her some paper napkins.

"So, I've been meaning to tell you this, but we've been so busy at work I felt I needed to make the trek." Her gaze avoided mine, which worried me.

I lived on Hound Island, which only had four ferries a day, two in the morning and two in the evening. It made visits challenging and usually an overnight affair. But if whatever Gabby wanted to tell me required a trip to see me, I wasn't looking forward to whatever was about to spill out of her mouth.

"I don't know how to put this," she began.

I bit the gingerbread man's head off and stared at her. Gabby's golden blond hair was in a thick braid and wispy strands framed her delicate features. Even after a long day running the bakery, she looked incredible. I, however, needed a date with my red hair dye to revive the dull color. I was born a brunette, but since my divorce I enjoyed being a redhead because my ex-husband hated the look.

She took a sip of milk, buying herself more time.

"Just say what you have to say. Is it the bakery? My job?"

Gabby shook her head and looked somewhat relieved by my guesses. "Not at all. The bakery is growing at an unbelievably great pace, and I can't imagine not having you there."

"Then spit it out." I let out the breath I'd been holding in.

"You know how we're having our bachelor/bachelorette party up at the lodge the weekend before the wedding?"

I nodded. "Do you need me to stay at the bakery after all?"

Truth be told, I wouldn't mind staying home one bit. Weddings and holidays weren't exactly my favorite things on earth. I was still in the baby-step stages of both. I did my best to fill my life with the joy of the season, but it was a feeble attempt at best. And weddings... Don't even get me started.

"No. Not at all. The bakery is covered. I'd be

traumatized for months if you didn't come."

My heart sank slightly.

"Then what's up?"

"Lily has a friend who she thinks would be perfect for you." Gabby bit her lip and waited.

"What do you mean perfect for me?" I asked, narrowing my eyes at not only my boss, but one of my closest friends. It was a tricky spot to be in. Not to mention Lily was one of Gabby's best friends and a bridesmaid. It would be impossible to ignore this mystery setup. And I certainly couldn't ditch the blind date at the last moment like I usually did. I was stuck.

Gabby fidgeted, but she couldn't hide her smile as she continued with the details of their plan. "Well, Lily thinks she's a matchmaker and has found someone she thinks you'll like."

The pit in my stomach grew to the size of a gully. Dating was not my thing.

"I told you about my online dating fiasco—"

"And how you canceled your profile after only two weeks. You didn't even give it a chance."

"Because the experience was horrible. I didn't even bother going on the last date I accepted with a new guy."

"Well, hopefully you at least canceled with the guy and didn't just stand him up."

My cheeks reddened.

"I'd forgotten to message him until the next morning, and I did feel horrible about it. But I got so busy at the bakery that when I got home, Bodie needed to go for a walk, and before I knew it, I'd crawled into bed with a good book."

"Are you serious?" Gabby's eyes widened. "That's horrible. He's probably wounded for life."

"Doubtful, but I do feel really bad about it."

"Yeah. It sounds like it." She rolled her eyes. "But you can't blame the bakery on forgetting that one. You're sabotaging yourself and your dating life. Plain and simple. Your subconscious has decided that dating isn't important."

"I'm not sabotaging myself. I'm content living a blissful existence on the island."

"On one of the smallest islands in Washington tucked away from most of civilization. It sounds to me like you're turning into a hermit."

"And precisely what would be wrong with turning into a hermit?" I crossed my arms and flashed a grin.

Gabby groaned and shook her head, but she pressed on. "Anyway, the guy will be at our party at the lodge."

"The bachelor/bachelorette party? Please tell me you're kidding." I slapped my head with my palm.

"Not kidding at all. Come on." She grinned. "It'll be good for you."

"It's one thing to be set up on a blind date over coffee, but it's quite another to be expected to see the guy for an entire weekend. What if we don't hit it off, and then forever after, we'll be dodging one another. Can you say awkward?"

"Not only can I say it, I can spell it." Gabby wriggled her brows, and I wanted to slug her, all in good fun of course. "And you'd only have to dodge one another for the weekend if it went belly-up. He's unable to make it to the wedding so don't be overly dramatic."

I groaned. Gabby was the sweetest girl I knew, but she also had a no-nonsense manner that kicked me in the gut at moments.

"Sometimes the best things in life blossom from getting out of your comfort zone."

"Seriously, this could go really wrong, and I'll be stuck up in the mountains with no way to escape."

"But we'll all be there with you," she assured me.

"Is that supposed to make me feel better?" I laughed. "My dating life has now become a spectator sport."

Bodie sensed my pain and jumped off the couch to waddle his way over to me. I bent down to give him a grateful scratch but realized all he had planned was to sniff out the cookie crumbs.

Traitor.

"It'll be fine. He's really cute, and he's a lawyer."

I cringed.

"What?" Gabby asked, almost offended.

"My ex was an accountant."

"So?"

"I tend to stay away from any men in suits."

"Who are you kidding?" Gabby chuckled. "You stay away from all men. Period."

"I'm not that bad."

Gabby's brow arched.

"Well, maybe I am." I sighed and shook my head. "I guess if he's a total dud, I can hide out with Bodie in my hotel room."

"Not on my watch, but yes. Tell yourself whatever you need to in order to get to the lodge. This gingerbread cookie is fantastic."

"Thanks."

"Not my recipe?" she asked.

"I added orange zest."

"Wow. We might need to include this in our daily selection." She grinned. "Would you mind?"

"I'd be flattered."

Gabby stood up and walked over to a painting I'd just finished for her and Jason. I'd propped it on a side table near the television. It was one of their wedding gifts, but I'd left it out to see if Gabby would gravitate toward it or not. Paintings were so personal, and what I felt they might like, they might hate. I was hoping my little test wouldn't backfire.

"Is this a new piece?" Gabby asked. Her eyes studied the watercolor in front of her. I'd found a photo from when Jason and Gabby went to Utah for a ski trip. I wasn't sure if she'd recognize the area, but I thought it was a perfect scene to paint with a rustic lodge centering the work, and snowflakes falling around the pine trees and cobblestone pathways.

"It is. I've finally gotten away from painting angry scenes," I said with a chuckle.

"I'm in love. Absolutely in love. It transports me to such a calm place."

"It's in a new series." My body relaxed, and my insides filled with joy. The wedding gift would be a success.

She nodded, still staring at the piece. "It's gorgeous."

"Thank you."

"Now, you have to promise me that if we do decide to move forward and open up another bakery and espresso shop here on your island, you won't hermitify." She came back over and took a seat.

"Hermitify? That's not even a word."

"It is when I use it with confidence. But seriously. I could see you never leaving the island."

"That doesn't make me a hermit. I'd see people every single day."

"That doesn't count."

"Yes, it does." I gave her an evil look.

She shook her head and let out an disgruntled sigh, her eyes falling to my tree.

"Did you know your tree has a certain tilt to it?" she asked.

"Thanks for noticing. If you move the branches, you'll see I tied twine around the trunk and nailed it to the wall so it should last through the holidays, tilt or not."

Gabby giggled, and I glanced around my tiny house. Actually it was more of a cabin—crooked tree included—and I loved every inch of it. I loved what I'd made of the place and how I made it just for me. Becoming a hermit sounded like an amazing existence. Was enjoying my own company more than others really a bad thing? I didn't think so.

Gabby caught my expression. "Anyway, don't

worry about this blind date thingy. Either it will work or it won't. Be yourself. Lily wouldn't lead you astray, or she'd have me to deal with."

"How good-looking is he?" I asked.

"That's the spirit." She batted her lashes. "I'd say he's an eleven on a scale of one-to-ten. And he's three years older than you with no kids and no ex-wives."

"Why hasn't he married?"

Gabby huffed a frustrated grunt.

"Sorry. You're right. I do sabotage myself," I said, realizing I'd already started looking for a reason to write him off.

She nodded in agreement. "Whatever the guy has in his past is the exact opposite of what you want, regardless of how contradictory it is."

"Alright. Alright. I get it." I waved my hands in protest. "I'll go into this with an open mind and an excuse to have a good time."

"I say you should go into the weekend with no expectations beyond having fun. No strings attached. What happens, happens. Even if it's nothing more than having a good time and never thinking about him again."

"So how does Lily know him?"

"He dated one of Lily's coworkers when she was in Portland back at the job she hated. Anyway, she heard about how amazing he was in bed every Monday morning, like clockwork."

"So that was why Lily thought of me?" I giggled.

It had been a really, really long time since I'd been with a man.

Like a really long time.

Years.

Many of them.

Combined to create a really long stretch.

Of time that made me forget what it was like to be with a man.

"So what happened with the girlfriend?" I asked. Not sure I wanted to hear the answer.

"She dumped him for the son of the boss."

"The dirtbag Lily told us about?"

Gabby nodded. "Some women just don't learn from others' mistakes."

"Or they think they can change the men."

"True. Anyway, the guy—his name is Eric—left Portland and wound up working for Lily's husband up here."

"Oh great. It keeps getting better and better. So if this goes haywire, I'm really in trouble."

"It's not like that. No one is going into this with any preconceived notions. I'm telling you, this guy is a great way to get back into the dating world."

"Maybe I could use a sexy guy to bring me out of..." I stopped myself. I didn't know what I needed to be brought out of.

"Out of your sexual hiatus." She finished for me.

"Exactly. Hiatus. That sounds planned and like I was in control."

"By all accounts, I think you've been completely in control of the hiatus. Since I've known you, I've seen the regulars who stop by the bakery to snoop around, and it's not only the cookies they're after."

I shivered at the thought. I had accumulated quite the assortment of flirters while working at Gabby's bakery. Most of them had canes and backup pairs of teeth on their nightstands.

"Are you talking about the seniors who show up during Senior Happy Hour who love to flirt with me?"

"Well, those fine gentlemen will be disappointed with your absence when we get this new location up and running," she teased. "But no. I wasn't referring to your elderly admirers. You're just too blind to see the ones who are more age-appropriate."

Gabby glanced at the clock. It was time for her to turn right around and catch the last ferry of the night. And contrary to my hermit tendencies, I was sad at the thought.

"Promise me that you're not mad." Gabby stood up and glanced at Bodie who'd wandered back to the couch.

"Not mad at all. I think it's sweet that you and your friends are worried about my dating life. I just don't want Lily to be devastated when this blind date backfires."

"Not when, my dear Emily. It won't." She grinned from ear to ear. Her happiness was infectious as was the hopeless romantic inside of her. "Because you're going into it with no expectations except to have fun."

"Right. Fun is exactly the word I'd use to meet a complete stranger that is a potential candidate for sex where I have to laugh at his jokes, stare into his eyes, and lick my lips seductively at all the right moments."

"Well, when you put it that way, there might be more reasons about why you're still single than I knew about."

"I still think Bodie is the ideal mate," I said, ignoring her latest assessment.

"And that, my friend, is the problem. Bodie is not a mate. Bodie is more like a child. There really could be more issues here than I realized."

I smacked her arm playfully, and we laughed on the way to the front door where she gave me another squeeze and headed off to catch the ferry.

Maybe she was right.

What if all I needed was a carefree weekend where I never had to look back? I'd certainly done enough rearview mirroring over the last six years and was ready for a change.

About the Author

Karice received an MFA in Creative Writing from the U of W. She has written over thirty novels, and she has several exciting projects in the works (or at least she thinks they're exciting). Karice lives in the Pacific Northwest with her awesome husband and two cute English Bulldogs. She loves anything to do with snow, and she seeks out the stuff whenever she can, especially if there's a toasty fire to read by.

Contact the Author

To contact the author, please visit her online at http://www.karicebolton.com or via

Twitter/Facebook/Pinterest @KariceBolton.

If you'd like to be included on her mailing list to find out about new releases go to Karice Bolton's at www.karicebolton.com

You can also text KariceBooks to 313131 to receive a message from her on release days!

www.ingramcontent.com/pod-product-compliance
Lightning Source LLC
Chambersburg PA
CBHW030155200626
46812CB00017B/2092